BEATEN PATHS

BEATEN PATHS

STEPHIE WALLS

Stephie Walls

DEDICATION

For Maggie...
Your endless faith in me drives me forward.
I'll always pick you.

Life isn't always about paved streets; the adventures lie on the gravel roads and beaten paths. Take the route less traveled.

PROLOGUE
CHARLIE

Hospitals do their best to be nice places. They keep the lobbies scrubbed, arrange leather furniture around fake hearths, and add little gardens to their walkways, but it is all still largely for the visitors. The cafés with their warm-coffee smells at the entrance, the small gift shops with fuzzy bears and big red hearts, and the fountains full of wishful pennies don't do anything for the people inside. Just like everyone else, I'd stopped to grab a snack before facing whatever lie upstairs.

People latch onto anything that allows them to forget the pain and misery while paying their respect. Everyone wants a distraction. No one chooses to think about what is going on a few floors above their heads. The patients are the ones who have to live with the buzz of bright fluorescent lights, the sanitized and sterile smell, and the constant hum of electronics. That is why no one likes hospitals. When a patient is there for the long haul, they are left staring at a white wall with their stomachs in knots, thinking about what will come next. Meanwhile, their families and friends are in the lobby, chugging lattes and wishing them the best.

Not that I had strong opinions.

I wasn't one hundred percent certain whether Jack would be at the hospital or not. But it was as good a bet as any. He was a difficult man to pin down, in general, and even more so these days. For good reason—not that any of us blamed him. But I couldn't seem to catch him at home, so it was easier to show up at the hospital. It was the one safe bet for finding him.

I had just finished my snack—the saltiness didn't bring nearly the pleasure I'd hoped it would before trudging down the hospital halls. I crumpled up the yellow-foil bag that had contained roughly a handful of chips and shoved it into a trashcan. I hated that I was as familiar with this place as I'd become in recent weeks, but I knew where Sarah's room was by heart at this point. I hated walking down the long white halls. Each noise I made seemed to amplify in the empty corridors, and I felt like an organism under a microscope, not that people were staring. It was quite the opposite; the halls tended to be rather vacant. Every now and then I'd pass a doctor or a patient. But for the most part, it was just one long, empty stretch after another. Grey door after grey door, surrounded by endless feet of white drywall. Somehow, I managed to miss the little gardens on my path to Sarah's room—no glimpses of flowers through the odd window, only flat concrete.

It was truly depressing. I tried to ignore it, and I kept

walking toward Sarah's room. I didn't really know her, even though we'd grown up in the same small town and gone to school together our entire lives. However, the two of us hadn't run in the same crowd, and I was closer to her younger sister than her. Coming here to talk business seemed like an invasion, but her dad needed my help with his cattle ranch while she was here, and I needed his answers to my questions.

There was no Jack Adams in her room. There was only Sarah.

She sat alone. If I had to guess, I'd bet that her dad had been there but had already left for whatever reason. Personally, I couldn't imagine what it would be like to leave my little girl alone after all she'd been through. It must have killed him to do it every time he had to step foot out these doors.

Sarah sat with one leg propped up on the edge of the mattress and the other hanging off. I assumed that to be a good sign. There'd been so many days that were touch and go that just seeing her off all the machines was positive. She reached down and stuffed her small hands under her thigh, moving her leg to prop it up next to the other one. It took effort, and I stood mesmerized by the willpower and determination she must possess to get through this. I wanted to help, but I wasn't sure how. I just stood frozen in the doorway. She hadn't seen me, and I wondered how long I could wait before it became too awkward for me to make my presence known.

She lifted her hand to her face and dragged her fingers across her nose. While I couldn't see her expression, there was no denying the tears that streaked her cheeks. Maybe she had been crying the whole time I'd watched her. A tear clung to the tip of her nose while others dripped from her jaw, but she hadn't made a sound. She did her best to keep her emotions under control, even when she believed she was alone. Her shoulders rose with each deep breath she took in what I assumed to be an effort to calm down, but every inhalation made her shudder, and her entire body shook.

I wanted to say something—needed to—but I wasn't sure where to begin. Part of me felt ashamed. I shouldn't be witnessing this extremely private moment. The other part of me felt guilty. There wasn't anything I could do to ease her pain. Another small part of me wanted to comfort her. Even knowing that I couldn't stop the discomfort or the struggle she faced, there had to be *something* I could do that was better than lurking in the hallway.

When I finally stepped into the room, Sarah lifted her head as I crossed the threshold. She immediately dragged her sleeve across her face, soaking up the tears with the arm of her cardigan. Her tiny hands furiously blotted a tissue beneath her lashes. I couldn't discern whether her expression was a scowl or something else akin to mildly distressed—but whatever it was, it obviously hurt. Sarah cleared her emotion and returned to the blank slate I'd become accustomed to seeing.

I rapped my fist on the doorframe despite the fact that she'd seen me staring. "Can I come in?" I slid my hands into my pockets as I waited and tried to keep my posture relaxed, inviting. I didn't want her to think that I was just walking in on her most vulnerable moment because I could.

Sarah nodded ever so slightly. "Of course, please." There wasn't a rude bone in the girl's body. It didn't matter how much pain she was in; she'd keep up the Southern demeanor of small-town Texas because that's how she'd been raised.

I didn't miss the way she flinched when she touched the tissue she'd used on her eyes to the angry red scars on her face. It appeared incredibly painful and tight, but I didn't know her well enough to ask and needed to stop staring.

I tried not to read too deeply into the meek tone in which she'd invited me in. It didn't take a genius to see that now wasn't an opportune time for company, but there was a reason for my visit. And while it wasn't Sarah, I did need to find Jack.

"Sorry to barge in. I was just looking for your dad." I tried to appear properly chagrined for my intrusion. I couldn't shake the feeling that she would rather be left alone.

Sarah hid her face, deliberately avoiding eye contact. "He isn't here." Even her swallow appeared labored. "If you hurry, you may be able to catch him at home."

I nodded, but I didn't leave. My feet were bolted to the ground, and something compelled me to stay. My boots were rooted in place, preventing me from leaving or moving closer.

"Is that all?" Her words broke the spell. They cut through the tension that lingered between us like a knife, but instead of pushing me back, they drew me a little closer.

The only time I'd ever seen something so fragile and defeated had been an animal in a trap. Sarah appeared to have lost her will to fight, and I had an overwhelming urge to pull her into my arms. Something in me wanted to whisper into her ear that she'd be all right, that everything would be okay. But despite just how downtrodden she appeared or how heavy her shoulders seemed, I wasn't the person to bring her hope.

"Yeah." I didn't want it to be, but I sounded like an idiot to my own ears. My mind raced to find something to talk about, something to lift her spirits, but I stood there like a mute. I couldn't imagine what she thought of me. "Are you doing okay?" *That was brilliant.*

She didn't respond other than to swallow hard. The tears welled up again. I could see them getting caught in her throat as she tried to swallow them down, fight them back. She bit her bottom lip and lowered her head, closing her eyes. The tears beaded on her lashes and then streaked down her cheeks.

I might not be great at offering comfort or support, but I couldn't stand to see a woman cry. "Hey." That one word lifted my feet from where I stood, and I moved to sit next to her on the hospital bed.

I took a seat on the mattress not too far away from her but not close enough to make her uncomfortable, either. Sarah grabbed her thigh and shifted her leg toward her to create space for me.

She rolled her lips into her mouth and waved a hand in front of her face. "I'm not trying to make a scene. Daddy would be so embarrassed for you to see me this way." It wasn't a bid for pity.

The idea of anyone trying to make her feel bad about what she was going through mortified me. This was one of the hardest times of her life; hell, she was lucky to be alive. If I were ever privy to anyone trying to tell her to suck it up, I'd give them a clear message regarding their behavior. I'd be damned if I didn't put them through a window.

"You're not making a scene." I wasn't great with words and even worse at empathy, so I tried to keep my voice gentle. I tended to have a fairly deep timbre, and in this stark room, it reverberated rather forcefully. The last thing I wanted to do was come across as condescending. "You've been through a lot. I think you're entitled to show some emotion." I needed her to look at me, to give me an indication that she heard me, but I got nothing. "Most people would have cracked under the pressure. You are an incredibly strong woman."

She shook her head, and her messy blond curls bounced with the movement. "I'm not." Her voice cracked, and I felt it like a knife to the heart. "I'm not strong. Not like everyone keeps telling me I am...." Her shoulders heaved and shuddered as she fought to remain composed. Each time she peered at me through her dark lashes, she'd quickly duck her head to avoid my stare.

Sarah wanted to hide her fear. She tried to mask her insecurity. Despite whether or not she felt strong, she needed people to continue to believe she was. I felt that in my soul. And then I realized, it wasn't just the weakness she hoped to shadow; it was the disfigurement. Her fingers hovered over the black thread of stitches where her head had been shaved for surgery, and she held her head at just the right angle to camouflage the scars on the other side.

My hand twitched. Before I even realized what I was doing, I reached out to touch her cheeks. But when she'd flinched, I rested it against her knee instead.

"Please, don't look at me, Charlie." It hadn't been an admission exactly, but the sentiment was still the same.

I hadn't been prepared for it, and I tried not to show her just how taken aback I was by her request. "Okay." I didn't want to push the issue, but I didn't want her to believe I agreed with her. "I don't have to look at you if you don't want me to. But for the record, I would *like* to." There was no chance I'd ever be accused of being smooth around Sarah Adams. This version of me was worse than the pre-puberty one.

She huffed out a hard laugh under her breath. It was fast and barely audible and clearly not born from humor.

"I'm not exactly at my best." Her words wavered at her insecurity, and they shook just like her spine did when she inhaled deeply. She licked her lips and then lifted her bright eyes to meet mine—like she dared me to see her flaws. "There's nothing redeemable about my face, anymore." She straightened her spine as if to brace herself for whatever harsh criticism she thought I might impart on her, and her words were strangled as her throat tightened.

I was so far out of my element that I didn't have a clue what to say, but I knew I wanted to keep her talking...about anything. "Is that why you're crying?" I asked. "Are you afraid someone might react to your face?" That hadn't come out as eloquently from my mouth as I had meant it in my head.

She shook her head. "It isn't just that. It *is,* to an extent. But," she sighed, "every day is harder than the last. Nothing gets any easier, and every time I think I'm making progress, I realize that I've gone an inch in an endless stretch of miles. I'm trying to stay positive. I want to be thankful that I survived and have the chance to recover. But today—heck, every day—is hard. So hard. And what's the point? The physical therapists' intentions are better than their capability. They aren't God, and they can't perform miracles."

I nodded and kept listening.

"I'm at the end of my rope, and I think I need to accept that I'll probably never walk again." She dropped her head into her hands, careful to avoid the stitches and the abrasions. "I'm drained. I don't have any more fight in me. I know that sounds like the biggest crock of bull you've ever heard, but..." Sarah stopped shaking her head long enough for me to really take her in—it wasn't nearly as bad as she thought.

My heart melted. I wanted to reassure her, but I kept my distance. My hand remained on her knee, and I found myself stroking her soft skin with my thumb. The desire to pull her to me nearly overtook my willpower. God, I wanted to protect her like a runt calf, but I didn't know this girl from Adam's housecat. And thus, I remained still.

"You wouldn't understand," she whispered. "No one does. Everyone keeps telling me that I'm lucky to be alive. And I *know* I am. No one is more aware of that fact than me. And when it first happened, that support was almost suffocating. But the world kept spinning for everyone outside these walls. The clouds rolled away, and the threat of my dying passed. People went on with their lives. They stopped panicking. But when the dust settled, it was just *me*."

I squeezed her knee, and she stopped talking long enough to give me a meager smile that hurt me more than it helped. But I didn't let her go, and I didn't stop caressing her skin. She might not realize how much warmth and life she still had in her, but I could feel it in the pads of my fingers.

"Other than Daddy, it's just me, the physical therapists, and countless doctors who won't remember my name the day I'm discharged. All I'm left with is grueling exercise that isn't producing results. I hope you never know what it's like."

I wondered if anyone else had given Sarah the chance to vent, or if they expected the same woman in here that she had been on the outside. I didn't know her well, but our families were intertwined. I knew how much she did for Jack and that she took care of Miranda after their mama left. She needed someone to take care of her for a change, and it didn't seem she had that. So, I just let her talk and tried to commit every word she uttered to memory.

"All the medication zaps my energy and makes me foggy, but without the pain meds, there's no way I can do the physical therapy. It hurts. All of it hurts so much." A tear slid down her cheek, but she didn't collapse. "What if I never walk again? What if this is the best any of this will ever get? I haven't managed a single step. Not one. I'm just ready to throw in the towel." And with that, she finally stopped. Her shoulders rounded, the tears streamed, and she appeared utterly defeated.

For a moment, my heart refused to beat, and I just stared at her. The absolute hopelessness created a fissure in my chest that cracked open. I ached for the woman in front of me, so much so that I reacted instead of thinking. My hands found her face, and I cupped her jaw without touching any injuries. My thumbs brushed aside the tears she couldn't stop, and I couldn't have torn my eyes from hers if I'd had to.

"Hey," I said. "Listen to me."

She didn't say anything. But she didn't look away, either. Her eyes held mine like she could see through them and into the very essence of me, deeper than anyone else had dared look.

"You can't give up, Sarah."

Her expression softened, but it changed, too. I couldn't pinpoint what it was, but if she weren't riddled with pain, I'd guess it was a hint of elation. I hadn't said anything earth-shattering. Hell, I hadn't even said anything poetic. I started to pull apart, but before my touch left her skin, she lifted her hand. Her braced and bandaged fingers rested on top of mine, and she leaned into my palm.

Her eyes smiled, but the tears came faster than they had since I'd walked in the door, and the salty brine seeped under my hands, captured against her cheeks. "What?"

I'd never heard someone sound so panicked in one word —much less myself. "What did I do?" My erratic heart had started beating again, and now my racing pulse was the only thing I could hear. I didn't have a clue what I'd said to upset her, but whatever it was, I'd move mountains to fix it.

She hiccupped in what had to be the cutest display of vulnerability I'd ever witnessed. "It's just..." Her blue eyes sparkled with the first glimpse of hope I'd seen since I stepped into her room. "I didn't even think you knew my name."

My lips turned up in a grin I couldn't resist. Despite the stitches and the scabs, the scars and broken bones, she was the most adorable thing I'd ever seen. Every fiber of my being wanted to pull her in close, to hug her, hold her. But for the first time in my life, I was afraid to touch a woman for fear of hurting her body and my open heart, so I just held her face in my hands.

I planned to stay there as long as she'd let me.

1

SARAH

There was a beautiful blue butterfly on the porch railing. I wanted to capture it and put it in a glass jar, even though I shouldn't. Daddy always told me that rubbing the powder off a butterfly's wings made it impossible for them to fly. I didn't want to hurt the thing; I just wanted to look at it a little longer. And as soon as I walked up the porch, it would fly off, and I would never see it again.

The butterfly flew away, as predicted, and I had only made it up the first step.

With the slight distraction gone, I was free to focus on other things. I had a mission in mind now that Miranda was home. Through the screen door, I could hear her rustling around in the kitchen like a raccoon.

Honestly, there were some days where she wasn't so bad. They were just buried underneath all of the other days where everything she did annoyed me.

She had her face stuck behind the fridge door, and I

waited—*patiently*—for her to pull her head out. I had no doubt she lingered on purpose just to irritate the snot out of me. When she finally straightened, she had a carton of orange juice in her hand. Randi pierced my stare and twisted off the cap. She lifted the jug to her mouth and wrapped her lips around the spout.

I *hated* that. It was disgusting and unsanitary, and I just knew she would backwash. Now, no one other than her could drink out of it again. As always, my sister didn't seem to care. She just burped and went back to drinking. Her thin throat convulsed with each swallowed mouthful. Then she burped again and set the juice on the counter.

Even though I couldn't see myself, I felt the twisted way my features mangled into an expression of disgust. "It's amazing you have any friends at all with manners like those." The words just jumped out of my mouth before I could sensor or soften them.

She shrugged and didn't respond. Randi would push every button I had right up until the point of detonation, but she never wanted to initiate a full-blown argument. I hated fighting with my little sister almost as much as I hated being the one to have to discipline her. But she was really good at careening us down a path toward a disagreement and then trying to deviate to save her own tail.

Randi popped back up and seemed disappointed that I hadn't gone away. She sighed again and set her elbows on the counter that stood between us. That counter had kept us from lunging at each other and prevented us from gouging each other's eyes out on more than one occasion, and today, it seemed to serve the same purpose—a barrier between the Adams sisters.

She squeezed her arms together in a sad attempt to make her breasts pop. They looked like biscuits exploding from the tube. I had no idea where she'd learned such crass behavior. Even before Mama had left, Randi had never been allowed to act like anything other than a young lady.

"I got a call from your coach this morning." I threw out the information I had and stood my ground, waiting to see what she did with it. I kept my jaw clenched and my chin high.

Miranda would take it as a challenge, a dare for her to retaliate or rebut. And when she stood straighter and squared her shoulders, I had no doubt that a screaming match was quickly becoming a very real possibility.

She muttered something about a violation of privacy, and I knew I had her. She was uncomfortable and squirming —she'd also lied.

"She said you didn't show up for camp yesterday, which is odd, since you left the house with your bag, and I specifically remember your telling me that was where you were going *and* why you wouldn't be home last night." The heat rose from my chest to my cheeks.

I was desperate to maintain my composure. I wasn't trying to lose my cool and let her gain a single inch of moral superiority. But here it was. Randi had noticed just how irritated I'd become.

"It's not a big deal, Sarah," she huffed. Randi waved me off in an attempt to dismiss her actions.

"It's a huge deal. You made a commitment to those girls." I couldn't stop my own hands from balling into fists. "Do you have any idea how bad it looks for the captain of the squad not to show up?"

She pressed her lips together. "Previous captain. And it's cheerleading, not the Nobel Prize." Randi lifted a shoulder with a shrug. "There are tons of other seniors there to help."

I hated how complacent she was about all of this, how it all rolled off her shoulders like water off a duck's back. It was entirely possible that I wanted her to be angry because *I* was angry. It built faster than a forest fire, and it was going to spread just as rapidly if she didn't start using language that made her seem like less of a self-serving prima donna.

"I'm going next week. Chill out." She started to move away.

Without even thinking about it, I reached out and snatched her arm. My anger boiled right in the center of my chest. I didn't want to do this. I wanted to have a reasonable conversation with my eighteen-year-old sister. But she refused to act reasonably. It was her MO. Randi took everything for granted—me, Daddy, everything we had worked for. She did nothing to pull her weight on the ranch, and she abhorred manual labor. Meanwhile, she trotted around, flashed her assets and stunning smile, and got away with murder.

Ever since Mama had left, Miranda Adams had refused to follow the rules and insisted on making her own.

I wasn't about to let it keep happening. It had to end sometime, and I chose today—*now*. If nothing else came out of this, she would give me a straight answer. One way or another, Randi would admit where she'd been. I refused to let her skip out on me this time.

"Where *were* you?" I demanded.

Even I noticed the chill that took over the hot Texas air. My voice softened in a frightening way the angrier I got, and it cast an icy haze over the conversation. I swore Miranda shivered.

She licked her lips, trying to buy time to formulate a lie. But the longer she searched for a way out, the less likely she was to find one. And when she dropped my gaze, I had her. "The lake," she said.

Bull.

I had to hold my breath and count to ten. If I didn't, I was liable to explode. "All night?"

"No." She was racking her brain as she spoke. My sister was a master at cutting up the truth to feed it to me in unrecognizable pieces. "There was a field party at Twin Creeks."

That explained it. I still wasn't happy about her sneaking around and offering me half-truths, but at least she had been in good hands.

"You were with Austin?"

Austin was a good kid who came from good people. The entire town was aware that the Burins were basically angels sent down to earth—Austin, Charlie...well, the whole lot of them.

"He was there. Along with two hundred of his closest friends." Her sarcasm wasn't winning her any brownie points. Miranda acted like she *wanted* a fight. The smug look on her face spoke of her resistance. She wasn't giving in easily.

I'd been so focused on keeping my breathing under control that I was on the verge of passing out. My head was starting to spin the way it frequently did where my sister was concerned.

"Was Charlie there?" I didn't want to ask and didn't know why I had; it wasn't like it mattered.

Charlie never remembered my name despite twelve years of school together and the fact that our families had Sunday lunch together more often than not. Charlie Burin wouldn't know me if I slapped him in the face.

"Yes." Miranda deflated a bit, but there was also a hint of pity in her eyes.

"You know he and Daddy are working on an irrigation project, right?"

"So?" She flashed back.

I was pressing too much, and I didn't like the look on her face. "Did he mention it?" There was a knowing gleam in her expression—she thought she was on to me. I didn't want to know what she thought I was trying to get out of this conversation. Heck, at this point, *I* didn't know what I was trying to get out of it.

"I didn't talk to him," she said.

I could feel myself losing steam. This conversation was going nowhere, and it was pointless. If she hadn't gone to the Burins' to talk about anything useful, then there was no point in her being there at all. That wasn't true—I knew exactly why she'd been there; it just wasn't something I would have done. It didn't matter that I wouldn't have done it because I was never invited and not because I wouldn't have wanted to be included.

I wasn't as naïve as Randi liked to believe. It wasn't a secret that my little sister judged me, but I often forgot just how deep it ran until she gave me certain looks or made catty comments. I might not have ever been popular or part of Mason Belle's social scene in high school, but I did have some worldly knowledge outside of my dusty *Farmer's Almanac*.

Miranda would never understand just how drastically my life had changed the day our mama left. Any chance I'd had at a normal childhood vanished just like the mother who'd abandoned us. I'd done my best, but I didn't want to be Randi's surrogate mother any more than she wanted me to be. The only thing I wanted from Randi was for her to do her part and act like she'd been raised with manners.

She would rather die, it seemed, than do something to contribute to the family in a positive way. Her association with the Burins was a blessing in a lot of ways, and I always prayed that Austin would be a calming influence on Randi's wild ways. Unfortunately, it seemed to lean the other direction. Rather than his good qualities rubbing off on her, she did her best to smear her worst traits all over him.

I hated that line of thinking. I was the last person who needed to give up on Randi, and I did my best to sweep my attitude under the proverbial rug...for now. Small-town gossip could ruin a girl like Randi and kill any hopes she might have of keeping a boy like Austin. Rumors could be brutal, even if they weren't true.

"Your reputation is already questionable." I had my own impulse control issues—they just weren't the same as my sister's. I couldn't help it; the words just sprang off my tongue. My own fury coiled tightly in my chest. "Pulling these kinds of stunts only cements what people in town think of you." I didn't want to hurt her, but I hated the way she looked at me like I was the pathetic one of the two of us.

She crossed her arms and narrowed her gaze. "No one in Mason Belle gives a flip what I do. And last time I checked, you weren't my mama."

Her words stung. Maybe it was the blatant, red-hot anger that colored them, but more than the anger, it was the contempt. It all hurt. And it had hurt since Mama had left, and I'd tried to fill in. Eight years of torture—not just for me, but Randi, too. Neither of us deserved the hand we'd been dealt.

This had gone beyond the scolding I'd intended and morphed into a full-blown fight, and I had no way of pulling it back. Words flew from my mouth in a way I didn't intend before I could stop them. "I'm the closest thing you've got, and I'm ashamed of who you're becoming. This is not how you were raised."

Her jaw shifted, and then she sucked on her teeth. I wondered for just a second if my sister was going to spit on me or hit me.

She did neither. "Are we done?" she snapped, having far more self-control than I wanted to give her credit for.

"Not quite."

Randi's nostrils flared, and she looked like a horse ready to paw at the ground.

I wanted to nail her down with one final comeback. I wanted to end this exchange and put her in her place. But more than anything, I wanted my little sister to see what she'd done wrong. For once, she needed to admit the error of her ways. But she was far too stubborn ever to give me that satisfaction. She always bested me in the end. Randi stayed one step ahead, regardless of how hard I fought to keep her in line. That bullheaded streak was as wide as a river, and there was nothing Daddy or I could do to take it out of her.

"You're grounded." The words tumbled out, and the weight they held went with them. It was a suitable punishment if it stuck. "You can go to cheer camp. That's it. There's plenty to do around here."

Her mouth fell open, and I felt an unsatisfying surge of victory. Not even the smile that lifted the corners of my mouth created a sense of satisfaction. There should have been far more joy in knowing I'd won the war.

She just looked so ridiculous with her flushed face and her jaw hanging open like a big-mouth bass. "For how long?"

I allowed myself a tiny shrug when I clasped my hands in front of me. Randi thought I took pleasure in disciplining her, but the truth was, I had to twine my fingers to keep her from seeing them shake. "Two weeks should make my point."

"Not happening," she muttered and pushed her way past me.

I called out just as she reached the bottom of the steps. "Don't test me on this, Miranda. I've already talked to Daddy." It felt a bit ridiculous pulling that card. We were both grown women—although one of us was a tad more mature than the other—and I shouldn't have to.

But Miranda forced my hand. She might not listen to me, but she wouldn't cross Daddy—*ever*. Whether or not I had actually spoken to him, all I had to do was mention his name, and it instantly made my life a little bit easier.

Her shoulders sagged as the wind left her verbose sails. "Whatever."

She stomped up the steps like a toddler pitching a tantrum; only, this child was my eighteen-year-old sister. But then again, it was Miranda. And I wasn't at all surprised by the way she acted. Seconds later, Randi slammed her bedroom door just to make sure everyone on the ranch and in the house knew exactly how unhappy she was. And while I didn't care to listen to her pout and throw things for the next two hours, at least I knew I'd made my point. It was bittersweet.

I made my way to the second floor and down to my room. I needed to allow myself time to cool down before I went back outside to work. It was hot and incredibly humid. I had closed the curtains over my windows, but that did little to keep the heat at bay. My covers were cool, however. My bed was tucked into a corner and cast in shadows no matter the hour of the day. I sighed and sank down onto the edge of the bed, putting my face in my hands to massage my temples.

I gave myself a few minutes to close my eyes and relax.

There was stuff that needed to be done around the ranch, but the heat was so oppressive that all I could find the energy to do was lie down. We hadn't seen a heatwave like this one in years. The air conditioner couldn't keep up in our old farmhouse, and the only time it was bearable, inside or out, was after dark.

My clothes clung to my sticky skin when I laid back on the bed, and my eyes swirled with the rotation of the fan overhead. The hypnotic spin coupled with the heat had my lids drifting closed in a short amount of time, and I allowed sleep to creep in.

What I'd intended only to be a few minutes turned into a couple of hours. I woke with a start and glanced at the clock on my nightstand. And then I realized what had brought me to consciousness so quickly. I scrambled to my feet and opened my bedroom door just as Miranda slammed hers behind her. She had a head start, and I wasn't going to be fast enough to catch her, but that didn't mean I wouldn't try.

"Miranda!" My voice rang out down the hall, but I might as well have whispered because Randi didn't stop.

Her flipflops clapped on the hardwoods beneath her feet with each step she took, and when she rounded the corner to the stairs, her dark hair flashing as it whipped behind her.

Heat fanned my face, but I couldn't tell if it was from my growing anger or the deadly temperatures in south Texas.

My sister took the steps two at a time, and I knew if I didn't catch her before she made it out the front door that I wasn't going to. I hated this cat and mouse game the two of us played. It wasn't fair to her or me. I had never wanted the role of surrogate mother any more than Miranda wanted me to have it. In my mid-twenties, I should be starting my own life, not picking up the pieces of the one Mama had left behind.

"Get back here, young lady." I sounded just like our mom had years ago, and it made me cringe. But I couldn't help myself. I wouldn't have to step in to fill that role that both of us needed to have filled if Miranda weren't so keen on acting like a child.

With every step my feet landed on, I was reminded of just how backward all of this was. Daddy should be chasing his daughter down. He should be doing the disciplining. But even if Randi wouldn't admit it, she needed me in this role. The problem was she needed me to be her sister, too. And I just wasn't cut out to be both. It wasn't possible. Mothers disciplined; sisters conspired.

If I were just her sister, I could encourage her to go out, have a good time. Defy the rules. Be with her boyfriend. I could help her sneak out, take her places she was too young to go, confide in her, share secrets with her. Despite how much I wanted that relationship with my little sister, we'd had that stolen from us the day Mama left us alone with a man who wasn't designed to be a single father of two girls.

Without so much as a glance over her shoulder, Randi grabbed the handle and flung open the door just as Austin's truck entered the circular drive in front of our house. Her friends shouted words of encouragement, and someone let the passenger door fly open. Randi leaped from the top step on the porch to the gravel drive below, took two steps, and reached out to grab her best friend's hand. The truck never slowed down, the kids only got louder, and Randi believed she'd won as she hung her head out of the window after closing the door. A wicked grin parted her lips, and her hair whipped around her cheeks.

I hollered her name one last time, but it was pointless. At the top of the front stoop, I watched my sister defy me with glee. My chest heaved from racing from my room to the porch, and I was so mad I could spit nails. And in that moment, with her friends hurling childish insults and my sister proud of what she'd done, I snapped.

Miranda Adams had gone too far this time.

Not only had she disobeyed me, but she'd defied Daddy, and I, for one, was tired of her immature antics.

My fists were so tightly clenched at my side that my nails broke through the skin in my palm, but I didn't notice until I grabbed my keys from the bowl by the door. I wiped the smattering of blood on my jean shorts and stomped out to my car. There was only one place Randi and her friends would go, and if I had to follow her there and make a scene, then that's what I planned to do. She'd be mortified, but it served her right.

The steering wheel was scalding hot, and I'd swear I heard the blood on my hands sizzle, but that might have just been my anger bubbling over. I rolled down the windows until the air conditioner had a chance to kick in and barreled down our long, gravel driveway. The crunch of the rocks under the tires normally soothed me, but today they were like grit in my eye and nothing more than an irritant that kept me from proceeding at the speed I preferred.

The wind did its best to rip at my ponytail, and the sun tried to blind me. The long, country road to the lake spread out ahead, and the heat shimmer created a mirage on the asphalt. I pulled down the visor to stop the light from directly hitting my pupils; those bright golden beams were just enough to obstruct my vision.

And then my world shattered.

I wasn't sure which happened first, or maybe it all happened simultaneously. Shards of glass rained on my arms and legs and lap and nicked at my cheeks, imbedding themselves beneath the skin. The whoosh of multiple airbags deploying rushed my ears just before the seatbelt locked, and I was pinned against the seat.

Everything hurt from my head to my toes, so much so that I couldn't identify where one ache started and another began. Each movement caused unfathomable pain, all while the smell of gasoline and an electrical fire singed my nostrils. I had to get free, but despite my best effort, there wasn't a single muscle I could move successfully. Either, I was pinned or paralyzed; I couldn't decide which.

Darkness crept along the edges of my vision as panic set in. I had to get out, but I couldn't formulate a complete thought much less escape. I didn't know what I'd hit or even if the car was upright. Based on the way my head spun and weight pressed on my shoulders, I had to be upside down. The strap across my chest pulled so tightly there was no other explanation, but it might have been my imagination.

I hung in some surreal dimension that had to be just short of hell. My ears rang, and a horn blared non-stop on top of the white noise I couldn't silence. Smoke billowed from somewhere, but I couldn't see beyond the crumpled metal to know if it came from the engine. I fought like crazy to pry my lids open, to stay alert.

But the darkness came in like a thief in the night, blotting out more and more of my vision until all that remained were silvery spheres that glimmered like bubbles. Just as my eyes closed, a piercing cry floated around me. It could have been a scream for help or someone writhing in pain. I wanted to holler, yell for someone to save me from this agony, but my tongue grew thick.

And then everything went black.

2

CHARLIE

This was the last place I wanted to be, but I had questions about the work I was doing for Jack on his ranch, and just because his life had stopped, didn't mean mine could. Someone had to keep his cattle and land watered, or he'd have far bigger issues than just Sarah when his ranch met its demise. My parents had thought it was a good idea for me to use this as an excuse to come check on Jack and Sarah. My mom had even sent me with a plate of food because she knew Jack wouldn't have eaten. That's what women in this town did. They fed people. A lady had a baby, they got casseroles. Someone got married, they catered the reception. Funeral—food. It was some Southern tradition that had passed from generation to generation, and I doubted I would ever understand it. But it did give me a reason to show up the day after the second tragedy of Jack's life fell on his shoulders.

I didn't have a clue where he might be. I imagined in

whatever waiting room was closest to Sarah, but this was so far out of my comfort zone that I was lost. I started in the emergency room since that's where Randi and Austin had last seen Jack. I didn't have the details of that encounter but based on what my little brother had told my mom, it hadn't been pretty.

The antiseptic smell singed my nostrils as soon as I passed through the sliding glass doors and into the emergency room—or maybe it was the death they were trying to cover up that made my head hurt. I hated this place. Time seemed to stop inside these walls. People could wait for hours with a broken bone while others were rushed in and out on gurneys. Nurses and doctors scurried about like their tales were on fire, but then the woman at the nurses' station barely batted an eye. Nothing about her demeanor or her day looked hectic or frazzled. For a place that handled emergencies, nothing appeared to move. No one seemed to go anywhere. And by the time a staff member finally acknowledged a patient, it was only to usher that person to another room to wait.

I glanced around the ER and didn't see Jack or anyone else I knew, so I stepped up to the desk to ask the nurse where I could find them. She pointed me toward the elevator and to the seventh floor where Sarah was in surgery.

Even if Jack hadn't been the only person in the waiting room when I made it onto the floor, he would have stood out like a sore thumb. The man looked like he'd aged a decade overnight. His eyes were weary, and bags clung to them. I'd never noticed the weathered appearance of his skin from years out in the sun, but today, every wrinkle, scar, and divot was prominently displayed. And his knee bounced like a jackhammer.

"Hey, Jack." I took a seat next to him with the tinfoil-covered plate of food my mom had sent for him still in my hand.

He turned toward me, patted my knee, and gave me the feeblest attempt at a smile I'd ever seen. Fear clung to Jack like a wet shirt, and it wasn't a pretty sight. "Hey, son."

It wasn't unusual for Jack to use terms of endearment with me. I'd grown up with him at my table, in the pew next to me at church, and I'd worked with him for the better part of my adult life. But somehow, it seemed odd when his daughter's life hung in the balance.

"How's Sarah?" There wasn't an easy way to ask, and ignoring the circumstances would just be rude.

He ran a frail hand through his greying hair. "She's in surgery, but she hasn't woken up since the accident." Jack tried to sound optimistic, but his eyes gave him away.

I handed him the plate and shrugged. "Mom thought you might be hungry."

"She means well, Charlie. It's just what women do." He brought the plate to his nose. "Fried chicken?" he asked, the corner of his mouth tipping up.

I chuckled. Mom was famous around here for her chicken. "Yeah. She made it just for you. There was a peach cobbler in the oven when I left there a little while ago." I shook my head. "Leave it to the women in this town and you'll be fatter than butter."

Jack stood abruptly. I watched as he traveled the length of the room and back. If he were here very long, he'd wear a path into the floor. I didn't do small talk, and I sucked at empathy. I had questions I needed answers to, but I couldn't bring myself to cut to the chase. Instead, I sat in awkward silence. Jack returned to his seat, and that knee went to bouncing. He propped his elbow on the other thigh and covered his mouth. I could only imagine the thoughts that crossed his mind and the emotion that squeezed his heart. He'd lost his wife when she'd just up and left him eight or nine years ago—losing his daughter would destroy him.

I wanted to ask if there was anything I could do—I knew there wasn't—but he didn't appear to want to talk. I respected that, and I just waited by his side. I had things to do, but at the end of the day, it all paled in comparison to Jack's daughter's life. I didn't have a lot of details, but I could only imagine what kind of shape she was in after her sedan had been T-boned by a semi.

I finally broke the silence. "Can I get you some water? Coffee?" The lazy pop music that was piped through the waiting room only added to the stench of death, and I needed to move.

Jack nodded with his face still in his hands. Sweat beaded at his brow and slid down his craggy cheek. I wanted to offer him more than a bottle of water from a vending machine, but right now, I didn't have anything of comfort to suggest.

I stood and brushed off my jeans, and when I turned to ask if he'd like anything else, he'd closed his eyes. I wished my parents had come down here to hold his hand and wait this out instead of me. God help us both if the old man started to cry—I'd be out. I didn't do emotions on women, and there was no way I could handle it on a man. I left him to his business and stepped out into the hall.

While every floor in this place was different, essentially, they were all the same. As I passed a handful of nurses, I opted to head back to the last vending machine I'd seen instead of searching for one up here. It would give me time to compose myself and a few minutes to breathe away from Jack. I circled my way around chairs and meandered down the hall to the alcove with walls of vending machines. And just before I stepped into the alcove, Miranda Adams caught my eye— Sarah's little sister and my little brother's long-term girlfriend.

There wasn't much to her on a good day. She had the petite figure of a cheerleader with tight, toned, and tanned muscles, but I doubted she weighed a buck fifteen soaking wet. But what she lacked in size, she made up for in person-ality. Hers was bigger than life, and everyone loved her, espe-cially my family. Yet, right now, she not only looked small, but she also looked lost—broken. Her eyes darted around the room as if she were searching for someone, and when she didn't find what she was looking for, she wrapped her arms around her middle and stepped up to the intake desk.

Jack had always spoken highly of her. They were tight, even though she tried his patience. She was Daddy's girl and had been going back as far as I could remember. Sarah was the one who always stood on the sideline, never engaging whereas Randi took the bull by the horns and held on for the full eight seconds.

But in the last twenty-four hours, that bond, that tether, that connection had snapped. Randi and Austin were somehow tied up in how the accident came to fruition, but my parents didn't have the big picture, and I wasn't asking Jack for clarification.

For the first time in all the years I'd known Randi—which had been her entire life—that spark was gone. Her flame had been extinguished. She didn't just look worried; she appeared sick—grey.

I couldn't hear what she said to the woman at the desk, but the lady never bothered to look up when she spoke. Not once did she even make eye contact with Randi. My brother's girlfriend trembled as she leaned in closer and spoke again. Then she righted herself abruptly like the sting of a slap had crossed her cheek, and the frustration on her face was evident. And then she lost her composure. "Can you give me *any* update about my sister? Please!"

God, I felt sorry for her.

I glanced around for Austin, unable to believe he'd let Randi out of his sight. Those two were like a matched pair, but I didn't see him. Even without a detailed account of what happened that landed Sarah here, I felt sorry for her sister. Anything she'd done hadn't intentionally brought Sarah here; unfortunately, reckless teenagers cause reckless repercussions. My condolences wouldn't be worth much, and I didn't have any reassurance to offer because I didn't know any more than she did—except which floor her sister and father were currently on.

The only thing the town knew for certain was that Sarah was in a bad way, and it wasn't a given that she would pull through. I hoped like hell Randi didn't have that burden to bear. She'd never be the same, and Jack would never forgive her. He'd all but blamed Randi yesterday, and Austin had stepped between them to keep the old man from hurting his girlfriend. It was best I stayed out of that drama.

I turned my back on Miranda in favor of the vending machines. I fed a few dollars into the machine and waited for the cans to roll out. I downed half of one as if it might provide some clarity or levity—it did neither. The sides of the bottle crunched as I swigged, and I thought about the irony of those sounds and the condition of the tin and wondered if Sarah had been aware of anything as it had happened.

When I left the vending area, Miranda was heading out the door. Her frustration was painted all over her body, and tears streamed down her cheeks. I didn't plan to tell Jack I'd seen her, but I felt a twinge of regret at not stepping up to offer her support. But she had Austin, and Mom had sent me here for Jack.

It dawned on me that in all the years I'd known Randi Adams, I'd never seen her cry.

~

I'd stopped by the hospital again to get Jack to sign off on a finance agreement for equipment he needed for the irrigation project I'd been working on in his fields. He'd barely been at Cross Acres since the accident, and the hospital seemed to be the only place I could track him down with any success.

I found him in the same place I had the other times I'd come for one thing or another. I felt like I spent more time on the road to and from the Anston Medical than actually accomplishing what Jack was paying me to do. But right now, this was the only option. I either came up here, or irrigation stopped. And it wasn't just Jack who was affected. His entire staff needed this monkey off their backs with the drought we were dealing with, I'd planned time away from my family's farm—and Twin Creeks needed me just like Cross Acres did.

No sooner had I sat down and started to explain the paperwork to Jack than a nurse appeared at the double doors that never seemed to open, or they hadn't when I'd been here.

"Mr. Adams?" There was no one else in the waiting room, so I wasn't sure who she thought she might be talking to when she spoke into the air, not once glancing our direction.

Jack's head turned quickly. The only word that described his expression was haggard. "Yeah?"

Her brows lifted a fraction of an inch, and a hint of a smile curled her thin lips. "Sarah's coming around a bit if you'd like to come back to see her." She stepped back to press her back against the door, holding it open for Jack.

Jack sprang to his feet, and before he got two steps toward the door, he turned back to me. "Charlie—"

"Go. We can do this later." It would set me back a day, but I couldn't argue that it was more important than his daughter coming out of a coma. That would have made me a selfish prick, and my mom raised me better than that.

He shook his head. "I was going to ask if you were coming." His energy was infectious, and I could see the gleam of excitement in his eyes—or maybe that was just the hope of an answered prayer.

I didn't know why he wanted me with him, but maybe he just needed moral support. To my knowledge, he hadn't seen Sarah since the incident, and if he had, it had been brief, at best. The doctors had kept her in a medically induced coma to give her body the best shot at survival, and twice, they'd had to revive her when she'd flatlined. No one knew how long any of this would last, and the doctors refused to speculate.

After five days, Jack had started muttering about brain damage and the lingering effects of being under that long. He worried that she wouldn't be able to do anything for herself, that her muscles would forget how to work. It was fear talking because Jack was alone. And it was irrational. But I guessed that was what happened when a parent faced losing their child. It wasn't supposed to happen that way. And while Jack faced losing Sarah, he'd all but run Randi off.

He didn't want my advice or my input, so I didn't offer it.

Jack had made a mistake with Randi. She wasn't to blame for the accident any more than Sarah was—it was just that, an accident. But he blamed Randi, and I wondered if he would ever forgive her. But even now, there wasn't anything I could say regarding either situation. So, I did what I did best; I kept my mouth shut and followed him behind the metal doors.

I should have considered what I was doing before I'd blindly allowed myself to be led into Sarah's new reality. I'd dealt with some pretty gruesome situations on ranches around town with cattle that had become prey, sick animals, traps, and everything in between, but there was something vastly different about an animal that had been mangled and a human.

Sarah was hooked up to every machine imaginable. Wires, cords, IVs, there was so much crap hanging from her body that it was almost hard to find her. And then I realized, I couldn't find her because I didn't recognize her. My stomach twisted and threatened to revolt at the carnage. There wasn't an inch of visible skin that wasn't marred by bruising, swelling, cuts, stitches, or some other injury I couldn't even define. The girl looked dead. The only life in the room was the constant hum and beeps of the machines that forced her to breathe. And I had no idea what they had stuffed in her mouth, but it looked like a torture device. It would hurt like hell when they took the tape off her cheeks.

"She's just starting to come out of the sedation," the nurse warned as she pulled a sheet over the thin gown that covered Sarah's lifeless body. "So she may not be very responsive. But you can say hello." The nurse patted my shoulder as she walked by. "She can hear you. Don't be afraid to talk."

Jack moved to his daughter's side with caution while I stood at the foot of the bed. He scooted a chair from the corner next to the mattress and took a seat. He hesitated, clearly unsure of where he could touch her that wouldn't cause her pain. In the end, he decided on her pinky and ring fingers that were already bandaged together. Jack held that section of her hand tenderly and stroked tiny circles on her knuckles, managing to ignore the wires that spiraled off the back of her hand and the oxygen monitor on her index finger.

"Sarah, sweetie." His voice cracked as he attempted to contain his emotion. It was barely a whisper. "It's Daddy. Can you hear me?"

The machines around her beeped a rhythm that would haunt me for the rest of my life. It wasn't the cadence of a strong heartbeat; it was like "Taps," marking her trail to death. I hated it, and I wanted the hell out of here. Yet, here I stood with a stack of papers rolled up in my hand at the end of a hospital bed, staring at a girl I barely knew. She'd always been so reserved and closed off. It hadn't mattered that she was pretty because she was a snob in high school. And even as that thought crossed my mind, the one that countered that wracked me with shame. Nothing about her current situation was pretty.

Sarah moved her head a little, and her eyes fluttered open. She stared up at him with big blue orbs the same color as an afternoon sky.

Just the sight of his daughter's eyes was nearly his undoing. Jack fought against the onslaught of emotions as he broke in front of me. But he didn't give a damn who saw it. After five days of not knowing, he held her hand and looked into her baby blues. That was all he cared about.

All of the pain, the waiting, the suffering...it came to a head in that moment, and I felt like a fraud witnessing this deeply personal scene between a father and his daughter.

Her lips were chapped, and she tried to speak around the tube in her mouth. When she realized it wasn't possible, her eyes filled with tears. And then she closed them as the machine inhaled for her. Sarah was confused, disoriented, and when her lids parted again, she didn't appear to recognize her dad or me. As she frantically searched the room, her bright blue irises dashing from one thing to the next, it dawned on me. It wasn't that she didn't recognize us; she didn't have a clue what was going on.

I nudged Jack's chair with my foot, not wanting to startle Sarah or draw attention to myself. Although the moment he turned toward me, I realized I'd done just that. "I don't think she knows what happened." I tried to whisper to keep Sarah from hearing me, but she stared at me, waiting for an answer.

It made sense. The last thing she likely remembered was a tractor-trailer slamming into the side of her car—or hell, she may not even remember that. And now she was lying in a dimly lit room, unable to speak, and likely in a shit-ton of pain. I didn't say anything, though. I didn't even move to the side of the bed. Sarah and I weren't tight regardless of the fact that we'd gone to school together since kindergarten and her family ate dinner at my parents' house more often than not. We didn't run in the same social circles, and Sarah Adams would never have sullied her name with the likes of me. In fact, my being here only added to her confusion. And again, I wanted to stop, drop, and roll—right on out of this room.

"I'm so glad to see you, sweetheart." Jack leaned over and kissed her forehead.

A soft mewl escaped from her chest, but I couldn't tell if it was happiness or pain that caused the noise. The nurses were already starting to close in so they could usher us out. All the cliché lines I'd heard uttered in movies came flying out of their mouths. *It had been a big day. She was confused. He could come to see her again in the morning.* I stopped listening after that. None of it applied to me, but even though I'd stopped listening, I hadn't stopped watching.

Sarah's eyes tracked my movement around the room, even as her lids grew heavy. I gave her an awkward wave, and she looked away. That one gesture—my poor attempt at being friendly—seemed to have caused her more pain than the poking and prodding the nurses did at her side. I tried not to overanalyze it. My attendance hadn't been intentional, and I'd give her space and privacy going forward...once I got Jack to sign the papers still wadded up in my hands.

~

B efore I drove out to Laredo, I decided to stop by Cross Acres to locate Jack. It was possible that one of his ranch hands knew where he was if he weren't on the ranch. When I turned down his gravel driveway, I passed the ornate wrought-iron gates that were always dripping with vines and colorful flowers. I'd asked once who kept them up, and Jack told me that was Sarah's doing. I wondered if Randi would take care of them in her sister's absence.

I breathed a sigh of relief when I found Jack's F-350 parked in the circle in front of the farmhouse. At the very least, it meant I didn't have to make the forty-five-minute trip to Laredo or traipse all over town to track him down. Instead of pulling into the drive behind him, I parked in front of the barn next to what appeared to be Austin's truck. I hopped out of the cab, wondering what my brother was doing here at seven in the morning. I knew he'd been spending a ton of time with Randi, but this was early even for them.

And then Austin came out of the barn, reins in hand, and Randi's horse behind him. The scowl that marred his brow didn't encourage me. Unfortunately, he stopped and waited for me to come to his side.

"Hey, man. What are you doing? Where's Randi?" I jerked my head toward the horse no one else ever touched.

His lip curled, an expression I'd never seen when his girl-friend's name came into play. That girl was the light of my little brother's life. They had been an item before they knew what an item was. In some twisted Harlequin-type romance, he'd claimed her when they were like ten, and he lived by that promise like it was an oath. "The million-dollar question." He took a step away as if that ended the conversation.

I grabbed his bicep. "What gives, man? You two okay?" They never so much as fought.

Austin cocked his head to the side and then looked around like I'd missed something written in the sky. "What do you think, Charlie? Does it look like shit's good?"

I'd stepped in something, and I could smell it. I just didn't know what it was. "You're being pretty cryptic—"

"She fucking left, Charlie. Gone." He threw his hands into the air, startling the palomino at his side. "*Poof*—like a damn magician." Austin seemed to think I should know who *she* was and what he referred to, but I was lost.

"What are you talking about?"

He clenched his fist at his side and gritted his teeth before he answered. "Randi!"

I couldn't have heard him right. "Adams?"

"Jesus, Charlie, are you listening to me? Yes! Miranda Adams."

"She'd never leave Mason Belle, much less without you. You sure she didn't just run off with Chasity for a night?"

His nostrils flared, and his eyes narrowed. "She's gone, Charlie. As in not coming back."

The screen door into the kitchen banged, and I turned to see who it was. Jack made his way toward us when I faced my brother again. "Says who? And if she's gone, what the hell are you doing here at seven in the morning, anyhow?"

He shrugged, some of his anger dissipating and kicked the gravel underfoot. "Jack needed help. He told Mom and

Dad last night. She just left. He doesn't know where she went."

"That doesn't make any sense." And it didn't.

Randi grew up in this town, and it was small. People never left Mason Belle, especially not the ones whose families had been here for generations, which hers had. They also owned the largest share of the county, had the biggest cattle ranch for miles, and everything she loved was inside our town limits—including my brother.

I clapped him on the shoulder when Jack joined us. "I'm sure she's just rattled about everything going on with Sarah. Don't get discouraged, Austin. She'll be back. She loves you."

I'd never seen my brother look so lost and downtrodden. He nodded, turned to Randi's horse, and mounted the beautiful animal. I shook my head and gave Jack my attention. "Randi's going to castrate him when she sees him on that horse." I chuckled, but Jack didn't join in.

Jack's stare followed Austin as he rode out into the pastures. "He's a good boy."

He was right; my brother was a good kid. Before I could ask about what had him in such a tizzy and why he believed Randi had left town, Jack motioned toward the house.

"I need to sign that paperwork for you. And I have a check inside." He led the way, and I didn't change the subject.

I'd been trying to track him down for deposits, signatures, and green lights for days. It had started to test my patience, but I tried my best to consider his circumstances anytime my temper started to flare or I got agitated.

We went in the same door he'd just come out. It clanged behind us, and I thought about how that noise was common to every house in this area. It was as familiar as Mom's fried chicken or apple pie.

"Have a seat, son. I'd offer you some coffee or breakfast, but Sarah does all that around here. I'm not one for the kitchen. Might make you sick if you ate after me." He chuckled, but the smile didn't reach his eyes.

I sat at the breakfast table and waited for him to join me. "How's she doing?"

"Sarah?"

My head bobbed.

Jack removed his cowboy hat and set it on the table next to him. His weathered hand pushed his hair back, and he let out a slow, low sigh. "She ain't good, Charlie."

"She's only been out of the coma for a little bit. Give her some time, Jack. That was a pretty serious accident."

"Doctors don't know if she'll walk again. I haven't had the heart to tell her."

I blanched. "What do you mean? Isn't that the doctor's job?" I leaned back in the chair and crossed my arms. "Plus, isn't it a bit early to start making those type of proclamations? Yeah, she's banged up, got some broken bones, stitches, and a hell of a lot of bruises, but she'll mend."

His Adam's apple bobbed heavily in his throat when he swallowed. And when his eyes pooled, I realized he'd had to swallow a large lump to speak. "It's the spinal cord injury they're worried about. Not the other stuff. Not to say that all of those things aren't concerns as well. But her back—it's bad."

"Can you get a specialist in? Make sure she gets the best money can buy?"

It wasn't like Jack didn't have it; the family was loaded. They owned their land, the house, and the cattle outright. He was the only man in town that didn't have a loan of any kind at the bank. He paid cash for everything. The paperwork he was signing for equipment wasn't because he couldn't pay his share, it was the other three ranchers around him that needed him to co-sign so he could help them irrigate *their* land. It benefited all of the property owners, but the fact still remained, Jack could have a back doctor here from Dallas or Houston in no time.

"It's in the works. As soon as she's stable enough, we're moving her to an in-patient treatment facility where she can get full-time, round the clock physical therapy and rehabilitation. It's the best chance she'll have at any type of normal life." He dropped his head, and I wondered if he was going to lose his grip. "I've contacted several plastic surgeons, too." There was shame in his eyes when he lifted his head. "A girl who can't walk in a ranching community needs brains and beauty to help land her a husband. I gotta give her the best shot I can."

"Huh?"

The old man had clearly flipped his lid. Maybe he was just sleep-deprived and hadn't gone batshit crazy, but this was insanity. He could not tell his twenty-four-year-old daughter that she needed plastic surgery just in case her legs didn't work when this was all over.

"She wouldn't have been in that car if I hadn't made her deal with Randi. I should have been the one chasin' my girl down. Not Sarah. Randi got off scot-free while Sarah's laid up in a bed, and God—" A sob ripped from his throat. He covered his mouth with his hand, and I sat in the most uncomfortable position I'd ever endured.

I didn't know if I should hug him, wait for him to stop crying, or what. I sucked at this type of thing; that's what women were for, but the only women in Jack's life were his daughters. Right now, both were unavailable. "It was an accident, Jack. No one's to blame. Not you, not Sarah, and not Randi."

"I wish I believed that."

3

SARAH

Time had slowed to a crawl once they transferred me to the rehab center. It wasn't like the hospital where people had come to visit and there were always nurses or doctors in an out of my room. The afternoons passed by hot and lazy because just like at home, the air conditioners couldn't keep up with the blazing summer heat.

I kept my single window at the facility open even if all it did was invite in the warm, sluggish breeze and humidity. But it brought the smells of home with it—cattle, dirt, fresh grass, all the things I missed. I wanted to be back out in the thick of it or as much as I ever was. I might not have been in the fields working the head, but I missed cooking for the hands, doing the books, keeping track of the business side of the ranch. Even the trivial things like community events were passing me by as I stared at four walls and endured hours of painful therapy and isolation. I'd give anything for my life to return to normal.

The reality of that never being a possibility stared me in the face, and it was a cold, hard fact I needed to address. My life would never be normal again; nothing about it would. All I could do was stare out the open window at the blue Texas sky and wish I were underneath it. Then the idea of that warmth hitting my skin while the backs of my thighs stuck to the seat of a wheelchair hit me full force. It wasn't the part about my life not being normal that bothered me; it was the never walking again that I couldn't bear.

Daddy, the doctors, the nurses—they'd all whispered and talked in hushed voices just outside my room. None of them believed I'd come out of this mobile. They just hadn't dared to say it to my face. They'd expressed their sympathy to Daddy but not once to me. And when I'd asked—countless times—I'd been patronized with a pat on the arm or shoulder and told no one knew what my body was capable of doing.

I couldn't conceive of a meaningful life in a ranching community where I couldn't be of service. Not walking in a ranch town meant not working, and that didn't leave much of an optimistic outlook. Men in Mason Belle married women who were valuable to their businesses, and their businesses were their land. I'd always prided myself on being an asset to Daddy and hoped that someday a man would see that and find worth in it. But being bedridden or wheelchair-bound would only make me a burden to a man who already had acres depending on him. And a girl without a husband in Mason Belle was as useless as a slaughterhouse without cattle.

Thinking about all of it was overwhelming, so I did the

best I could to keep my thoughts to myself, to cry when I was alone, and pretend like I was unaffected by the hidden prognosis. Daddy didn't need to know where I was mentally, no one did. The last thing he needed was for me to fall apart, and it would kill him to think I was so unhappy. I should be grateful to be alive, but the truth was that I wasn't. Even Daddy had a hard time disguising his disappointment when he'd come to visit and find out that my physical therapy had been no more productive today than yesterday. I saw his unspoken pain at the scars the plastic surgeons hadn't been able to remove and my inability to stand from my wheelchair.

He couldn't take care of me for the rest of his life. Ever since Mama left, it had been my job to take care of him. That's what daughters do when their fathers are older and single. They make sure they eat, that they have coffee, that the bills are paid and the house is clean. I was failing at such basic tasks, more and more every day. I had to find something. A solution. This wasn't sustainable.

It also hadn't escaped my attention that I hadn't seen my sister once. I wanted to believe it was because she was filling in for me at home, but I doubted that very seriously since Daddy hadn't once mentioned it. In fact, he hadn't brought up her name at all. Part of me wondered why, but a greater part of me didn't care to hear the answer. Any time I'd tried to broach the subject of my little sister, Daddy had avoided the topic or changed it altogether. Once or twice he'd muttered a bitter reply that I hadn't been brave enough to challenge, but what it boiled down to was she wasn't here.

And he never insinuated she would be—not now or later. Daddy didn't offer to find her or bring her by. And now that I thought about it, he typically ended up leaving shortly after her name was mentioned. He'd tell me not to worry and get some rest. I heard that ten times a day if I heard it once.

All the rest in the world wasn't going to fix my back or make me walk again or erase the visual reminders of all I'd been through. And it certainly wouldn't repair my relationship with my sister, which, I had a sinking feeling, had been irreparably damaged. Whatever little had remained between us had gotten flipped by the semi and shattered like the glass in the car. I'd do anything to remedy it if I could.

But I didn't know why Miranda was avoiding me in the first place. Maybe she felt the same guilt I did over that day, or maybe she blamed me for how it changed her life after. She'd always been Daddy's little girl, and all of his attention now seemed focused on me. I didn't even want to consider the financial burden this put on our family—maybe she resented me for that. It was nothing more than a guessing game I couldn't win since Miranda wasn't around and Daddy refused to talk about her.

There was a tap at the door. "Hey, sweetheart. What's got you so deep in thought?" Daddy came into the room with an easy grin on his face, carrying a bag of food that smelled delicious.

That was one nice thing about the rehab center; they didn't care about food being brought in; whereas, the hospital insisted patients ate the food they served...gross.

In his other hand, he held a beer bottle with a few sprigs

of daisies and marigolds coming out the top. He'd likely cut them from the gate at the front of the property. I hoped someone was taking care of my flowers, or they'd be a lost cause when I finally got to them. I couldn't help but chuckle at his choice of containers, but that was Daddy.

"Thank you." The reminder of home was perfect. "They're beautiful. Is Miranda helping to keep up with them?"

He set the bag and the bottle onto the table tray that pivoted across my lap. "You're welcome." And he promptly evaded my question.

"Daddy?"

"Yeah?" He continued to fiddle with moving the tray so I could reach the food, and then he found a seat in the corner.

"What's going on with Randi?" It was time we faced this head-on. I wasn't going to let him off the hook.

I searched his face for any signs of what he might be hiding, but his rugged features gave away nothing. He just held my gaze, gentle around the corners of his watery grey eyes.

"Sarah." He dropped his elbows to his knees and his head into his hands. "We need to talk about your sister."

My heart stopped. The last time I'd seen that haunted look in my father's eyes—the one I'd caught just before he'd hidden his face—was the day he had told me Mama wasn't coming back. *Ever.* And to this day, I'd never seen or heard from her again.

I nodded, terrified of what he had to say. "Is she okay?" I almost couldn't bring myself to formulate the words. They had stuck to my tongue like peanut butter, and I'd nearly choked when they finally came out. I searched his face, hoping that if there were any bad news, a single twitch might betray it early.

Daddy didn't pick up his head. He didn't meet me eye for eye. "She left, sweetheart."

"What do you mean she left?" I bellowed so loudly I was certain the patients in the rooms on either side of me not only heard my shout but likely felt it. "How could she just leave?"

He finally met my stare, but I was so livid and full of disbelief that I didn't let him speak before I continued my tirade.

"So once again, Randi makes a huge mess and just waltzes away from it without a care in the world? Is that how things work?" I winced when I slammed my hands down on the mattress, jarring my still sore fingers. "That girl is so irresponsible. A minute in the pressure cooker and responsibility kicks her tail so hard she runs out of town. And what about Austin? Did he go, too?"

Sadness clung to my father's expression, but he didn't say a word. He just shook his head.

"Unbelievable. Only Miranda Adams would have the balls to think she can just up and leave to make it on her own, without so much as a goodbye. Poor Austin. I bet he's heartbroken."

Daddy's knee bounced in the corner, and I knew he was upset. They were close, always had been. Regardless of how angry I was at Randi, I couldn't imagine the strain it put on

Daddy. The second woman in his life walked away from him, right after the only other had almost died.

I shook my head and blew out a heavy breath. "She's selfish, Daddy. But don't worry, she can't make it on her own. She barely even has a high school diploma, and we both know she won't do manual labor." I half chuckled at the thought of my sister trying to find a job and a place to live. It was laughable, but I was too ticked off to give it any real consideration. "I bet she's back in a week.

I nodded at my own suggestion of Randi's reality. I could concede to that, make that my truth. Still, it hurt...a lot. Maybe I was the problem. I'd like to think my little sister had grown a conscience the day of the accident and she was just so overcome by guilt that she had to get out. Miranda had never been good at facing consequences, only living in the moment. And whether that was a blessing or a fault, it didn't matter. My gut twisted with guilt.

I had driven my sister away. I searched Daddy's face to see if he blamed me, too. I couldn't see anything past the morose expression that pulled his mouth into a forlorn frown.

"It was my fault, wasn't it?" I couldn't stop myself from asking. I needed to know if this, my being here, was what had caused her to run.

"Oh, no." He sat up and ran his hand through his hair, and it wasn't until that moment that I realized how old my father had gotten. "It's not your fault, Sarah. Your sister..." He stopped to consider something. "She was always going to go her own way. We both knew that."

We did. I'd just never considered that her way would be out of town and alone. No part of me ever believed she'd do anything without Austin. They were inseparable and had been since they were kids. They were more than just high school sweethearts; they were best friends, the epitome of soulmates. They'd both be lost without the other.

Before I could ask about Austin, Daddy stood and came toward me. He pushed my hair back from my face and leaned down to kiss my forehead. "I'm going to get out of here. Get some rest, sweetheart."

And just like that, the subject had once again been closed.

The next morning a new physical therapist came for her first visit. The first of many. And I knew the moment I saw her that I would hate every single one. She just looked severe. There wasn't a soft edge to the woman, and when she opened her mouth, she only confirmed my suspicion.

"Hey, Sarah. I'm Karen." She had a tight red bun perched at the crown of her head, and her nose was as straight as her thin lips. Frankly, she was a bit scary.

"I'm not going to like this, am I?" I didn't mean to sound ornery right off the bat, but she could have given me a little friendlier introduction, one that consisted of more than four words.

Her green eyes met mine, and her pupils were tiny. The

way she looked through me sent a shiver up my spine. "Not if you're looking for an easy fix." Well, that was pointed. "But if you're serious about the possibility of regaining mobility, then you'll suck it up and put in the work." Karen gave me the once over, and apparently didn't seem to think I was up for the task. "You need to be committed one-hundred percent. If not, you're wasting my time and yours."

I didn't even know what I was committing to being all in for, but I was afraid to tell Karen no. I bit the inside of my cheek until I tasted blood and nodded.

"I hoped you would be because today we're getting you upright and taking some steps." She flipped open her clip-board and clicked the end of her pen. She checked off a few boxes and then set it all down on a table.

She had to be joking. No one believed I'd ever walk again, much less a couple of months after the accident. This couldn't be right, but I refused to open my mouth to challenge her, either.

"Today we're going to work on some basics. I know you're in pain, but you're going to need to figure out how to harness that into motivation. I want to push you right to the edge of unbearable." Her eyes met mine, and for a second, there was a softness there. "You with me?" She didn't really leave any room for argument.

"I can try." I wasn't convinced, and my tone conveyed that. It wasn't that I didn't want to be up and moving. I did. But nothing worked right on my body, and I had an immobilizer on my back that made me stiff as a board.

But when I set aside all the excuses, the only one that I

had left was fear. Up until this point, it had all been speculation. No one knew for certain what my body might do. This was the pivotal point. This was where I found out what kind of courage and strength I really had...and I was worried it wouldn't be enough.

Karen didn't give me an inch and certainly didn't attend my pity party for one. She pulled out what looked like a giant green rubber band. "Here's how we're going to start."

When Karen left an hour later, my whole body felt like it was on fire. There was not a part of me that didn't hurt, ache, or burn—and not in that good way that made me feel like I'd accomplished something. I didn't think the staff would give me enough narcotics to make the rest of the day bearable. And I knew it wasn't over. Karen wouldn't be the only therapist that graced me with her presence today. I wasn't that lucky.

4
CHARLIE

Jack Adams was getting harder and harder to pin down. And when I was able to locate him, his mind was everywhere but on the task at hand. We didn't live in a huge town, but that man was covering more square miles than everyone else in the county combined.

I wound up at the hospital because I couldn't find him at home, the bank, the hardware store, or my parents' house. It had been almost a week since Sarah's last surgery, and Jack was scrambling to keep things in order. Sarah was back in the hospital, recovering. I didn't know when they'd move her to the therapy center again since they had her in physical therapy at the hospital. I just knew it would happen because Jack had said it would.

I'd done my best to avoid the hospital since the day she'd woken up, but after the surgery to try to repair her spinal cord, Jack was practically living here again. I think it had more to do with Sarah's mental state than his need to be present for anything going on. He floated back and forth to check up on her and keep her company. I knew that was the case, and I still went looking for him like a fool.

I should have just picked a spot and waited for him to come to me.

I wound through the hospital's impossible walkways until I finally found Sarah's room. They had moved her for the umpteenth time. Every time I'd finally memorized the path from the parking lot to the elevators and through the corridors that all looked identical, the nurses moved her to a different room or facility altogether. And with each move came a more obscure location. I was beginning to believe there was a conspiracy to hide her from Jack and in turn, torture me when I went looking for him. Although, now that I thought about it, it might have been a ploy to distract Jack. He was getting more and more difficult, if the nurses' gossiping in the hallway were to be believed.

He was just wound a little tight, that was all. It was his little girl in that hospital bed—his firstborn. And with Miranda gone, well, he had even less help than he did before. But that was a topic I didn't dare broach with him or my little brother. The entire town was up in arms about Sarah's accident and Randi's disappearance, but I knew to leave well enough alone. My mom didn't raise a fool—gossip was better left to women.

Austin and I did all we could to help Jack out around Cross Acres. Sometimes it didn't feel like enough. Sometimes it felt like all I could do was watch from a distance as the family played out their misery in front of me. I knew that even with Sarah's improvements, Jack was not very happy. He had thought he was going to lose one daughter, and he ended up losing the other, instead. In an entirely different way. But the one time I'd been around to hear anyone ask Jack about Randi, the expression on his face said more than words ever could—she might as well have been dead. That distant look that washed over his eyes was the same kind that people got when reminiscing about a grandmother who had long since passed.

It was a strange set of circumstances and getting more bizarre every day. I took a deep breath when I got close to Sarah's door, bracing myself for whatever stood on the other side.

She sat alone. If I had to guess, I'd bet that her dad had been there but had already left for whatever reason. Personally, I couldn't imagine what it would be like to leave my little girl alone after all she'd been through. It must have killed him to do it every time he had to step foot out these doors.

Sarah sat with one leg propped up on the edge of the mattress and the other hanging off. I assumed that to be a good sign. There'd been so many days that were touch and go that just seeing her off all the machines was positive. She reached down and stuffed her small hands under her thigh, moving her leg to prop it up next to the other one. It took effort, and I stood mesmerized by the willpower and determination she must possess to get through this. I wanted to help, but I wasn't sure how. I just stood frozen in the doorway. She hadn't seen me, and I wondered how long I could wait before it became too awkward for me to make my presence known.

She lifted her hand to her face and dragged her fingers across her nose. While I couldn't see her expression, there was no denying the tears that streaked her cheeks. Maybe she had been crying the whole time I'd watched her. A tear clung to the tip of her nose while others dripped from her jaw, but she hadn't made a sound. She did her best to keep her emotions under control, even when she believed she was alone. Her shoulders rose with each deep breath she took in what I assumed to be an effort to calm down, but every inhalation made her shudder, and her entire body shook.

I wanted to say something—needed to—but I wasn't sure where to begin. Part of me felt ashamed. I shouldn't be witnessing this extremely private moment. The other part of me felt guilty. There wasn't anything I could do to ease her pain. Another small part of me wanted to comfort her. Even knowing that I couldn't stop the discomfort or the struggle she faced, there had to be *something* I could do that was better than lurking in the hallway.

When I finally stepped into the room, Sarah's lifted her head as I crossed the threshold. She immediately dragged her sleeve across her face, soaking up the tears with the arm of her cardigan. Her tiny hands furiously blotted a tissue beneath her lashes. I couldn't discern whether her expression was a scowl or something else akin to mildly distressed—but whatever it was, it obviously hurt. Sarah cleared her expression and returned to the blank slate I'd become accustomed to seeing.

I rapped my fist on the doorframe despite the fact that she'd seen me staring. "Can I come in?" I slid my hands into my pockets as I waited and tried to keep my posture relaxed, inviting. I didn't want her to think that I was just walking in on her most vulnerable moment because I could.

Sarah nodded ever so slightly. "Of course, please." There wasn't a rude bone in the girl's body. It didn't matter how much pain she was in; she'd keep up the Southern demeanor of small-town Texas because that's how she'd been raised.

I didn't miss the way she flinched when she touched the tissue she'd used on her eyes to the angry red scars on her face. It appeared incredibly painful and tight, but I didn't know her well enough to ask and needed to stop staring.

I tried not to read too deeply into the meek tone in which she'd invited me in. It didn't take a genius to see that now wasn't an opportune time for company, but there was a reason for my visit. And while it wasn't Sarah, I did need to find Jack.

"Sorry to barge in. I was just looking for your dad." I tried to appear properly chagrined for my intrusion. I couldn't shake the feeling that she just wanted to be left alone.

Sarah hid her face, deliberating avoiding eye contact. "He isn't here." Even her swallow appeared labored. "If you hurry, you may be able to catch him at home."

I nodded, but I didn't leave. My feet were bolted to the ground, and something compelled me to stay. My boots were rooted in place, preventing me from leaving or moving closer.

"Is that all?" Her words broke the spell. They cut

through the tension that lingered between us like a knife, but instead of pushing me back, they drew me a little closer.

The only time I'd ever seen something so fragile and defeated had been an animal in a trap. Sarah appeared to have lost her will to fight, and I had an overwhelming urge to pull her into my arms. Something in me wanted to whisper into her ear that she'd be all right, that everything would be okay. But despite just how downtrodden she appeared or how heavy her shoulders seemed, I wasn't the person to bring her hope.

"Yeah." I didn't want it to be, but I sounded like an idiot to my own ears. My mind raced to find something to talk about, something to lift her spirits, but I stood there like a mute. I couldn't imagine what she thought of me. "Are you doing okay?" *That was brilliant.*

She didn't respond other than to swallow hard. The tears welled up again. I could see them getting caught in her throat as she tried to swallow them down, fight them back. She bit her bottom lip and lowered her head, closing her eyes. The tears beaded on her lashes and then streaked down her cheeks.

I might not be great at offering comfort or support, but I couldn't stand to see a woman cry. "Hey." That one word lifted my feet from where I stood, and I moved to sit next to her on the hospital bed.

I took a seat on the mattress not too far away from her but not close enough to make her uncomfortable, either. Sarah grabbed her thigh and shifted her leg toward her to create space for me.

She rolled her lips into her mouth and waved a hand in front of her face. "I'm not trying to make a scene. Daddy would be so embarrassed for you to see me this way." It wasn't a bid for pity.

I was mortified at the idea of anyone trying to make her feel bad about what she was going through. This was one of the hardest times of her life; hell, she was lucky to be alive. If I were ever privy to anyone trying to tell her to suck it up, I'd give them a clear message regarding their behavior. I'd be damned if I didn't put them through a window.

"You're not making a scene." I wasn't great with words and even worse at empathy, so I tried to keep my voice gentle. I tended to have a rather deep timbre, and in this stark room, it reverberated rather forcefully. The last thing I wanted to do was come across as patronizing. "You've been through a lot. I think you're entitled to show some emotion." I needed her to look at me, to give me an indication that she heard me, but I got nothing. "Most people would have cracked under the pressure you've been under. You are an incredibly strong woman."

She shook her head, and her messy blond curls bounced with the movement. "I'm not." Her voice cracked, and I felt it like a knife to the heart. "I'm not strong. Not like everyone keeps telling me I am...." Her shoulders heaved and shuddered as she fought to remain composed. Each time she peered at me through her dark lashes, she'd quickly duck her head to avoid my stare.

Sarah wanted to hide her fear. She wanted to mask her insecurity. Despite whether or not she felt strong, she needed people to continue to believe she was. I felt that in my soul. And then I realized, it wasn't just the weakness she hoped to shadow; it was the disfigurement. Her fingers hovered over the black thread of stitches where her head had been shaved for surgery, and she held her head at just the right angle to camouflage the scars on the other side.

My hand twitched. Before I even realized what I was doing, I reached out to touch her cheeks. But when she'd flinched, I rested it against her knee instead.

"Please, don't look at me, Charlie." It hadn't been an admission exactly, but the sentiment was still the same.

I hadn't been prepared for it, and I tried not to show her just how taken aback I was by her request. "Okay." I didn't want to push the issue, but I didn't want her to believe I agreed with her. "I don't have to look at you if you don't want me to. But for the record, I would *like* to." There was no chance I'd ever be accused of being smooth around Sarah Adams. This version of me was worse than the pre-puberty one.

She huffed out a hard laugh under her breath. It was fast and barely audible and clearly not born from humor.

"I'm not exactly at my best." Her words wavered with her insecurity, and they shook just like her spine did when she inhaled deeply. She licked her lips and then lifted her bright eyes to meet mine—like she dared me to see her flaws. "There's nothing redeemable about my face, anymore." She straightened her spine as if to brace herself for whatever harsh criticism she thought I might impart on her, and her words were strangled as her throat tightened.

I was so far out of my element that I didn't have a clue what to say, but I knew I wanted to keep her talking...about anything. "Is that why you're crying?" I asked. "Are you afraid someone might react to your face?" That hadn't come out as eloquently from my mouth as I had meant it in my head.

She shook her head. "It isn't just that. It *is,* to an extent. But," she sighed, "every day is harder than the last. Nothing gets any easier, and every time I think I'm making progress, I realize that I've gone an inch in an endless stretch of miles. I'm trying to stay positive. I want to be thankful that I survived and have the chance to recover. But today—heck, every day—is hard. So hard. And what's the point? The physical therapists' intentions are better than their capability. They aren't God, and they can't perform miracles."

I nodded and kept listening.

"I'm at the end of my rope, and I think I need to accept that I'll probably never walk again." She dropped her into her hands, careful to avoid the stitches and the abrasions. "I'm drained. I don't have any more fight in me. I know that sounds like the biggest crock of bull you've ever heard, but..." Sarah stopped shaking her head long enough for me to really take her in—it wasn't nearly as bad as she thought.

My heart melted. I wanted to reassure her, but I kept my distance. My hand remained on her knee, and I found myself stroking her soft skin with my thumb. The desire to pull her to me nearly overtook my willpower. God, I wanted to protect her like a runt calf, but I didn't know this girl from Adam. And thus, I remained still.

"You wouldn't understand," she whispered. "No one does. Everyone keeps telling me that I'm lucky to be alive. And I *know* I am. No one is more aware of that fact than me. And when it first happened, that support was almost suffocating. But the world kept spinning for everyone outside these walls. The clouds rolled away, and the threat of my dying passed. People went on with their lives. They stopped panicking. But when the dust settled, it was just *me*."

I squeezed her knee, and she stopped talking long enough to give me a meager smile that hurt me more than it helped. But I didn't let her go, and I didn't stop caressing her skin. She might not realize how much warmth and life she still had in her, but I could feel it in the pads of my fingers.

"Other than Daddy, it's just me, the physical therapists, and countless doctors who won't remember my name the day I'm discharged. All I'm left with is the grueling exercise that isn't producing results. I hope you never know what it's like."

I wondered if anyone else had given Sarah the chance to vent, or if they expected the same woman in here that she had been on the outside. I didn't know her well, but our families were intertwined. I knew how much she did for Jack and that she took care of Miranda after their mama left. She needed someone to take care of her for a change, and it didn't seem she had that. So, I just let her talk and tried to commit every word she uttered to memory.

"All the medication zaps my energy and makes me foggy, but without the pain meds, there's no way I can do the physical therapy. It hurts. All of it hurts so much." A tear slid down her cheek, but she didn't collapse. "What if I never walk again? What if this is the best any of this will ever get? I haven't managed a single step. Not one. I'm just ready to throw in the towel." And with that, she finally stopped. Her shoulders rounded, the tears streamed, and she appeared utterly defeated.

For a moment, my heart refused to beat, and I just stared at her. The absolute hopelessness created a fissure in my chest that cracked open. I ached for the woman in front of me, so much so that I reacted instead of thinking. My hands found her face, and I cupped her jaw without touching any injuries. My thumbs brushed away the tears she couldn't stop, and I couldn't have torn my eyes away from hers if I'd had to.

"Hey," I said. "Listen to me."

She didn't say anything. But she didn't look away, either. Her eyes held mine like she could see through them and into the very essence of me, deeper than anyone else had dared look.

"You can't give up, Sarah."

Her expression softened, but it changed, too. I couldn't pinpoint what it was, but if she weren't riddled with pain, I'd guess it was a hint of elation. I hadn't said anything earth-shattering. Hell, I hadn't even said anything poetic. I started to pull away, but before my touch left her skin, she lifted her hand. Her braced and bandaged fingers rested on top of mine, and she leaned into my palm.

Her eyes smiled, but the tears came faster than they had since I'd walked in the door, and the salty brine seeped under my hands, captured against her cheeks. "What?"

I'd never heard someone sound so panicked in one word —much less myself. "What did I do?" My erratic heart had started beating again, and now my racing pulse was the only thing I could hear. I didn't have a clue what I'd said to upset her, but whatever it was, I'd move mountains to fix it.

She hiccupped in what had to be the cutest display of vulnerability I'd ever witnessed. "It's just..." Her blue eyes sparkled with the first glimpse of hope I'd seen since I stepped into her room. "I didn't even think you knew my name."

My lips turned up in a grin I couldn't resist. Despite the stitches and the scabs, the scars and broken bones, she was the most adorable thing I'd ever seen. Every fiber of my being wanted to pull her in close, to hug her, hold her. But for the first time in my life, I was afraid to touch a woman for fear of hurting her body and my open heart, so I just held her face in my hands.

I planned to stay there as long as she'd let me. Over the conversation that followed, I determined that there were several things about Sarah that I hadn't realize before. First and foremost, she was beautiful. And it was so blatant and obvious that I wondered how I'd never noticed it before. Of course, she had those big, beautiful, doe-like blue eyes that were like pieces of the sky. But there was so much more to it than that. The scars and the bruises, the stitches and casts— they all faded away the longer we sat and talked. Her heart-shaped face came to a point at her cute little chin, and her dirty-blond hair had streaks of sunshine running through it. It was the way she crinkled her nose, the way her mouth moved when she tried not to smile and even worse when she actually parted her lips into a full-blown grin. Christ, she had sensuous lips...as pink as summer flowers and probably just as soft.

Sarah Adams was gentle at her core. And somehow, I'd managed to miss *all* of that for twenty-four years.

"Knock, knock." One of the nurses peeked her head in Sarah's door. "I hate to interrupt, but we need to take you for a scan."

I glanced at the nurse and then back to Sarah. I hated to leave, but I had work to do, and so did she. "I'll get out of your hair."

"It was good to see you." Her tone was fragile as if my response to that statement might somehow break her, and my heart leaped at the notion that I might hold that significance in her life unknowingly. "Daddy should be back soon if you want to stick around. But I don't know how long I'll be."

I rubbed the back of my neck and ducked my head. "Oh, yeah. Well, I'll catch him eventually. I know he'll want to talk to you more than he'd like to talk to me." I smiled sheepishly. "But tell him I stopped by. I'll catch you both later, yeah?" I was already backing out the door too fast; I was going to trip or something on my way out.

A totally graceless exit.

5

SARAH

That moment—time with Charlie—stayed with me long after he had left. I couldn't stop thinking about him. The way he had touched my face, how his gaze almost caressed my soul, and when he parted his lips and my name flowed past—I didn't even realize he *knew* my name.

He'd been under no obligation to stay. I wasn't delusional enough to believe he'd been there for me in the first place. Heck, he'd flat out asked for Daddy, but he hadn't left. Charlie Burin had seen me at my lowest, yet instead of turning up his nose in disgust at my injuries and the aftermath of what the accident had left behind, he'd been tender, gentle, kind. It was a side of Charlie I didn't know existed, and I fell that much harder for the boy whose heart I'd never win. Either way, it had been enough to carry my spirits through the rest of the day, and I woke up today filled with more hope than I'd had since I came out of the coma.

And then, there he was. He appeared early in the

morning with two cups of coffee in his hands, fresh from the cafeteria. The smile that spread across my face was almost embarrassing, but there was just something about Charlie Burin that had always pulled me in, enticed me. Before yesterday, I'd believed it was simply his good looks, incredible body, and Southern charm, but now, it was so much more.

"Is one of those for Daddy?" I teased, hoping he hadn't come to find my father.

He chuckled and shook his head, his sandy brown hair falling into his soft brown eyes. "No, one of these is for you." He extended it to me. "I didn't know how you took it—but I took a stab in the dark and went with black. I can go back down if you want cream and sugar."

"Black is perfect." I was thrilled that he had guessed correctly. I wasn't one of those twelve-creams-and-six-sugars types. I accepted the coffee, nearly dropping it when my hands wouldn't wrap around the cup normally. As I tried to make an accommodation for that malfunction, the immobilizer on my back kept me from reacting quickly.

Charlie didn't miss a beat when he reached out to steady my grasp until I had control of the drink. The cup heated my palms while the simplicity of his action warmed my heart. I knew he wasn't here for me, but the fact that he *was here* kind of made all of this a bit more bearable. His Mama would be proud.

I didn't know what to say when Charlie didn't make himself comfortable. I mean, it was a hospital; there weren't a lot of options for lounging around. I'd give him the bed in favor of being discharged any day, but I didn't think that was going to happen anytime soon, either.

I brought my gaze back to his and peered at him through my lashes as I blew on my coffee. "Daddy stopped by last night and said he was sorry he missed you. He swore up and down that he'd catch up to you." I pursed my lips and made a face that caused him to grin. "Of course, I guess by your being here that I can assume that hasn't happened." I felt bad. I knew Charlie needed my dad's attention to keep Cross Acres running, and our ranch wasn't even his responsibility.

"Not yet, but he's busy. I get it." Charlie took a seat in a chair beside my bed and blew the steam away from the surface of his cup. "I'll pin him down eventually. But I didn't come here looking for Jack."

I lifted my brows in surprise, and I tried to keep my eyes from going as wide as my brows had high.

Charlie didn't miss my shock. He took a sip of his drink, swallowed, and then held his cup on the armrest of the chair —cool as a cucumber and casual as could be. "I came to see you." He was smooth and experienced. Charlie Burin was a practiced flirt, while I, on the other hand, was a novice at best.

Heat rose in my cheeks, which meant a pink blush did as well. And then the vein in my neck began to throb as my heart rate increased at the thought of Charlie Burin driving from Mason Belle to Laredo to check on me. "*Oh.*"

He had game that I didn't know was possible to play. Watching him eye me with confidence almost made me uncomfortable until the right side of his mouth lifted into a sexy smirk. Charlie ran his hand through his overgrown hair and responded like he hadn't just rocked my world. "Yeah."

That was it? I needed way more than one word to carry on a conversation, especially when that one word had not only rendered me stupid but speechless as well.

"I wanted to check on you. You looked pretty bad yesterday."

Insert needle, pop balloon. "Oh." And that one word said more than his "yeah" had implied.

Charlie's smile wavered at my deflated tone, and he realized what he'd said.

He leaned forward and wrapped his fingers around mine, and when I winced, he dropped them as quickly as he'd sat up. "Shit, Sarah." He stared at my hand like it was on fire and he didn't know how to extinguish the flames. And then when he made eye contact with me, he stumbled even more. "That came out wrong." He ran a hand down his face before his shoulders sagged, and he gave me the most innocent look I thought I'd ever seen from Charlie Burin. "I meant I thought you could use some company. Damn. Did I hurt your hand?"

I shook my head and remembered his hands on my jaw, and the temperature in my cheeks rose as I drank from my cup and imagined all the things I wanted those calloused fingers to do to me. I wanted to talk about it—to find out if yesterday meant anything or if it was just a sympathy visit—but I also desperately wanted to stuff down the feelings. Drowning that emotion would cause me far less pain than addressing it. Charlie Burin had made it painfully clear throughout high school that I was *not* the type of girl he took an interest in, and that likely hadn't changed eight years after graduation. I settled on focusing on my expression, stilling it. The less emotion I showed, the safer my heart would be.

Unlike Charlie, I had no experience with any of this. I didn't know if he was flirting or if I was reading his signals wrong. I had never dated. I'd spent my high school years raising my sister after Mama had up and run away. Between that, school, church, and my community obligations, I didn't catch boys' eyes. And at twenty-four-years old, never having been on a single date, I was more like the town spinster. Men didn't look twice at me unless they needed something, and it was never my company.

"Do you have physical therapy today?" He kept his tone light, conversational. Charlie didn't seem to sense my discomfort or chose to ignore it.

I felt a little defeated just by the thought. "Yeah. There are a couple of different people that come in every day." I'd been shocked by how fast the physical therapists started showing up. "They don't want me to get comfortable doing nothing." I giggled, but my chuckle was more of a nervous laugh than brought on by anything funny. "They work my arms, legs, my back—although that's a tough one with the spinal cord injury." I thumbed over my shoulder as if Charlie didn't know where my spine was located and immediately felt stupid.

"Doesn't sound like a lot of fun, but I'm sure the faster they get you moving, the sooner you'll be up and walking. Right?"

The sigh escaped before I could stop it, and my eyes filled with the same stupid tears he'd witnessed yesterday.

As soon as the first one slid down my cheek, Charlie raced to find a safe place to set his coffee and moved to sit next to me on the bed. He used his thumb to swipe under my lashes gently. "What'd I say?" He searched my eyes, clearly confused. "I didn't mean to make you cry. *Shit*." His strong hand lingered on my jaw, and I leaned into his touch, selfishly soaking up his attention. "Talk to me, please." Charlie had never been this flustered in any situation I'd been privy to.

I took a deep breath and readied myself to admit my truth out loud for the first time. Once these words passed my lips, I couldn't retract them, and I feared it would make them true. "There's no guarantee, regardless of how many hours of excruciating therapy I endure, that I'll ever walk again."

He huffed, and a smile replaced the frown on his lips. The muscles in his tanned forearms pulled tight, and I wanted to trace the vein that bulged as he moved. His hand slid from my jaw to the nape of my neck; then he held my stare for one beat longer than was comfortable and leaned in to kiss my forehead. And when he pulled back, there was something—an emotion I'd never seen—glimmering in his chocolate eyes. "But there's no guarantee you won't, either." ·

I wondered what the nurses had given me in my prescription cocktail this morning. I had to be hallucinating because Charlie's Burins lips just touched my body, and it wasn't due to a dare or a drinking game gone wrong. Yet, when I blinked, he was still there, and the coffee on his breath tickled my nose he was so close.

This had to be a dream. Not even Daddy had pretended to be optimistic. He played the role of the realist, following the doctors' and nurses' lead on expectations. He hadn't discouraged me, but he hadn't signed me up to run a marathon, either. Charlie was the first person who'd fool-heartedly believed in me.

He carefully stroked my hair, and his eyes never left mine. "You've got the power to control this outcome, Sarah." He shook his head and raised one shoulder. "What do you choose? Are you going to let it beat you? Or are you going to make therapy your bitch?"

Any other time, Charlie's language would have made me giggle for the sheer fact that it made me uneasy. It was also part of the reason I'd never fit in. Everyone thought I was a goody-goody, but they'd never been responsible for raising their little sister. Today, however, it just made me want to roll my eyes—but I didn't.

"It's not that simple."

The moment he pulled his hand from my neck and set it in his lap, I missed the heat, the encouragement of his touch, and I realized I'd disappointed him. "No. Nothing worth having is ever simple or easy. But I think God gives us the will to move mountains—"

"If only I had the faith of a mustard seed."

He chewed on his lip for just a second before responding. "I think you have the fire and grit to prove everyone wrong."

I let out the deepest laugh, and it rattled my entire body. It hurt in the best possible way. But even through the grimace and the pain, I couldn't help but giggle as I talked. "No one has ever used the word grit to describe any part about me. Miranda, yes; me, absolutely not."

Charlie smirked, and God, I wanted to keep that look on his face forever. "Your little sister is a piece of work. But don't sell yourself short, Sarah. You've got gumption. If you want it, take it. Make it happen." It was as easy as that in Charlie Burin's mind. "Find your piss and vinegar. For God's sake, you're Jack Adam's daughter. It's in there somewhere." He winked, and I gushed.

Something inside me clicked, and I wanted to prove him right—make him proud. It might not have been the right motivation, but it was the only motivation I had. For the time being, I'd take whatever I could get. "Just like that?" I grinned.

He shrugged. "Just like that." Charlie leaned back and used his hand to support him on the mattress. His bicep bulged, and the vein that ran along the top popped out. I'd never salivated over an arm, but I'd be danged if Charlie didn't have me all kinds of bothered in the best possible way. He had the most masculine, rugged body I'd ever seen, and every part of me wanted to trail a finger over every part of him. And he wasn't the least bit affected by my staring. In fact, he seemed to enjoy it. Something passed between us, but I couldn't speculate what it was.

I swear, I felt like he'd summoned the warden. No sooner had he issued me his pep talk and topped it off with a panty-dropping smile than one of the therapists knocked on my door to put me into the torture chambers. It was a slight exaggeration but not by much.

He went to get up. "I'll get out of your hair—"

But I grabbed the tips of his fingers—it was all I could catch with a limited range of motion—and looked up into eyes that could tempt me to lie, cheat, and steal. "Stay?" I didn't know what had come over me. "Please..."

He blinked. Twice. "Stay?"

I licked my dry lips and pulled the bottom one between my teeth as I nodded slowly. "Please." It was pathetic, and I felt like I'd just begged the man to take pity on me. It was stupid, but somehow, Charlie had become my champion in the span of five minutes. I bet he'd think twice about ever bringing an invalid a cup of coffee again.

"Of course." There was zero hesitation.

He didn't even take time to consider what it would do to his day. The man had work to do—more so than normal because my father couldn't be tracked down so Charlie could finish the project on our ranch. He didn't say he needed to make a call or change plans. He just sat in the chair he'd been in before I'd cried and now made himself comfortable... or as comfortable as one could be in a plastic hospital chair.

I really hadn't thought that request through. Initially, I'd believed having someone here, even someone I barely knew, would be a welcome reprieve from the monotony of the therapist and the exercises. And if nothing else, I'd have someone to bear witness to just how awful all of this truly was and possibly confirm that it was terrible. What I hadn't considered was *why* all of this was so horrible. I struggled with everything Michael—the therapist sent by Satan—asked me to do, and I was embarrassed by the number of exercises I couldn't perform while Charlie witnessed my failed attempts.

Michael lowered the bed and helped me onto my side. Once he had me in the position he wanted, he took hold of my leg, gently lifting the dead weight. He cradled my knee in one hand and my calf in the other. His firm grip gave me confidence he wouldn't drop my limb, but as soon as he extended my knee and then bent it back, pain ran up my side, or maybe it was my back. I ground my teeth together, trying to stifle the hiss that passed my lips before I could seal them. To anyone else, this was child's play, but for me, that simple elongation caused my back muscles to engage and fire to burn beneath my skin. Regardless of how hard I gritted my teeth, I couldn't fight the tears when they welled. Crying in the middle of therapy—in front of Charlie— would be beyond humiliating, but no matter what I tried, I couldn't put a damper on the pain. I was seconds away from releasing a blood-curdling yelp when Michael found my eyes.

"Focus on breathing." His instruction was firm and left little room for discussion. "Deep, even breaths." He didn't move my knee while he spoke, waiting for me to align myself with what he'd told me to do. "When I bend your knee, I want you to take a deep breath in, and then as I straighten your leg, release the breath, trying to make the exhale last through the entire movement. Time your intake and exhale with each repetition, focusing on filling your lungs. It will bring oxygen to the muscles and help with the pain."

All I could do was nod. The truth wasn't I didn't know if I could do it. I didn't deal well with pain, and this went beyond anything I'd ever experienced.

"Ready?" Michael waited for my hesitant confirmation. "Here we go, then. Deep breath in, fill your lungs with as much air as possible. In, in, in, in." He chanted as he bent my knee to a ninety-degree angle, pressing my lower back into the immobilizer and my hip into the crummy hospital mattress.

A dull, awful ache shot up my thigh, and my leg began to tremble.

Michael held my knee in that position for just a moment as my back began to relax. "That's perfect. And slowly release it." He extended my knee, straightening my leg as I released the pent-up air from my lungs.

I fought the pain, desperate to show Charlie—and Michael—I wasn't a quitter. Mind over matter, but that wasn't the case. Charlie witnessed an intensely personal, awful, intimate thing that I struggled to endure. The grunts. The groans. The tears of frustration and discomfort. But the sharp little cries of pain were what drew him out of his seat. And when I cursed at Michael, Charlie's neck corded and veins bulged at his temples when he restrained himself from —I didn't know what...reacting, maybe. I let out sharp cries, and I swore at my physical therapist more than once. I didn't seem to be so self-conscious when thinking of Charlie having to bear witness to all of that. I couldn't remember a time I'd let a bad word come from my mouth, but I'd managed to call Michael every name I could think of until he moved on to something else.

My mind was wandering, and I had gotten wrapped up in my insecurities. It was a bad habit, yet one I couldn't seem to shake. I didn't know if it was my growl or the apologetic smile that I offered Charlie afterward that drew him to my side, but I slumped against the mattress with a sheepish sigh.

Charlie nudged Michael. "Can I?" He motioned to my hand that Michael now had his fingers intertwined with as he rolled my wrist.

Michael released his grip and stood to give Charlie his seat. "Put your fingers between hers, but be careful not to push them apart or squeeze. They're still healing."

I'd entered the twilight zone. My therapist was teaching Charlie how to do the exercises that I'd nearly lost my composure over.

"Support her elbow and forearm, and slowly, rotate the wrist in smooth circles."

Charlie's touch was different. It still hurt. My bones felt like a ratchet, fighting against each other with each twist, but somehow, the warmth from Charlie's fingers and the heat of his stare made it a little more tolerable—or maybe it was the gentle gaze in his eyes that distracted me from the pain.

I let him follow Michael's instructions, which enabled me to zone out. My mind opted not to focus on the pain of what Charlie did with my hand, wrist, and arm, and instead, my attention wandered over his handsome features. Handsome didn't do him justice—the man was gorgeous. He'd always been good looking, yet sitting here with him as he helped me with therapy took his attractiveness to a whole new dimension. Just when I'd started to believe the fluorescent lights made everyone look like a zombie that had just crossed over into death, Charlie had to shatter that theory for the rest of us.

He was beautiful in spite of the horrible fluorescent hue. And all this time, I'd thought his eyes were a rich brown, but up close I could see just how green they actually were—a deep and unusual shade. I wished my hands worked better and that my fingers weren't taped or secured by splints so I could run them through his perfectly shaggy hair. Over the years, I had focused so much on his handsome face with that strong jawline and chiseled cheekbones that I'd missed all the other subtle features. The rugged stubble that peppered his cheeks held an appeal all its own. But it was his big, broad shoulders that made me want to get lost in his embrace. He was all man, and the tan he sported from hours out in the sun on a ranch only added to his appeal.

I tilted my head to the side to consider the difference in his appearance now versus the last time I really looked at him. It was like he'd *grown*, but he was an adult—he couldn't have changed that much. It was ridiculous to even consider; maybe my mind was playing tricks on me. The doctors had ruled out a brain injury after the accident, but maybe they'd missed something and this was the first sign—memory failure. I shook off that thought as quickly as it had come.

Charlie hadn't changed; I had.

I hadn't bothered to look in a mirror since I'd woken up. I

didn't want to see what remained. I could feel the places where my hair had been shaved for surgery and stitches; I could see the raised scars on my hands and arms from where they'd picked shards of glass from my skin. I had more broken bones than I could count, bruises that had turned green and a hideous shade of yellow, and nothing moved the way it once did. I hadn't had a shower since I'd gotten here—sponge baths were *not* the same—and I smelled like betadine and rubbing alcohol. There were likely prettier girls in drawers in the morgue downstairs.

Absentmindedly, I lifted my free hand to my lips and touched the places I knew would always have visible signs of what had happened that day. I didn't have to see them to know they were there. The list of injuries had been so long that it was easier to note the parts of me that hadn't been damaged. And I wondered what I was thinking, having Charlie stay. I shouldn't have asked him to linger. He didn't need to watch me endure this.

"Have you ever heard of FES?"

I hadn't been paying attention when Michael spoke. I was too homed in on Charlie's face, the feel of his skin against mine and the gentle way he worked my arm to notice the physical therapist—whose voice was rather gruff anyway—speaking.

Once I pulled my dopey gaze from Charlie and redirected it to Michael, my thinking resumed, and I was able to breathe normally. "No. What's that?"

"Functional Electrical Stimulation. It is a type of treatment that uses electrical pulses to improve muscles that are weak or paralyzed. In a nutshell, it helps the brain learn new pathways to get your muscles to engage again."

Something about using shock therapy didn't sit well with me, and it must have shown all over my face.

For the first time since I'd met Michael, a full smile lifted his lips, and he shook his head. "They're gentle pulses. No one is going to be electrocuted or anything. You'll get to try it out next week. We're going to make it part of your therapy routine next week to see if it helps. It adds about thirty minutes to each session."

Michael might as well have been speaking a foreign language. New pathways, muscle engagement, paralysis— none of that sounded good. The words didn't make much sense. My head still spun from the exercises and the narcotics. My arms, legs, back—it was all on fire. I was overly tired from the workout I'd just received. My knees felt swollen, and overall, I was just miserable. It made anything that required attention difficult to process.

"How does it work?" I tried to situate myself on the mattress to get comfortable, but not much helped.

"It's a little machine." Michael held up his hands to indicate the size. "There are several electrodes attached to wires, and I'll place those down both sides of your spine. It's just a padded sticker, nothing fancy. We'll start off on a low frequency, but the FES will deliver a shock or impulse to your muscles."

"Sounds pleasant." I fumbled for the controls on the bed to sit myself up, but Charlie beat me to the remote. I gave him a tired smile.

"It's not nearly as bad as it sounds, but we don't want those muscles to go too long without stimulation. Your team of physicians agrees this is the least invasive and most promising course right now. You're facing additional surgery —likely more than one, and we need to keep your body in the best shape we can to make each of those successful." Michael patted my leg—it was awkward. Then he looked at Charlie. "Do you have any more questions for me?"

"No, thank you."

"Of course. Charlie, it was nice to meet you. Sarah, I'll see you tomorrow." He left before I could object to his returning, not that it would have mattered.

Charlie scooted his plastic chair next to the bed. "Is there anything I can get you? How do you feel?"

"Sore." Now that the therapist was gone and the pain had set in, the tears were back with a vengeance. I reached up and dashed the back of my hand under my eyes. I hated for him to see me so weak, unable to control my emotions, but I couldn't stop the flood. "If you could put me out of my misery, that would really be appreciated."

The softness I'd admired in his expression not so long ago was replaced by a rigid, unforgiving stare. "Not gonna happen." His tone was as firm as his face. "You survived for a reason, and I don't believe you're just gonna give up. Instead of thinking about the big picture, maybe you should just focus on today. Focus on what you've accomplished. You just made it through another therapy session."

I scoffed, and I could tell that belittling what I'd done irritated him.

He rolled his lips between his teeth and then took a deep breath. "Okay, so it was tough, but you made it. It might not have been pretty—and I won't tell anyone you cussed Michael out." His expression relaxed along with his shoulders, and then his tone softened. "And you'll make it through the next one and the one after that—one session at a time. Exercise by exercise, you'll regain mobility. And I'll be here to help."

"Why?" It came out before I thought through what I'd asked.

"Why not?"

I shrugged hoping to get out of answering. I didn't want to tell him his commitment surprised me. And I wanted to believe it was more than just a motivational speech, but Charlie had a life, and it did not include me. He'd made that abundantly clear for the better part of twenty-four years. And while I believed that he believed he meant it, I didn't necessarily believe that he would be able to follow through. Once Charlie realized what he was promising, the time commitment involved—not to mention the driving—he'd split.

There was no doubt in my mind that he'd remember a dozen other things he could be doing that didn't involve caring for a scarred up and broken invalid. I could think of several women right off the bat who could turn his head and occupy his time if given the chance, and they had all their hair and full mobility. Not to mention, none of them were outside of the Mason Belle town limits.

Still, I gave him credit for the encouragement and

offered him the sincerest smile I could muster. But it was easier to close my eyes and tilt my head back against the bed.

"Thank you for staying today. It helped to have someone else with me." I meant that. I wanted him to know that I meant it.

"Of course." He gave my fingers a gentle squeeze.

Each day was a repeat of the last, and Charlie kept showing up for every one of them. Therapy session after therapy session, he never missed one. I didn't have any idea how he managed to work at his parents' ranch or Daddy's along with being with me daily, but selfishly, I feared asking would alert him to the fact that he could be doing something else. Every morning, he appeared with two cups of coffee, and recently, he'd added breakfast. I didn't know the why behind that, either. And I almost didn't *want* to know the answer. If he was doing this out of pity, or out of deference to Daddy, or even if he just somehow didn't have anything better to do...

I couldn't bring myself to believe that Charlie would have any ulterior motive for his attention. His attitude and actions went far beyond helping a family friend, especially one he hadn't previously been close to. He got along well with the therapists, and he made friends with the doctors. Just like in high school, the guy made friends every-where he went because everyone loved him. He just had that personality that drew people to him—they *wanted* to be around him. I swore, I wouldn't be surprised to find out they were going out for drinks when the guys got off their shifts.

But it was more than just his comradery with the staff. Charlie made my comfort his top priority, but more than anything, he paid attention—first and foremost—to me, and then the physical therapists, nurses, doctors, anyone who might have insight into my healing process. He soaked up information like a sponge, and what he couldn't remember, he wrote down. The man took notes—about my recovery. Me —Sarah Adams—the girl he hadn't known existed until a tractor-trailer hit me going eighty-four miles an hour.

When the FES had been introduced, Charlie stayed quiet in the corner and watched. He made sure to ask questions before and after about how to hook up the machine properly—although, it seemed fairly straightforward to me. He took notes on how to store it, how to keep it clean, and how to make sure it was working. Michael assured him that it was unlikely I would take a unit home. But Charlie made sure he had all the information just in case. I didn't have the heart to tell Charlie that the machine wouldn't be going home because if it didn't work here, there was no point in continuing down the road. He got upset if I was negative, so I kept that bit of knowledge to myself.

I was grateful for everything he did, and, for him in general. Between Charlie and Daddy, I spent very little time alone. I wished my sister would stop by, but that was another issue I wasn't ready to address. I wanted to tell Charlie how much all of this meant to me, but I wasn't certain I could convey the message without confessing more than I cared to.

A guy would take my heartfelt sentiment and gratitude as an admission of something...needy. The last thing I wanted was for him to believe I'd become dependent upon him in any way, regardless of the fact that I was. The moment Charlie found out that I counted down the minutes until his arrival or that I endured physical therapy just to see him would be the moment he took off and I didn't see him again. I was absolutely certain of that much.

Even when I wasn't in physical therapy, Charlie still came by or hung out. He brought me coffee from the cafeteria and cinnamon rolls—oh my gosh, his mama's cinnamon rolls were to die for. And somehow, he'd sweet-talked a nurse into finding a more comfortable chair that had a place next to my bed.

He leaned back, kicked his feet up on the side of my mattress, and crossed his arms over his broad chest. "Austin got roped into helping with the Mason Belle parade. Charity has him building their float."

"Aww. That's sweet of him." I loved that the two of us could talk about life in town like we'd done it a hundred times before. "What are they making this year?"

The town parade wasn't really much of a parade. It was an excuse for the citizens to come together in a show of support and community...and to eat—because that's what the men in Mason Belle liked to do, and the women loved to feed them.

"A cow."

I couldn't hide my laughter. "A cow? How big?"

A smirk tickled his lips, and his eyes glittered with

amusement. "Apparently, Charity didn't really understand what she was asking for when she suggested Austin make the frame ten times the size of a real cow."

I covered my mouth when a little gasp escaped. "That would be enormous! Would it even fit under the stoplight on Main Street?" We only had one.

Charlie shook his head. "Austin had to cut it off at the knees. Needless to say, his cow is ridiculous looking, and he's less than happy."

"Bless his heart. Does he have anyone helping him?"

"Brock. And I talked Mike into trying to see if he can help them fix it. Austin's not doing all that well without Randi around, so his temper tends to flare. Mike said he loses his cool pretty fast these days."

I didn't know who he was talking about. "Mike?"

His brow dipped a bit not understanding my question, and then the confusion cleared. "Bell. My best friend."

At that moment, I realized just how little the two of us knew about each other. I didn't really spend time with Charlie unless it was at his parents' house, and I hadn't seen Mike Bell in ages. They both lived in the heart of Mason Belle, but Mike worked on his family ranch just like the rest of us. There hadn't been a need for our paths to cross. "Oh, I didn't realize you two were still close."

Charlie picked up the remote to the TV but kept talking. "We're tight."

But I didn't want to let the conversation go. I wanted to know everything there was to learn about Charlie. He was far more interesting than anything that played on the television in my room.

He held the remote in his lap and turned the questioning back to me. "Have you met anyone here?"

I didn't want to admit that I wasn't good at making friends. I was a loner, not by choice but by design. "Not really." That was vague and not an outright lie.

I just wasn't interested in hanging out with other patients. Either they were overly optimistic and tried to cram sunshine down my throat, or they were so depressing that I wanted the world to end by the time I finally got away from them. So even though I craved human interaction, I was picky about who it was with. And Charlie was my number one pick, not that I could tell him that.

"Daddy comes by a good bit. So, between the two of you, doctors, and rehab, there's not a lot of time for socializing."

Thankfully, Charlie wasn't the type of man to pry. I was amazed at his ability to talk for hours without really revealing much about himself or really saying anything at all. We'd both grown up in Mason Belle, our parents were friends, our siblings were sweethearts—he shared the town gossip like he was one of the ladies down at the A & P. But I was quite certain it was for my benefit and not because he cared about what Harriet Hillman did last Saturday night while her husband Wade was out in the fields. Those little tidbits made life bearable, almost normal, like I was still part of things going on at home. And hearing them from Charlie Burin's point of view made them funny regardless of whether or not the gossip was true.

Yet somehow, in all those conversations and all the happenings around Mason Belle, Charlie never talked about himself. I didn't get the impression he was hiding anything, just that he was a bit closed off. I'd never realized how reserved he was, borderline shy. Yet the more time I spent with him, the more I noticed that growing up—and as an adult—I'd mistaken quiet confidence for swagger and arrogance. The guy I believed Charlie to be in high school wasn't at all who he was today and may never have been that person. Women had always flocked to him, and guys wanted to be his friend, but he'd never been the type to seek an audience. Just like Austin, he was typically the center of attention, but I realized now that likely wasn't so much by choice any more so than it was for his little brother. They both just drew people in—quietly.

I watched him without *watching* him. I reached for a snack just to be able to take in the full view without being obvious. It was highly probable that I wasn't as smooth as I thought I was, but Charlie didn't so much as bat an eye. He still sat with his feet up on the bed and his arms crossed with his stare trained on the screen on the wall.

"You've gotta be the bravest person I've ever met." His comment was completely unprompted, and he'd said it while watching a daytime talk show.

I paused with a spoonful of applesauce halfway to my mouth, not sure if he was talking to me or the man on the screen—since I'd been studying Charlie's face and not the show—until his gaze left the TV and locked with mine.

"What do you mean?" I set the spoon down clumsily and

waited for his response. There was no need to choke on whatever he had to say.

"You've survived this." His expression was stoic, but that emotion I'd seen in his eyes once before had returned, not that I could identify it. "Not only have you survived it, but you're *beating* it."

It was a good thing we weren't sitting on the porch at Cross Acres, or I'd have a mouthful of flies the way my jaw hung open. And my eyes would be burned by the sun the way I stared without blinking.

He chuckled. "Don't look at me like I have two heads."

I closed my mouth but started to choke and cough at the absurdity of all of this.

Charlie muted the TV and tossed the remote onto the table. When he set his feet on the floor and leaned forward, I was quite certain I'd stop breathing. His eyes were intense and set on me. "I see the improvements you make every day. In physical therapy...it's amazing. I just..." Charlie shrugged and then rubbed the back of his neck, suddenly uneasy. "I don't think I could do it."

"You're the one who told me it was mind over matter."

"And that's true. I'm just not sure that my mind would be strong enough to overcome the matter. I don't think I could do what you've had to. And I sure as hell wouldn't have a great attitude."

I felt the unease wash over my face as I processed what I presumed to be an attempt at a compliment. I had no idea where he was going with this, but I kind of wished he'd stop. He'd convinced me there was no other option than through it. Charlie had made me believe that if I wanted it bad enough, I could make it happen. But if he thought I was beating this, then there would be no reason for him to continue to visit. It was a double-edged sword. He had no idea that he was my motivation. If he quit coming, I'd be alone most of the day. Daddy was great, but Charlie was a lot easier on the eyes even if he was harder on the heart.

Charlie turned in his seat, bringing the chair near the bed. He took my hand closest to him, picked it up, and kissed the misshaped, knobby knuckles. My chest constricted in pain as I waited for him to leave, yet my pulse rose at the feel of his lips on my skin and the way his warm breath tickled my fingers. I wanted to stop time right at this moment so that it wouldn't be ruined.

"You're in a lot of pain, but you stay strong. Every day you choose to survive instead of giving up. And I think that makes you the bravest person I know." And again, he kissed the top of my hand, but this time, he held my eyes in the most intimate exchange I'd ever experienced.

I flushed as the heat of a blush swept up my neck and across my cheeks. I knew I had to respond, but I wasn't sure what was appropriate under the circumstances. "I don't think I have a lot of choices. This," I waved my free hand around the room, "isn't much of a life. I certainly don't want to be here any longer than I have to. And the only way out of here is through this." I shrugged and dropped my focus to his knees. "You make it sound like I've actually accomplished something when really, I'm not in any better condition than I was after the accident. I'm just trying to make, or at the very least, fake it until I do."

His fingers found my chin, and he lifted my face until I met his stare. Charlie's eyes were a warm forest green, and his pupils grew just before he spoke like they were drawing me in. "I think that's all any of us are trying to do." It was sincere, heartfelt, and I wanted to curl up in his voice like it was a warm blanket on a cold winter's night. "I admire you, Sarah."

I dared to touch his jaw and cringed when I saw how my slightly crooked fingers appeared against his perfect features, but Charlie didn't pull away. "You're a good man, Charlie."

He huffed out a bit of a laugh, and I dropped my fingers from his chin. "I wasn't fishing for compliments."

"I know, but that doesn't make it any less true." I swallowed past the knot in my throat and dared to utter the thoughts that had plagued my mind since he'd started showing up at the hospital. "No one else—other than Daddy —has sat here, entertaining me or helped me with physical therapy. You probably know more about the process than I do at this point, and I'm the one who has to go through it. My own sister hasn't shown her face, but you've come every single day. Do you have any idea how much that helps me when I'm trying to get through a PT session?"

Charlie didn't comment, but he also didn't look away or dismiss me. He was just as interested in hearing what I had to say as I was his response.

"When you're not here, I feel like I'm in a vacuum, Charlie. Life just becomes a monotonous void." That might have been too much, but it was true regardless. "Daddy means well, but he's old school, and honestly, he doesn't get being a girl, much less a girl who's been through this." I didn't have to detail the account; Charlie knew what I meant without my pointing out all of my now visible imperfections. "But you've been here. And when you're here, I don't feel like it's just me against the world…" I trailed off, but he maintained eye contact. "I don't know if that makes any sense." I was just babbling at that point, but somehow, it had needed to be said.

I hadn't garnered the courage to ask the why behind his attention, but I had conveyed that it meant something. That was a huge step for a girl who'd never held a boy's hand, much less his attention. "You're just…thank you."

The happier Charlie was, the more green showed through the brown in his irises, and today his eyes were a field a clover. His lips lifted into a bright smile, and I swore, it was better than the sun breaking through the clouds on a stormy day.

6

SARAH

Daddy sat in the chair that Charlie had managed to finagle out of the nurses, and he'd pulled my swinging table up to use it as a desk. There were papers scattered all over it, and he had his checkbook out and a pen stuck in it.

"Daddy, why don't you let me help you with that?" Cross Acre's books had been my responsibility since I was in high school. "I can write checks and pay bills." My handwriting might not be pretty, but if a doctor got away with chicken scratch, surely no one would question my wobbly script.

He ran a hand through his grey hair. I didn't think I'd ever get used to seeing Daddy without a hat. There were rarely times I saw him without one—church and supper; that was about it. But in the hospital, he never brought one, although I could tell he'd had one on in the truck from the ring it left behind. "I've got it, sweetheart."

I sighed. "You're being silly. Just because my body isn't working right doesn't mean my mind won't function." I waited for him to lift his chin to meet my eyes, but when he didn't, I kept going. "It would be nice to feel useful. Since I've been in here, all I've done is sit around."

"Not your job to focus on bills, Sarah. You need to focus on takin' care of you." Spoken just like a bull-headed Southern man.

Before I could insist further, a woman walked in the open door, tapping on the wood as she approached. "Good morning." Her voice was more like a coo than words, and I'd learned in the time I'd been in these facilities that that was never good. They'd been trained to soften blows with melodious tone.

"Mornin'." Daddy didn't bother looking over at the lady in a suit.

I did my best to give her a welcoming smile, but since I didn't know her, and she appeared far too formal to be a new therapist, I struggled with putting forth anything genuine. "Hi."

She stood at the end of my bed with a folder clutched in her arm, now held close to her chest. "I'm Chantel Stafford."

"It's nice to meet you. I'm Sarah Adams, and this is my dad, Jack."

When she crossed her other arm over the folder and took a defensive posture, I realized she wasn't just going to deliver bad news; she was going to turn my world upside down. "Sarah, I'm your case manager."

Somehow, that got Daddy's attention. He stopped what

he was doing and stared the woman down like she'd just introduced a virus to his livestock. I ignored his sudden bristliness and tried to figure out what that meant.

"I didn't know I had one."

A practiced smile turned up the corners of her mouth. "I'm here to assist in situations like yours." She grabbed the folder with both hands, and I saw just how thick the stack of papers was inside it. "And hopefully find solutions to get you the treatment you need." None of that sounded good.

"Doesn't my insurance cover most of it?" It wasn't the greatest policy on the market, but Daddy paid a pretty penny to ensure we had some sort of coverage in cases like this.

The woman looked confused but then shook her head. "Oh, yes, the driver of the other vehicle had insurance that has covered your stay and surgeries. Unfortunately, when we start talking about long-term care in rehabilitation facilities, insurance companies stop responding as quickly as they did when we were trying to save your life."

I was pretty smart, but what I was reading into what she was saying couldn't have possibly been what she meant. "What does that mean exactly?"

Chantel took a deep breath and released it on a sigh. "Well, for now, it means that we need to find therapists for you and get you set up with a treatment plan outside of these walls."

"Does that mean you're sending me home?"

Daddy sat up straighter, and the tic of his jaw caught my eye. When I glanced over, anger brewed all over his face, and he was doing his best to maintain his composure.

She set the folder on the end of my bed. "The insurance company doesn't believe you're making enough progress to warrant continued in-patient care. So, unless something changes, you will be discharged at the end of the week."

"But I can't walk!" I shouldn't have shrieked; it brought a nurse in to check on me and only served to upset Daddy further.

Chantel traced circles with her well-manicured, fake nail on that folder still sitting on the end of my bed; I wanted to pick it up and smack her with it. "That's why I'm here. I've put together an out-patient regime with your doctors through our state-run program. You'll still work with the same therapists in the same facility, but instead of your staying here every day, you'll come in for appointments."

I didn't know what to say. None of this made any sense. I'd been hit by a truck. The guy had insurance. This shouldn't be an issue. "Daddy?"

My father was less than impressed, but even as country as he was, he recognized the limitations put on him and the woman at the end of my bed. "Let's hear her out, darlin'."

What? No. I didn't want to hear her out. There was no way I could go home in this condition. I couldn't imagine traveling back and forth to Laredo for appointments. This place was forty-five minutes from home, and I couldn't drive.

I sat there, wide-eyed, and stared at Chantel while she talked. Daddy asked a bunch of questions, but at the end of it, the decision still remained. Our choice was to go along with what the insurance company was willing to continue to pay for—out-patient treatment—get an attorney to fight on my behalf—which still wouldn't guarantee I didn't go home at the end of the week—or pay out of pocket.

"How much would it cost per week to stay?" It was the first question I'd asked since they'd started talking. "I mean out of pocket." My eyes lifted from my hands to my father and then Chantel.

Her eyes shifted from me to my dad and back. "Fourteen thousand."

I nearly choked on my own saliva. "Per week?"

She nodded. I didn't have that kind of money, and I wouldn't ask Daddy to spend that, not when everyone here thought I'd never walk again anyhow.

"So, what now?" I resigned myself to this fate.

Chantel picked up her stupid folder—I still didn't know why she'd brought it. She hadn't so much as opened it. "We need to get you outfitted with a wheelchair, and I need to make sure your dad knows what needs to be done to prepare the house for you so you will be able to get around."

"In a wheelchair...." It was kind of a question but more of a smart-aleck statement that Daddy would have chastised me for any other time.

She patted my foot, and if I could, I would have kicked her. It was juvenile and immature, but I didn't care. I didn't understand how someone could be sent home in the condition I was in. I didn't have a nurse to help me. Daddy was... Daddy. He was a man. I didn't even have anyone to help me shower or change. I certainly couldn't count on Miranda since I hadn't seen or heard from her and based on what little I'd been able to garner, neither had anyone else.

"I'll get someone in to get you fitted for the wheelchair. And I'll be back to help get you situated before you go home.

~

C harlie tossed out a card and then laid his hand on the mattress. "Royal flush." He was proud of himself and fought the smirk that indicated just how much.

"Flush? I thought we were playing gin." I didn't really, but seeing his expression fall was nothing short of adorable. "I'm kidding." I tossed my cards onto the pile. I didn't have a clue about how to play poker. He could have had four of a kind and told me it was a straight, and I wouldn't have known the difference.

"Another hand?" He had already started to shuffle the cards, and then as he started to deal, I picked them up one by one. "You're supposed to wait until the dealer's done before you pick up the cards."

I rolled my eyes. "Remind me of that if we're ever in Vegas. I don't think anyone on the ward is going to call the poker police."

"For some reason, I don't ever see you on the strip in Vegas." He chuckled and kept doling out cards before he stacked the remainder of the deck between us.

I shrugged and cocked my head to think about it. "Yeah, it would probably be difficult to navigate in a wheelchair." As I tried to sort my cards, Charlie's hand covered the fan I'd spread out and pushed them down. "Hey!"

His eyes met mine, but instead of the hazel green I loved

to see, they were more brown than normal. "That's not what I meant."

"I wasn't offended, Charlie." I tried to pull my cards out from under his grasp, but he wasn't relenting.

"I didn't say you were, but I was referring to the fact that someone as pure as you should never be sullied in Sin City. I wouldn't want you to go to Vegas." He spoke slowly. His tone was soft and truthful.

I sighed. "I'm sorry. I'm just on edge."

He took my cards and his and added them back to the deck. When he placed the stack on the table, I guessed we were done playing cards. "Talk to me." Charlie joined me on the bed, sitting in front of me and holding my hands. His thumb stroked my knuckles without purpose, yet that simple gesture eased my anxiety if only briefly.

"I'm scared."

"Of what?"

My lungs inhaled, pushing my chest forward, and when I finally let out that labored breath, it came in a rush. "Have you talked to Austin about Randi?"

"What does that have to do with your being scared?"

I bit my lip and turned his hands over in mine. There was nothing sensual in his touch, but God how I wished there were. I appreciated the comfort, but I wanted so much more. That was one part of my fear that I couldn't express, at least not directly. "Have you thought about what I'm going home to?"

"More than I probably should have."

I didn't know what that meant, and I wasn't going to ask.

"I have help here, Charlie. When I go home, there's no one but Daddy."

"That's not true. What am I?"

I huffed and met his stare. "A man."

He squared his shoulders and puffed up with pride. "Well, yeah."

"My sister isn't home."

"You're going to have to spell this out for me, Sarah. I'm not following what you're saying."

"You and Daddy can't help me shower or bathe. You can't help me change clothes. There are things I need my sister around for since there won't be a nurse at the house for those types of things. I don't even want to think about the fact that the house isn't wheelchair accessible or that my bedroom is upstairs. It's the little nuances of life that I won't be able to navigate on my own. So, have you talked to Austin about Randi?"

The vein in his neck began to throb, and when he dropped the hold he had on my hands, I knew there was something he wasn't telling me. The question became, would he tell me now. It was one thing not to offer information voluntarily, but I'd asked flat out, and I didn't believe he'd lie. His bicep flexed, but for the first time, it wasn't appealing; it was a distraction.

"Austin hasn't heard from her. He's been at Cross Acres every day taking care of her chores and her horse."

I blanched unsure of what to do with this. I'd been gone for weeks. "Why?"

"He wants her to know that he still took care of her when

she wasn't there. That he didn't lose faith that she'd come back to him."

"No, I don't mean why is he at the house. I mean, why hasn't he heard from her? She's just a kid. Where could she have gone? We don't have any family outside of Mason Belle."

Charlie was as lost as I was, and the pained look on his face told me just how much he hated to be the one breaking this news to me. "No one has seen or heard from your sister since she took off, Sarah. Not even Austin."

It didn't make any sense. Miranda was a hothead, but she loved Austin more than life. If the two of them had run off into the sunset, I wouldn't question it, but Randi Adams could no more survive on her own than a baby bird without its mother.

"If my sister hasn't come back, then there's something wrong. Why hasn't anyone looked for her? Surely, Austin knows where she would go." My heart pounded as I thought about all the ways I'd failed my sister by not being home to take care of her. "Charlie, you have to convince him to find her."

"Babe, he's tried. He's gone everywhere he knows to look for her. He's talked to Charity, and he even threatened Brock because he figured if anyone would have helped her leave it would have been him. They got into a fistfight over it. At the end of the day, she just left. No one has heard from her."

I couldn't accept that. There wasn't much I could do from here, but when I got home, finding Miranda would become a priority. My little sister was a pain, and she grated on my every nerve, and truth be told, had she done what she was told I would never have ended up here. But this was my fate—my destiny. All the anger in the world wouldn't change that, nor would it alter my circumstances. We'd been through too much together just to let her walk away.

7

CHARLIE

After basically forcing Sarah out, the rehab facility took its sweet time actually releasing her. Maybe that was just how it felt, but between the time the decision was handed down, Jack delivered the message, and Sarah physically left, it had been days of wondering when it would happen. I couldn't say I was upset that she was going home, although I knew she wasn't looking forward to it. The drive to Laredo every day was a killer in a huge truck, and I was at Cross Acres every day anyhow. Even if I weren't, it was only a couple miles from my parents' property. I felt like I'd lived in an uncomfortable chair in a sterile room in Laredo for the last couple of months, and *I* got to go home every day. I could only imagine how Sarah felt. She seemed to have mixed emotions regarding the whole thing. Part of her wanted to be back in Mason Belle, part of her was afraid she wasn't ready to leave, and there was a part of her that believed I'd quit coming to see her—even if she hadn't verbalized that fear.

She'd hinted at the last without coming right out and saying it.

Nevertheless, the day had finally come—release day. Jack and I pulled up to the facility to get her out of this place. He parked under the awning in front of the building, and just as I hopped out of the cab of his truck, the glass doors parted, and a nurse escorted Sarah in a wheelchair toward us. And then I noticed the other three staff members behind them, pushing carts. I hadn't realized how much stuff Sarah had accumulated here since she'd had the accident. Between Jack bringing her clothes from home, books and magazines she'd requested, and well-wishers who'd brought things to brighten her day, I wasn't sure where we were going to put all of it. But that part didn't matter.

My lips lifted into a grin that only Sarah seemed to earn, and her face lit up like a morning sunrise, slow at first and then warm and inviting. "Hey." I ran my hand through my hair, not really sure how to go about this. "You ready to get out of Dodge?"

Sarah bit her bottom lip and gave me an uncertain nod.

I kissed her forehead and patted her shoulder—because those two actions didn't contradict each other at all. "Sit tight. Let me help Jack get this stuff in the truck, and then I'll get you situated."

Never in my life had I had a problem talking to women. Not a single one had ever left me tongue-tied or tripping over my feet. That was until recently. Something about the strawberry blonde had me more twisted up than a tie on a loaf of bread. I said stupid things, did even dumber ones and made myself look like a total fool. Yet somehow, it didn't seem to bother Sarah in the slightest.

Jack and I unloaded the carts into the bed of Jack's truck, and one by one, each of the women said goodbye to Sarah and retreated back inside. Sarah sat patiently with her hands in her lap—although, I could see the anxiety hiding beneath her stilled expression—and Jack clapped me on the back.

I squatted next to her wheelchair. "You ready?" It was me that had to get ready, mentally. The doctors had told me repeatedly I wouldn't hurt her by picking her up, but the fear remained.

Sarah placed her hand on my forearm with a gentle squeeze, and I wanted to close my hand over hers and escape into a moment where everyone else disappeared. "You're not going to break me, Charlie."

I prayed to God she was right. I'd never forgive myself if I caused her any more pain than she already endured daily. I slid my forearm under her knees and my other behind her back. And when her arm curled around my neck, my heart raced. She'd lost weight since the accident—weight she hadn't needed to lose—and was now light as a feather. When I lifted her from the chair, her slight intake of air scared me until I realized she wasn't holding her breath in fear. Sarah was perfectly content in my arms.

"Come on, you two. We're burning daylight." Jack held the passenger door open.

I took the couple steps toward the truck to place Sarah in the seat and maximized the close proximity and time I got to touch her by fastening her seatbelt for her. She didn't complain, and in fact, she managed to hold my free hand while I got her situated. Secretly, I enjoyed it. I liked being her safe place. I wanted to be her fortress. I'd kill anyone who tried to get near her. But she didn't need that added pressure right now. She didn't need me being a jealous buffoon. The last thing on Sarah's mind was my libido.

Sarah squeezed my fingers the best she could when I stood back up. "Thank you."

Before I could say anything else, the nurse pulled me aside to show me how to fold up the wheelchair to get it into the truck. I put it in the bed with the rest of Sarah's things and then fastened the cover over the back to keep everything safe from the wind.

By the time I came back around to get in the back seat, Jack had gotten in behind Sarah and closed the door. I couldn't imagine why he wanted me to drive his truck, but since he'd made the decision—and left no room for argument—I rounded the hood to the driver's side.

I pulled myself into the cab. "You don't want to drive, Jack?"

He waved me off. "It's been a long day. I'm just gonna rest my eyes on the ride back. You youngins can chatter." And just like that, he leaned back, tipped his hat to cover his face, and crossed his arms over his chest. *Crazy old man.*

Sarah giggled under her breath, and her cheeks warmed to the softest shade of pink I'd ever seen. She shook her head at her father's blatant push for us to interact, and then she turned toward the passenger window.

She didn't say much throughout the drive back to Mason

Belle, but I didn't miss the little gasp when she saw the town limit sign.

"Nervous?" I asked.

Sarah shifted in the seat next to me, and her anxiety was written all over her face. "A little, I guess. Just not sure what to expect."

I covered her hand with mine on the console and did my best to lace my fingers through hers. "Nothing's changed."

"That's what worries me." She took a deep breath, and I expected her to elaborate. Instead, she rested her head against the seat and stared at me through those beautiful blue eyes.

I didn't follow her line of thinking. "What do you mean?"

She huffed like she thought my ignorance was cute. "I mean Mason Belle hasn't changed, Charlie, but I have." Her lips pressed together, and that was all the knowledge I needed.

It wasn't worry. It was fear. And as soon as I turned off the rural road and into Cross Acres, that gorgeous pink tinge left her cheeks, and all color washed away. She was at a point of no return. She couldn't go back, and moving forward was likely scary as hell. There was no normal here—not for Sarah —even though it was home. Every acre of this ranch and every inch of that farmhouse were now treacherous where they'd once been familiar and comforting. Couple that with her father's inability to help a lot and her sister's sudden disappearance, and there was nothing safe here.

It was hard to imagine much less believe that Sarah's life

had changed in a handful of minutes and a few split seconds. A series of unfortunate choices by her sister, Sarah, and the truck driver had irrevocably changed her life; whether or not that was for the better remained to be seen. For the foreseeable future, it had definitely put a wrinkle in her way of life in this town.

Jack and I had done all that we could to make the transition easier, but there was nothing I could do to make this less challenging. Several of the ranch hands and I had spent the better part of last weekend moving Sarah's furniture downstairs and into Jack's old room and moving Jack upstairs to Sarah's. My mom had come over with a couple of other ladies from town to make the room more feminine—girl it up a bit. Despite the gentle touches from the fairer sex—clean sheets, a new comforter, fresh flowers—the room just appeared lifeless. While we'd moved Sarah's things, there was no real sign of her in the space, and to top it off, Jack hadn't told her what we'd done.

As we pulled into the circular, gravel driveway, it became painfully obvious we'd missed a very critical detail. It was only five steps up the front porch to the door, but those were five steps Sarah couldn't maneuver in a wheelchair or on her own. And looking around, it became more obvious just how much of the property was no longer accessible to her.

I glanced over to see her eyes glistening with unshed tears, and I watched her hide her emotions. She was a pro at concealing what she didn't want the world to see, and Sarah refused to allow anyone to believe she was weak, needy, or down. She was a nurturer—she was going to struggle with being the one who required care. I stroked my thumb over the top of her hand in quiet reassurance and then lifted it to kiss her knuckles. I didn't have to say anything. The quick glance she gave me told me she heard me loud and clear.

Reluctantly, I released her hand to put the truck in park in front of her house. It had never seemed as massive and daunting as it did today, not even when I was a kid and my parents had dragged me over here.

Jack stirred in the back seat, but I didn't take my eyes off Sarah. "You're home." Jack patted Sarah's shoulder from behind. "How's it feel, sweetheart?"

"Good," Sarah said.

Jack would have had to have been deaf, blind, and dumb to have missed the lie in that one word. It was flat, monotone. It was as lifeless as the bedroom she was about to enter. There wasn't an ounce of joy in her eyes, and I recognized the meek smile she put on for people she didn't want to burden. For a brief moment, she met my eyes, and her brilliant blues shined back at me. Understanding passed between us, and I hoped like hell she realized I was here to cheer her on, not let her fall.

Her dad hopped out of the truck and closed the door, but I lingered.

"You okay?" I knew she wasn't, but I wanted her to recognize that I saw what she didn't admit.

A hint of a smile lifted the corners of her mouth, and she gave me a nod. Her blond curls bounced with the movement, and I wanted nothing more than to grab the back of her neck and pull her to me. Press my forehead to hers, stare her in the eyes, and promise her the moon. But I did none of that.

"Sit tight." I opened the door and dropped onto the gravel driveway. The crunch beneath my feet was as familiar as the smell in the air. This was life in the country.

By the time I rounded the hood, Jack had already pulled the bed cover back and had the wheelchair out. He fiddled with it, trying to get it to open. Before he got frustrated, I stopped him.

"Jack."

He jerked the handles unsuccessfully and used his foot to try to pry apart the bottom, effectively ignoring me.

"*Jack.*" That time I got his attention, and when he looked up, I pointed toward the steps. "That wheelchair isn't going to go up stairs very well."

He cursed under his breath and kicked at the rocks underfoot. "Need a ramp."

"We can deal with that later." I knew he was right, but it wasn't going to happen while Sarah sat in the truck. "I need to get Sarah inside."

He tipped his hat back. "Oh. Right, right." Jack grabbed the wheelchair—still closed—and made his way toward the door while I turned back to Sarah.

Sarah looked at me from the passenger seat once I'd opened the door, and it was written all over her face—embarrassment, shame. But she bit her bottom lip and refused to cry. I watched as she swallowed past what had to be a huge lump in her throat. I knew better than to make a big deal out of this.

I gave her a half-bow and my best smile. And she rolled her eyes when I extended my hand, but she couldn't hide the grin that tugged at the corners of her mouth. She eased her delicate hand into mine, and I used the motion to run my hand up her arm and rest it against her back. I slid my other arm underneath her knees and shifted her toward me. It was a little trickier with the truck, but it gave me an excuse to get her close, so I'd make do. I loved the feel of her in my embrace, cradled against me—her weight, the heat from her skin, the breath she blew across my neck unknowingly. And then, Jack chilled those thoughts with his icy stare as he watched me move his daughter. I had no doubt that if Sarah so much as winced, he'd leap off that porch and come after me. And I pretended like he couldn't sense the pleasure I got out of having her pressed against me because that would be a death sentence in itself. Nevertheless, for a few brief moments, I got to enjoy the way her arms wound around my neck and what it felt like to hold her.

Her breath hitched, and I pulled back to see if she was in pain. She closed her eyes, tears seeping between her lashes.

"Sarah?" I whispered so only she could hear.

She drew her lips into her mouth and shook her head. I guessed the entire experience was a bit overwhelming, so I made a point of getting her up those steps as quickly as possible.

Once we crossed the threshold and moved into the house, she let her arms drop from my neck. She rested them in her lap, one hand crossed over the other. The loss of her touch was like a knife to the heart, and disappointment hung heavily upon my shoulders until she leaned against my chest, resting her head against my shoulder. I looked down my nose, trying to catch a glimpse of how she looked nestled next to me. Signs of pain started to show on her brow, and I picked up my pace.

I went straight down the hall to her new bedroom with Jack leading the way. Sarah didn't ask where we were going. I'm sure she knew a move was inevitable. Thankfully, the room was on the backside of the house shadowed by trees, which helped block the heat of the sun. It had to have been ten degrees cooler in the master bedroom than the hall we'd just stepped out of. And unlike the rest of South Texas, this space wasn't blistering hot. Jack moved ahead of me and pulled back the comforter and sheets and then arranged the pillows to give her some support. I set her down on the mattress, fluffed the pillows a bit behind her, and pressed my lips to her temple. She held onto my elbow with one hand and my forearm with the other. Sarah didn't need to grab hold of me with force. All it took was her to acknowledge she wanted my touch, and I lingered.

When she released my arm and I pulled back, her face was poised, but her eyes were miserable. Sarah and I hadn't been close long. I wasn't sure I could say we were *close* now. But I'd known of her long enough and spent enough time with her in recent weeks to be certain she hated every bit of this. If she could have shooed us away and managed on her own, she would have.

Jack clapped me on the shoulder in his own protective way of asking me to step back, which I did. "There it is." Jack was proud of what we'd been able to do for Sarah while she was gone. "How's it feel?" Jack was as lost as I was about what to say. He'd started repeating himself—maybe he'd hoped for a different or more heartfelt answer the second time around.

Sarah shifted a little, attempting to get comfortable. "Good to be home, for sure." Pain flashed over her face again, although she tried not to let it show.

Jack seemed to have missed it. I, on the other hand, noticed every cringe, twinge, ache, and hidden emotion. I'd never fancied myself as an observant man, and I'd never seen myself as oblivious the way Jack appeared. Somehow, I believed myself to be in between, but when it came to Sarah Adams, suddenly I was acutely aware of every emotion, feeling, and sensation that passed through her body and mind.

God, this woman was strong. I admired her more every day. Other than the time I'd found her in tears at the hospital, she'd kept dry eyes. Sarah did whatever she had to do to keep from breaking down, even on the days it probably would have served her better to let go. But here she sat, in a room that had belonged to someone else only days ago, she couldn't walk, she was in pain, and the list just kept going. And other than me, I hadn't noticed she spent time talking to anyone else.

Based on what Austin had told me in the past, Sarah had never been tight with her sister, but even now, when Sarah could have used Randi the most, her sibling was nowhere to be found. Sarah had sacrificed her teenage years for Miranda only to have Miranda act like Houdini when times got tough and Sarah could have used her help. Her sister was gone, and there had to be resentment piled up. It was just Jack and her, now.

Well. And me. But I wasn't sure I counted that much. It had never been a secret that Sarah carried a flame for me. Now, however, I wondered if that hadn't fizzled into nothing. Her issues were so much bigger than anything I could possibly offer her.

I didn't know what to do with Jack in the room. Typically, we took turns at the hospital and the rehab facility, so she wasn't alone all that much. Sarah and I had our own routines that didn't include an audience—other than doctors, nurses, and therapists—and now, I was all kinds of awkward and out of place. This was Jack's home, and I was the visitor.

"Can I get you anything before I get the stuff out of the truck?" I needed to breathe and regroup. That would give me the chance to do both while helping Jack.

"Some water?" Sarah peered up through her dark lashes to stare at me like I'd hung the moon and named the stars.

My heart swelled, and my chest expanded to accommodate the growing size. That one look had killed the notion that Sarah's flare had been extinguished. There was passion in her eyes, and her full lips begged to be kissed. And I needed to get out of this room, quickly.

"Sure." I nodded to Jack and ducked into the hall.

Getting a glass of water didn't provide anywhere near the time I needed to breathe through the thoughts pummeling me and slow my racing heart. Unfortunately, the stroll back down the hall didn't grant me the peace I searched for, either. Sarah had me all jumbled up in ways I couldn't begin to understand. I'd dated my fair share of women in this town—none of them had ever done this to me. Not one.

Sarah accepted the drink with a grateful smile. And I kept my hand hovering underneath the glass until I was certain she had a good hold on it. Her grip was still weak, and it was possible it would never get any better than it was currently. But I hadn't filled it to the top so it wouldn't be as heavy.

She sipped from the water and took a deep, shaky breath. "Thank you." She sipped again and then awkwardly managed to set the glass on the nightstand.

I had a hard time breathing with the tension in the room. The best thing I could do was make myself useful, and that would not happen, standing around, watching Jack and Sarah.

I thumbed over my shoulder toward the door. "I'm going to unload the truck."

Sarah's expression pleaded with me not to go, and Jack encouraged me to make myself scarce.

"Just set it all in the living room. I'll figure out what to do with it later."

I accepted that and stepped out of the room again. Jack closed the door behind me. I took the gesture with the intended hint. He needed some time with his daughter, and I appreciated that as well as respected him for doing it.

The truck sat where I'd left it in the driveway. The faster I got this done, the faster I could get out of the heat. No sooner had I started to unload the bags from the bed than my little brother wandered out of the barn toward me.

"What are you doing, Charlie?"

I hadn't been out here five minutes, and sweat already ran down the side of my face. I wiped it off with my shirt sleeve and turned toward Austin. "I think I should ask you that. What are you doing out here?"

He jerked his head toward the barn and brushed his hands on his jeans. "Trying to help in the barn."

My little brother had been devastated by his girlfriend's just up and leaving. And I'd been a shit big brother for not making more time to help him deal with it. But Austin had always handled things his own way, and when he was ready, he'd come to me.

"Randi?" Her name held as much weight as my question. I didn't have to say anything more.

Austin reached up and pulled on the bill of his ballcap. Since he was little, he'd done that very thing to hide his emotions, and that emotion had always surrounded Miranda Adams. "Just making sure things are the way she wants them."

"So, when does she comes back?" I let the question drift into the air.

He crossed his arms over his chest, and it was the first time I realized how big he'd gotten. The guy was cut and had filled out his senior year. "She'll know that even though she wasn't home, I still took care of her."

And therein lied the rub. I wasn't sure Randi was ever *coming* home...primarily because I didn't know why she'd left, and neither did Austin as far as I knew. "You wanna help me grab this stuff?"

Austin answered by reaching over the edge of the truck bed to grab a load. I grabbed the bags and followed him inside. We set stuff on the couch and the floor in the living room, and when Austin went back outside, I stared at the crap I'd piled up. There was a lot of stuff Jack wasn't going to keep. Random things. Sarah had gotten ahold of a huge cup. I didn't even know how she held the thing. There was a whole bag of hideous socks the nurses kept on her feet because she got so cold. And then there were the plants, balloons, and knickknacks people had brought her.

"Thanks for your help, Austin."

"No worries. I'll see you at home later." Austin didn't stick around to make any plans or give me the chance to dive into what was going on. The door slammed behind him almost as quickly as he'd turned away.

I left the piles as neatly as I could without going through everything and circled back around to the hall. Jack was emerging as I approached Sarah's room, and he pulled the door closed behind him.

"She's not feeling much like herself, son. Needs some rest."

"Yeah, of course. I was going to head out anyhow."

The two of us strolled back down the way I'd just come and stopped at the front door.

"Jack, if you need anything, don't hesitate to call."

He clapped me on the shoulder. "You're a good man, Charlie."

8

CHARLIE

This was the first time since Sarah had started physical therapy that she would have a couple of days off. Even in the rehab facility, she'd had standing appointments on the weekend. It was a complete submersion into healing. Now she'd had the weekend without anyone poking or prodding her. I didn't know what Jack's plans were, and I hadn't asked. I just knew Sarah had to be back in Laredo for most of the afternoon, and I had more leeway with my time than he did. At some point, her dad had to get back to business. His business was cattle ranching, not hospitals and doctor's appointments.

He hadn't called me, although he did look relieved when I hopped out of the truck in front of the barn. It was an expression I'd never seen much growing up—not from Jack—and saw it just about every day now.

"Hey, Jack." I closed the truck door and walked over to

the horse Jack had in hand. "Is Sarah about ready for her appointment?"

He patted the horse's neck and smoothed its mane. "About as ready as she's gonna be." He could have been talking about the mare, but I assumed he referred to Sarah.

"You mind if I take her?" It took everything in me not to kick the dirt like a kid waiting for his parents to give him the green light to go play.

"Don't mind at all." He brushed off his hands. "Been getting a lot done 'round here this mornin'. I'd hate to break my stride. Would, to get Sarah where she needed to go. But it's good a you to offer. Sure Sarah won't mind, either." Jack tipped his hat the way old cowboys did; it was a respect thing the younger generations had shied away from.

I smiled. "I'll go get her, then."

He stuck his foot in the stirrup and mounted the horse. "Her wheelchair's in the living room. Last I checked she was on the couch."

With a nod, I made my way into the house, and Jack took off into the pastures. Sarah was right where Jack said she'd be with a book in hand. She hadn't seen me come in, which gave me a minute to watch her unnoticed. She flipped through the pages anxiously. There was no way she was actually reading at the speed she turned the paper.

I pushed off the door frame I'd propped myself against to watch her. "Hey, Sarah." There was just something about this girl that put the broadest smile on my lips.

"Hey, Charlie." She looked up and appeared genuinely glad to see me.

Her eyes lit up in a way I hadn't been expecting, and her smile was radiant. I reached out and leaned over the sofa. I want to offer her a hug, but again, I stopped myself. She lifted one hand and brushed it over the length of my arm in a familiar gesture. I wanted to kiss her on the forehead or the cheek—really more like her plump, red lips—but I held back. It had been a couple of days since I'd seen her, and I didn't want to push my luck. Sarah hadn't been expecting me anymore than Jack had, and I didn't want her to feel like I was encroaching on her territory without permission.

She pushed her strawberry blond curls away from her face, and I noticed her fingers moved a little better than they had been. "I wasn't expecting you."

"I thought you might need a lift to Laredo." In my mind, this had been the right thing to do, and Sarah had been over-joyed at my surprise visit. In reality, I wondered what I'd been thinking, not telling her I was coming.

"That would be nice."

"You sure you aren't sick of me yet?"

Her pretty lips twisted up, and she shook her head. "Don't be silly, of course not."

"That's a surprise; you're way ahead of most people." I joked. "Are you ready to get going?"

She set down her book and motioned toward the wheel-chair. "Can you help me?" Sarah didn't meet my eyes when she asked.

I took a chance and reached out to lift her chin with my fingers. "I'd love to."

And instead of treating her like she was made of glass, I

swept her into my arms like I would any other girl. Her arms flew into the air unexpectedly and then around my neck as she laughed. When I spun in a circle and stopped, our mouths were mere inches from each other, and God, I wanted nothing more than to press my lips to hers—taste just how sweet she was, feel her tongue tangle with mine. Sarah felt it. I felt it. The sexual tension couldn't have been cut with a chainsaw.

I cleared my throat and did my best to adjust myself without letting her go. Sarah didn't need to see the evidence of my excitement, and I didn't want Jack to catch a glimpse of it, either. Despite the draw I felt toward her and the gravitational force of our bodies and the magnetic pull, I placed her into the wheelchair.

"You realize there are steps outside, right?" Her tone was light, but there was no doubt it held no humor. "I can't exactly get down them."

With both of my hands on the grips behind her, I ignored her comment and tilted the chair backward so I could stare down at her. "You can with a little help." God, I wanted to taste her lips.

Sunlight poured through the windows and cast the most angelic glow around her face. She was beautiful. I couldn't get over the subtle things like the soft curve of her jaw, the shape of her supple pink lips, and her bright blue irises almost hidden by thick, dark lashes. When she looked up at me, I got lost in her eyes every single time. With little effort, this girl could own me in ways I'd never dreamed possible.

I caught myself thinking about what it would be like to

kiss up her neck, across her jaw, and beneath her ear. To run my fingers through her soft curls and hold her close. And each thought led me down a more treacherous path. That slippery slope was one I needed to avoid for the foreseeable future. Her dad would hogtie me and bury me on one of his hundreds of acres of land. No one would ever find my body. The way my mind wandered, before long, there would be physical evidence I wouldn't be able to refute. I wouldn't have to admit to Sarah I was incredibly attracted to her. All she'd have to do was look down to the ridiculous bulge in my pants—there would be no amount of adjusting in the world that could hide my desire for Sarah.

Thankfully, I had a moment to will my erection away as I pushed her out the front door toward the truck. "How are you feeling today?" I probably should have asked that question before I picked her up like she didn't have spinal cord injury and twirled her around like we were on a dance floor.

She peeked over her shoulder with a shrug. "Some days are better than others. I feel like all I do is take medication, lie around, and sleep. I hate the burden I'm putting on Daddy."

"Jack doesn't see it that way, Sarah. He just wants to do anything he can to help you get better." I tilted her wheelchair back when we reached the steps on the porch, and she stared up at me—God, she was gorgeous. "Ready?"

Sarah grinned and nodded. One by one, we descended the stairs until we reached the driveway. It was easier to keep her tilted and roll the chair on the back wheels, plus I got to have those blue eyes focused solely on me even if it was only for a few seconds. I stopped just short of my truck, opened the door, and turned to face her. In one fluid motion, she was back in my arms, and I lifted her into the truck. Her hands on my skin were like jolts of electricity that revved my heart and got my blood pumping.

At that moment, I realized I'd never felt alive—until I felt it: the energy, the chemistry, the everything. And for a moment, I forgot to breathe.

I closed the truck door and went to my side. I got in and stuck the key in the ignition. This wasn't supposed to mean anything. We were just driving to physical therapy. Yet somehow, it meant everything. Having her beside me just felt *right*.

Five weeks and countless sessions later, Sarah was starting to show signs of improvement. I hadn't missed a single visit and drove her to Laredo every day. I was grateful I worked on my parents' farm and that they valued the Adams as much as I did. They encouraged me—and Austin—to do whatever it took to help Jack at Cross Acres. I didn't think they had any idea that would include falling for his daughter, but since they hadn't specified that was off-limits, I hadn't discussed it. Jack and Sarah needed help. Austin was working on his ranch, and I made sure Sarah was taken care of. I never asked again; I just showed up. It hadn't taken long for Jack to stop asking why I was there, and he quickly reached a point where he simply kept working. Lately, he wasn't even around when I arrived, and if he were, he would just raise a hand in "hello." Jack trusted me to take care of her, and somehow, that was a reward in itself.

"Sunshine?" I called out for her as soon as I stepped into the foyer.

Sarah had gotten better about getting around on her own. She could move herself to and from her wheelchair, and Jack and I had built a ramp for her to get outside as well. Now, I never knew where I'd find her. I wasn't surprised by her resilience or the fact that she'd found ways to do what she wanted like cooking and taking care of her dad.

"I'm back here." Sarah's voice came from her bedroom down the hall.

A few long strides took me to her open door. She sat perched on the edge of her mattress with a bright smile that I wanted to believe was just for me. I couldn't prove it, but I was pretty confident that seeing me made her feel better. Stronger. Not invincible, but like she could conquer more, knowing I was by her side with each step.

That made my heart swell. I'd never wanted to be a man a woman could be proud of until I started spending time with Sarah. I wanted to be that for her. Her rock. The one person she could depend upon no matter what. And when she looked back at this, I wanted to be the one she remembered having at her side through the darkest days.

"Hey, you." She beamed, and the way she looked at me was why I called her sunshine—that look right there could light up the darkest sky.

I leaned down and kissed her cheek. One of these days I'd get up the courage to plant one on her lips, but I didn't need to be her focus right now. The only thing she needed to worry about was getting stronger. The rest could wait. Sarah Adams had lived in Mason Belle, Texas, her entire life, and so had I—we both had nothing but time on our hands. Patience wasn't one of my virtues, but I would wait a lifetime for her. "You about ready?"

Sarah shifted from the bed to her wheelchair, and I beamed with pride seeing how much strength she'd gained in the few months since the accident. It was the little things that had the biggest impact like the playful way she swatted at my chest when I irritated her and the fact that she was getting dressed on her own. The first time I saw her holding a coffee mug by the handle, my heart burst with satisfaction. But the day I walked in to homemade biscuits baked by her hands, *that* was the day I knew I was a goner.

"I guess." Sarah situated herself in the wheelchair, and her tone gave way to the lack of enthusiasm she had for making another trip to Laredo.

I stepped aside so she could roll out of her room. "It is PT you don't want to do? Or is it being locked in the truck with me for forty-five minutes?" I flipped her ponytail from behind.

She swatted behind her head at my hand and giggled. "You're so immature, Charlie. Didn't boys stop picking on girls in like fifth grade?"

I shrugged even though she couldn't see me. "I missed out on those years with you."

"That's your own fault. But to answer your question, no. It's not you. I'm dreading the FES."

The electrical stimulation device might be her least favorite part of physical therapy, but it had proven to be the most beneficial. There were days she was sick as a dog by the time she finished her sessions from working out so hard. I'd spent far more hours than I cared to count, holding her hair back while she puked into a bucket.

"Is it the FES? Or the walking?" I coddled her when she needed it, and I called her out when she needed that, too.

The scowl I received when she peered back at me over her shoulder told me I'd hit the nail on the head.

"Has anyone ever told you that you talk too much?" Sarah pushed her wheelchair over the threshold and out onto the front porch.

A laugh rumbled through my chest and out of my mouth; she was so damn cute when she was angry. "You. Just about every other day."

"Can't you just leave me be about this?"

I opened the truck and helped her in before folding the chair and placing it into the back. "Not a chance." I popped another kiss to her cheek and shut the door before she could respond.

It was no secret just how grueling physical therapy had become. They'd quit playing around and really focused on harnessing her mobility. I'd seen the agony of what she endured. I'd witnessed her try and fail—multiple times—to put one foot in front of the other. Sarah would work so hard that she'd reach exhaustion mentally and physically. Some days it resulted in tears of anger, and others had physical—like vomiting—repercussions.

"I don't want to go."

I hadn't even gotten my seatbelt buckled. This was a side of Sarah I hadn't seen. Even when she'd resisted, she'd never flat out said no. "Too bad this isn't optional, huh?"

She crossed her arms with a huff, and in any other situation, I would have chuckled. This time, she was serious. My making fun of her or joking would only result in an argument.

"It's pointless." Ah, so she was having one of those days. It didn't happen often, but when she felt hopeless, everything was a struggle.

With nothing to do on these drives back and forth to Laredo, we spent a lot of time talking. There hadn't been a pep talk in a long while, so I guess this was overdue. "You can't say none of this has been beneficial, Sarah." I glanced over at her and then returned my attention to the road. "You've regained strength, flexibility, mobility. You're not in as much pain—"

"That was before we started walking." The impatience in her voice, the need to rush out that sentence was the warning a breakdown was on the horizon—it was coming. "I just wish everyone would give up on it." She heaved in a breath, trying to stave off the tears. "The doctors already said I'd never walk again, so I don't know why they keep pushing this. There's no reason to keep trying. It's punishment for the therapists who never see results and torture for me."

"Sarah—"

"Don't you get it, Charlie? I'm like a lab rat. They keep trying all this crazy crap with no inkling as to whether it will work. I get my hopes up, and then it dawns on me; it's never going to happen."

I hit my fist on the steering wheel, startling her in the seat next to me. "No. I don't get it. And I'm not going to get it. Because the second I give in to that way of thinking there's no one fighting when you don't have the energy to do it for yourself." I ran my hands through my hair, pulling on the roots. "You *can* walk again. I believe that with every ounce of who I am. If you want it, Sarah, you can have it." I strained to keep my voice even and not raise it, but it was difficult. I wanted to shake her and force her to see what I saw when I looked at her. I wanted her to see the strength in who she was. "I know you can do it."

"No, *Charlie*," she snarled my name. "I can't!"

Her anger wasn't about me, and I refused to allow it to affect me. I wouldn't give in to that any more than I would concede that her walking was impossible.

She dropped her face into her hands, and her shoulders shook with emotion. "It hurts so much. I swear, I give it all I have, but you don't know what it's like." She was right; I didn't have any firsthand experience, but watching her struggle gave me enough insight into her battle to know none of this was easy.

Sarah swiped under her eyes to catch the tears she's allowed to fall. I hated to hear her sniffle, and I wanted to pull her into my arms to comfort her. But I couldn't do that driving down the highway.

"It's humiliating, Charlie. Stumbling around like a fool, clinging to a bar and having someone hold me up by a strap—

it's the most degrading thing I've ever endured. I'd rather be in a wheelchair for the rest of my life."

"You don't mean that."

Her gaze snapped in my direction when she turned her head sharply to stare at me; thankfully, I couldn't really look back and keep the truck on the road. "Maybe I do."

A funny thing happens when your heart takes up residence with another person's—their hurt becomes your own. I racked my brain for something to comfort her, but so far, I felt like a CD on repeat.

"It's going to get easier." I reached across the console to take her hand. I rubbed my thumb across her knuckles, hoping to ease her frustration. "Your therapists say you're doing great." I lifted her hand to my lips and kissed her fingers. "Don't give up, sunshine. I know you can do this."

Typically, anytime I called her sunshine, she became putty in my hand. It didn't have the desired effect today.

"You don't have to comfort me," she chided. "I know I have to keep going back. I'm fully aware that I don't have a choice. But I *wish* I didn't have to go back." Sarah pulled her hand from mine and twisted her fingers together in her lap. "I wish it were my decision and Daddy wouldn't force me to continue. I wish the rehab facility didn't have this stupid program. And I wish you weren't so dang optimistic all the time."

I couldn't tell if she'd just growled or mumbled, but either way, her frustration was clear. I didn't take any of this personally. Sarah needed a safe place to let off steam, and I was honored to be the person she felt she could do that with without repercussion. So, I let it happen.

The highway between Mason Belle and Laredo was rather desolate and really nothing more than a two-lane country road. The silence rested between us for a lot of miles, and it had started to rain. Neither of us had turned on the radio or tried to make idle conversation, and oddly enough, that was one of my favorite things about Sarah. The two of us could sit in silence comfortably. She wasn't like other women who filled space with mindless chatter.

And when I felt like enough time had passed between her jerking her hand from mine, I reached over and rested my hand on her thigh. The little gasp that escaped her lips at the touch was soft but there. I squeezed her knee gently, and she placed her palm on my fingers, finally giving me a squeeze.

She couldn't stay mad. "I'm sorry." And she never had a problem apologizing.

"Don't be," I told her. "I know it's frustrating."

"It is," she said. "But that doesn't give me the right to take it out on you. You don't deserve that."

"There's a difference between taking it out on me and venting. I'll always be your sounding board. That's what I'm here for." I looked over long enough to give her a smile. "To listen."

~

The rehab facility had an entire room with different machines and contraptions specifically designed to assist with walking. The space was large, and multiple patients worked with different physical therapists at the same time. And while I'd thought that would give Sarah hope and encourage her to see other people struggled, too, somehow, it only made her struggles worse. Her insecurities were preventing her progress as she worried more about what other people saw than focusing on the task in front of her. No one inside these walls other than her own team paid the least bit of attention to her, yet in her mind, they were all staring.

Her eyes scanned the perimeter of the room as the therapists got her into position between two bars. She held on for dear life to keep her balance, although she zoned in on everything else going on. Kappi—the newest therapist to her crew —was getting frustrated by her inability to reach Sarah. It was like Sarah had a wall up that she couldn't see past or hear beyond. Kappi tried to walk with her while an assistant stayed behind Sarah, holding a belt around Sarah's waist along with the brunt of Sarah's weight. It was an incredibly physical task for the two women. Add to it that Sarah wasn't paying attention, and it was like cats in a bathtub fighting against each other to get out.

We'd been at this for weeks, and I was nearing my breaking point. I didn't have a clue how Kappi and company were dealing with Sarah's insecurities. Nevertheless, Kappi would ply one leg, gently lifting from behind the knee, then set the foot on the floor, then repeat on the other side. It was slow and agonizing with a patient who *wanted* to do the work. It was brutal with Sarah.

I didn't know the assistant's name—they constantly changed—but I knew I had to save her to help Sarah. I stood and joined them at the bars. "You want me to take over for a bit?"

The assistant looked to Kappi, who gave her a nod of agreement. I could see the appreciation in the girl's eyes as I freed her from the responsibility of dealing with her patient. I wanted to tell the girl she might want to pick a new profession if she couldn't stand Sarah. I'd witnessed some nasty confrontations in this room, and Sarah didn't hold a candle to some of these grouchy old men.

I assumed the spot she'd been standing in while Kappi set Sarah up to get moving again. While the therapist got situated, I pulled Sarah close to me. Close enough for her to feel my breath on her skin and the strength in my hands.

With my mouth almost pressed to her ear, I whispered. "Sunshine, you've got to focus." I watched her knuckles turn white, and I could feel her jaw tense against my cheek. "I know you can do this. But baby, you're the only one who can make it happen."

The word "baby" did more to her than "sunshine." Her face relaxed, and she practically melted into my hold.

"I'm right behind you."

She turned into the heat of my words.

"I won't let you fall."

Sarah leaned her head against the side of mine.

"Just forget anyone else is here. It's just you and me." I felt her nod and then kissed her temple.

And for the first time since we'd stepped foot into this room weeks ago, Sarah zoned in on the task at hand. I'd never seen her so determined. She forgot about the other people in the room and just listened to Kappi. I stayed right with her where I'd promised to keep her safe.

We went through the motions as Sarah took a few assisted steps. They were ugly, and her knees snapped back, but they happened all the same. The goal was to get to the other end of the walkway between the bars. Before she'd gotten halfway, her legs started to shake.

Sarah stopped for a moment and leaned back onto my chest. She looked up at me, and the second I locked onto those bright blue eyes, I wanted to give her the world. "I can't do it, Charlie," she whispered.

I bent my neck, keeping the words between us. It was our world, and no one else existed in it right now. "You are so close. You can totally do this." I squeezed her waist for reassurance, and I hoped it gave her the extra oomph she needed to keep pushing.

She took a deep breath, but she seemed encouraged. She took a few more steps forward with the help of her therapist. We reached the end of the walkway, and I gave her hips another happy squeeze. Sarah was visibly exhausted. Her arms and legs trembled under the strain, but she hadn't given up.

"That was awesome." I couldn't be more proud.

"You're helping." She sighed. "You're helping *a lot*." She

acted like my assistance somehow negated her accomplishment, and I disagreed.

Thankfully, Kappi called for a break, so I didn't have to have that discussion. It would be nice to pump Sarah up, but it would take her seeing what she could do, not hearing it from me. I helped her to a seat, and then I went to get her a bottle of water while she rested.

"We are going to try it one more time." Kappi rubbed Sarah's calf muscles as she spoke, massaging out some of the fatigue. "Then we are going to do some joint manipulation, and you'll be done for the day. You're barely going to be able to move tonight."

"I'm not sure that's a good thing," Sarah muttered.

Kappi motioned for me to stay where I was while she helped Sarah up and got her back into position with the bars. "All right, we're going to try it a little differently this time."

There was a slight edge of panic in Sarah's voice. "What do you mean?"

Kappi winked at Sarah. "I mean, I want you to do exactly what we've been doing...just without our help." There was a gleam in her eyes, and I wondered if she was sadistic or just delusional.

"On my own?" Uncertainty laced Sarah's voice, and panic crinkled her brow. "Like by myself?" Her eyes darted to me, and when she didn't get the response she'd hoped for, she looked back to Kappi.

"Exactly. You can do it. I believe in you. Charlie believes in you." Her smile got wider. "At some point, Sarah, you have to learn to believe in yourself."

"She's right, sunshine," I added to back her up. "Mind over matter. Mustard seed."

Sarah gave me an evil glare and pursed her lips. If I didn't shut my mouth, her shaking hands might collide with my teeth. But Sarah didn't say anything; she just turned her attention back to the task at hand.

"You can do it, Sarah." Kappi's reassurance did nothing for Sarah. "Use the bars for support like usual—"

But Sarah didn't wait for Kappi to finish her instruction. Her knee wobbled, and her hands slid just a bit on the bar. And I'll always believe, she moved her foot just to get us to shut up. Irritation was a great motivator. It was messy, and Sarah was nearly out of breath, having barely moved more than a couple of inches. But she'd done it.

Sarah had just proven all the doctor's wrong with that single movement. I was out of my seat faster than my heart leaped into my chest. My entire body flooded with a sense of immense *pride*. All I could think when I looked at her was, *that's my girl*. And just as gnarly as the first step had been, Sarah made it two and then three.

Her arms were about to give out, and I couldn't hold myself back anymore. Kappi saw me moving and got out of the way. I swept Sarah into a hug, lifting her off the ground. I squeezed her without hurting her but didn't want to let her go. She clung to my neck with the same vigor that I held her.

I buried my face next to her ear. "I'm so fucking proud of you, sunshine."

When I finally set her down, I still steadied her with an arm around her waist—her front pressed to mine.

I couldn't stop myself. I didn't even try.

My free hand slid into her hair, tilting back her head, and I got lost in the ocean of blue when her eyes met mine. I gave up the fight that had waged inside my head for weeks and pressed my lips to hers. It was soft and warm and inviting, but as classic as Sarah herself. In essence, it was perfect.

I leaned in and pressed my face close to her cheek with my nose against her ear. "I love you." I hadn't intended to make that confession regardless of having known it for quite some time.

For a moment, she was still in my arms, but then she melted and leaned against my chest, pushing her face into my shoulder. "I love you, too."

9

SARAH

I couldn't get him out of my mind. And that kiss. As far as kisses go, the steam level might not have been that great for anyone else, but for *this* girl—who'd never been kissed—it was amazing. Not only was it a welcome relief from all of the worry, all of the stress that had weighed me down the past few months, but it was Charlie *freaking* Burin. His mouth had touched mine; his tongue had parted my lips; his fingers had dug into my neck. It was just—*ah*. A girl could die happy after that exchange.

Charlie had managed to nudge his way into my world without my really noticing that he'd come in, and he'd never left. It was Charlie who encouraged me through physical therapy. It was Charlie who picked me up when I was down. It was Charlie who believed in me when I didn't believe in myself. At my lowest points, he was always there to get me through. He marked every bit of progress as a triumph, and he tallied all the wins. One unassisted step at a time. And while it might not have been many, the progress was definitely there. In my mind, I owed the victories to him. Even when doctors hadn't thought I'd walk again, Charlie had believed in me.

He showed up faithfully every day. No one had ever asked him, to my knowledge. But once he'd started, Daddy supported him, and his parents did, too. Looking over at him, I couldn't help but be grateful. Not just for what he'd done for me but for him in general. And then I got lost in staring at him.

A grin tickled his lips as the corner started to turn up. He knew I was watching him, and I think part of him secretly loved it. Charlie was no stranger to women's attention and affection, but sometimes I thought it embarrassed him when it came from me. But I could spend hours memorizing the details of his handsome features and days getting lost in his eyes. What I couldn't figure out was what he saw in me. Self-doubt had become a nasty demon in my head. It would take years for my hair to grow out and just as long for the scars to lose their angry hue. And even if I did manage to walk again, it would always be with a limp. My fingers looked like I'd suffered from years of arthritis, and I'd lost so much weight I appeared anorexic. But when Charlie's eyes met mine, I didn't feel like he saw any of that.

When I turned my attention back to the road, I realized he had veered off the highway toward Mesa, a little town not far from Mason Belle. "Where are we going?"

"Mesa." A dimple appeared in his cheek.

I couldn't help the grin that lifted my lips. "You think you're pretty cute, don't you?"

"Most days."

I shifted in the seat to face him better. "What are we going to Mesa *for?*"

"Have you ever been to the Sock Hop?"

Embarrassed, I shook my head. "I've never been to Mesa."

Charlie turned his eyes to me, and they were as green as grass on a summer day, not even a shimmer of brown remained. "Really? Not even in high school?"

"I've been to Laredo with Daddy for cattle auctions, but other than that, I've never left Mason Belle."

"At all?" Charlie kept shifting his attention back and forth between the road and me, but I couldn't help but laugh this time.

"You act like it's a big deal. Lots of people never leave Mason Belle." I shrugged. "I happen to like our little town." And I did. I loved that I knew everyone in the county and that I'd grown up with generations of people who would always be there. There was comfort in that type of familiarity.

He moved his hand to my thigh and squeezed. "So, you'd be happy living there for the rest of your life?"

"Of course. Why would I ever leave? Who would take care of Cross Ac—" I didn't bother to finish that sentence.

It wouldn't be me.

I couldn't take care of myself much less a cattle ranch, and at twenty-four and single, it was unlikely I'd marry someone who'd work another man's ranch in hopes of gaining it in an estate later. Cattle ranching wasn't for the faint at heart. It was also passed down through generations of men. Neither of which my daddy had at his disposal. Austin had been the closest thing Daddy had to a son, and with Randi gone, that didn't bode well for either Austin or him.

"Sarah, Cross Acres is in good hands." He slid his palm down my thigh and squeezed my knee. "But it's good to know you don't want to branch out to a city somewhere."

I held his hand and bit my lip. "Nah, I'm a country girl. I couldn't survive in someplace like Laredo."

Charlie turned into a parking lot, and as he pulled into a spot, I realized the Sock Hop was an old fifties diner complete with girls on roller skates and curbside service for those who didn't want to get out of the car.

"Wow. This is so cute. How'd you ever find it?" I ducked down to see out the window and above the truck. This place was as authentic as it could be without a time warp—someone had done an amazing job of keeping up the original décor and design.

He put the truck in park and barked out a laugh. "Everyone came here on Friday nights after football games in high school. Where were you then?"

"At home, raising my sister."

Any other man would have let that dampen the mood, but not Charlie. "Well then, today's a first. The burgers are amazing, but save room for a chocolate malt."

"Do they have fries to dip in it?" Who wouldn't want that triple threat? Death by fat.

A smile rose on his lips that reached his eyes, and he leaned forward. Charlie captured the back of my neck and pulled me to him. "And *that* is just one of a million reasons why I love you. Of course, they have fries."

I'd never tire of hearing him say it, although he didn't use those words often. I could count on one hand the number of times he'd paired *I* with *love* and *you*, and each one had more meaning than the last because they had become more personal, more detailed, more specific. "Oh, yeah? Will you love it if I gain a hundred pounds on greasy burgers and fries?" I giggled.

"Seeing as how you've never really left Mason Belle, I think it's safe to say I don't have to worry about you and fast food."

"Mason Belle could have a population boom, and corporate conglomerates could take over Main Street. There could be a McDonalds in the works right this very second. Who knows? Don't be so sure of yourself, Charlie." The tsk that followed made him laugh.

He pecked my lips. "Sarah, you've got a smokin' hot figure, but it's not your body I'm after."

I didn't know how to take that backhanded compliment.

"You make me a better man, and I want to be that for you. I don't care what shape or size that comes in as long as you wrap the package."

My jaw dropped. Yes, Charlie had told me he loved me. And yes, we had kissed several times. And yes, Charlie Burin had been the love of my life since, well, forever. But somehow, I hadn't allowed myself to believe any of this was more than just a favor to Daddy or an obligation to please our families.

Before I had a chance to gather my wits and formulate a coherent sentence, a cute blonde on skates knocked on the window. Charlie rolled it down while she chomped on her gum and lifted a pad and pen to take our order.

"What can I get you?"

"Two chubby checkers and a chocolate malt."

She winked, tucked her pad and pen into her pocket, and gave her gum one final chomp. "Sure thing, sweetheart." And then she pushed off on one foot and bent over to skate away with her ruffles underneath her skirt barely covering her butt.

Part of me was envious, not just of her perfect little tush but of her agility and confidence. She knew she was gorgeous, and she worked it for tips. Yet Charlie barely seemed to notice her, and he hadn't so much as grinned when she'd flirted with him. He'd been polite, and then immediately returned his attention to me. It was then that I noticed his hand still on my thigh. And I realized he hadn't hidden his affection, either.

"You're going to love this place."

My heart swelled just being in his presence. "Is that so?"

Charlie leaned back in his seat and rested his head while looking at me, into me. "Yup. You're going to beg me to bring you here for a chubby and a malt every day after physical therapy."

"A chubby and a malt, huh?" Laughter bubbled up from my chest and out my mouth.

God, he was adorable. "Just wait. You can thank me later."

His green eyes glimmered, and I thought about how that must be the color of Irish luck. It was stunning and magical wrapped into one.

The mirth didn't stop dancing in his irises when he spoke. "You've got a mischievous look on your face. What are you thinking about?"

I didn't think he'd understand my leprechaun analogy, nor did I want to divulge just how much I enjoyed being with him, staring at him, loving him. Because I was in way too deep. I'd landed in the part of the pool where I had to tread water, and I couldn't swim.

"Two chubbies and a malt? Do you guys need ketchup?" Thankfully, the waitress saved me from having to answer.

And for the next thirty minutes, all I did was praise Charlie's burger choice and moan at just how good it was. The thin cut-cut fries were perfectly salted for dunking in the malt. I could have died and gone to heaven—right here, right now—a happy, happy girl.

"You're welcome." Charlie wiped his mouth with a napkin, but it didn't remove the I-told-you-so smirk from his kissable lips.

I swatted at his bicep playfully. "You were right. It was the best burger I've ever had." I also liked that for once I felt normal. Like this was a date. Except Charlie hadn't had to help me out of the truck and into a wheelchair. We'd been able to enjoy a meal in the cab, listening to music, talking, in our own perfect bubble.

He kissed my cheek. "I need to get you back before Jack starts to worry."

That was the problem with having almost died in a car accident; it left everyone on edge if I were five minutes late. Daddy would start texting and calling if he didn't know where I was. "Oh God, I need to call him."

"No worries, sunshine. He knew we were stopping. You're in good hands."

A wave of heat crept up my cheeks as they flushed with a blush. "You asked my dad if you could take me out?" That had to be the most chivalrous thing a man had done this century, and I swooned.

Charlie put his hand behind my head on the seat as he looked over his shoulder to back out. "Why does that surprise you?" He shifted gears and straightened out the truck.

I shrugged. "Austin never asked Daddy to take Randi out."

He didn't take his eyes off the road, and I noticed he'd moved both of his hands to the steering wheel instead of having one on me. "Yeah, well, I'm not Austin, and you sure as hell aren't Miranda."

There was a hint of animosity in his tone when he said my little sister's name, but I let it go. She wasn't high on anyone's list these days, but I still hadn't figured out what was going on. And anytime I tried to get information, Austin would snap at me, Daddy would find a way to change the subject or leave the room, and Charlie didn't know any more than I did. Or I didn't think he did.

"You didn't have to say it back, you know?" He broke the silence, but I wasn't sure what he referred to.

I looked over at him, furrowing my brow. "What do you mean?" I was lost. "Didn't have to say what?"

"*It.*" His ears were pink, and it was easy to see he was flustered—I just had no idea why. "I didn't want you to feel obligated."

"Charlie, I'm not following you."

"The other day after physical therapy—"

I thought back to what he might be referring to, and there was only one culprit. "When you told me that you loved me?" And now I was flustered. If I'd confessed how I felt to Charlie Burin only for him to back out and tell me it was something he'd said in the moment, I might throw up that burger and fries I'd just inhaled.

He nodded and swallowed hard like he had a boulder in his throat. That was not good.

"Did you not mean it?" I didn't mean to screech, but I'd gone from confused to mortified to panicked, and I was about to settle on heartbroken.

Charlie's face scrunched up into an indescribable expression, and it was one I couldn't place. "What? No. I mean, yes." He took a deep breath. "Yes, I meant it. But I sprung it on you. Like out of the blue without warning, and I just want you to know you didn't have to say it back...if you didn't mean it. I kind of put you on the spot." He paused. "Sometimes it's just natural to respond or easier. Hell, I don't know. I'm sorry, Sarah."

"Do you?" I'd turned completely in the seat, so I didn't miss a single tic in his expression.

He glanced away from the road and at me for a second, then back to the road and then me. "Do I love you?"

I nodded.

"Of course, I do. I didn't say it without thought. I mean, it was kind of spontaneous, but I've spent a lot of time thinking about it. About you." He ran his hand through his shaggy hair and then down his face, and I smiled. Any time Charlie got nervous, that was his tell, and I secretly loved that I affected him that way. "I'm not good at this kind of thing, Sarah."

I shouldn't find humor in any of this, but now that I knew Charlie felt the way I did, my stomach had stopped churning, and my dinner had settled. For once, I wasn't the only one in uncharted territory. "Really? I never noticed that. You've always been quite the lady's man."

He groaned, and I burst out into laughter. "Are you kidding? You realize I haven't dated anyone seriously? Ever."

"I hadn't noticed that." That wasn't a lie. There were always so many women clamoring for Charlie's attention that I'd always assumed he'd had one after another. Although, now I wondered if that had been an unfair assessment.

The man appeared miserable, waiting for me to stop giving him a hard time and respond to his initial comment.

I reached over the console and wound my hand under his arm and around to his forearm. "I didn't feel obligated to return the sentiment, Charlie." I'd sobered a bit trying to get the next part out, and the laughter had died on my lips. "I love you, too. I always have."

"That was just infatuation in high school, Sarah."

I shrugged. "Maybe to you. But my feelings haven't changed; they've just matured." And that was the simple truth. "I don't have any experience," I rolled my eyes, "like at all. But one thing I do know is how to love. And I'm confident in the fact that I love you."

He moved his arm to take my hand and then lifted our twined fingers to his lips. I adored the way he kissed my knuckles like I was delicate, cherished. *His.* And somewhere in that conversation, I thought there had been an unspoken change or commitment between us.

Charlie didn't drop his hold on my hand when he lowered the windows in the truck and let in the fall breeze. The wind whipped through my hair, and for the first time since the accident, I felt free. I was filled with hope and love, and that might all come crashing down in a devastatingly painful way, but for today—*today* it was liberating, exhilarating. The best part was that it was all with Charlie. He'd helped me find the girl I'd lost years before the accident, and regardless of what ended up happening between us, I'd forever be grateful for the second chance at life.

When we got back to Cross Acres, that sense of freedom felt a little more fleeting. Daddy sat in one of the rocking chairs on the porch, waiting. My bubble was about to burst, and I wanted to hover in it just a little longer. I didn't want to go back to being dependent upon other people when I got out of this truck. I didn't want to go back into the house. More than anything, I didn't want Charlie to leave.

I stared at Daddy while Charlie parked in front of the barn. "Are you going to stay for a while?" I couldn't bear the thought of his going. The day had been too good. Somehow, in my mind, if Charlie left, so would that feeling.

"I wouldn't mind helping with dinner."

I glanced back over my shoulder at Daddy, still sitting in the chair. "I'm sure Daddy would love having you around, too. Does he look upset to you?"

Charlie peered through the back window of the truck. "He's definitely got something on his mind." He patted my knee. "Come on. Might as well find out what's going on." Then he leaned over the console and kissed my temple before he hopped out.

Seconds later, he appeared at my door. Once he'd opened it, he gave me his back.

"What are you doing?"

He reached over his shoulder and patted his back. "Hop on."

I huffed out a laugh. "Are you kidding? I'll kill us both in the process."

Charlie faced me, turned my legs on the seat so my knees pointed out, and then he turned around. He grabbed each of my knees with his hands. "Put your arms around my neck." He waited, but I hadn't moved. "Sunshine, your dad's watching. Come on."

I did as he told me and wound my arms around him. He pulled me snuggly to him, and I realized how much better this was than being carried like his bride everywhere I went. This was fun and playful, and it didn't make me feel like an invalid or a hundred years old. I giggled when he hopped on one foot to close the door behind us.

"Whoa." I slipped just a hair, but that inch might as well have been a mile when I wouldn't be able to catch myself if I fell.

Charlie pulled my legs tighter around him and leaned his head back. "I've got you, baby. Always." He popped a kiss on my cheek and then hollered at Daddy. "Hey, Jack. What are you up to?" I didn't have to see the smile on his face; I could hear it in his voice. It was fast becoming my favorite sound—Charlie happy.

"Just enjoying what's left of the evening. Glad you two are home. I need to talk to you." He stood and then opened the front door for us. "How was physical therapy?"

"Cut the small talk, Daddy. What's wrong?"

My dad was a man of few words. If he needed to talk, it wasn't to chit chat about the sunset or the weather. Charlie followed him into the kitchen and set me down on a stool and then took the one next to me. Whatever was going on wasn't good. Part of me wondered if it had to do with Randi, but I didn't dare mention her name without risking upsetting Daddy. If it were related to my sister, I'd find out soon enough.

Daddy busied himself in the kitchen, clearly wasting time and dragging this out. Charlie got up and got a glass of tea and brought me one as well. But when he returned to my side, he didn't sit. He stood behind me as if he were afraid that whatever Daddy had to say might send me flying backward.

And then his strong, solid baritone floated into the room. "Jack? What's going on?"

Daddy's hands shook when he faced us. He finally set down the glass and wrapped his fingers around the edge of the counter. "Doc Hammond called today while you were gone." That wasn't good.

Charlie's hands landed on my shoulders with a squeeze, but he didn't say anything.

"Wanted to talk about your next surgery."

I'd known it was coming. I'd had more discussions than I could count with numerous surgeons. This one wouldn't be the last either. I'd just hoped to have more time between making progress and having to start over again.

Somehow, in the back of my mind, I'd known it would be soon, but I wasn't ready to face it. Today was the first glimpse of freedom I'd had, and another surgery would put me out of commission for an undetermined amount of time—again. "Already?"

"Yeah, sweetheart," Dad said. "But it ain't gonna be as bad as the last one. Doc said it won't bring you down for long."

I'd played these games for weeks. Physicians regurgitated whatever they needed to in order to motivate a patient; afterward, they'd say there are no guarantees, and everyone's body is different. That meant *my* body was different when I was slow to heal. "How long?"

"You'll be out of physical therapy for a week." Daddy

didn't sugarcoat it, although he'd never been that kind of man.

Charlie leaned down and wrapped his arms around my neck to whisper into my ear. "I'll be here to help you, sunshine."

I watched Daddy's eyes for any reaction to the man behind me who touched me without hesitation in front of my father, but if it bothered him, he didn't even flinch. In fact, that might have been a hint of a grin on his weathered cheeks. I'd just gotten Daddy's acceptance in that one gesture, and that meant the world.

"When is the surgery scheduled?" Charlie asked the question with his cheek still pressed to mine, and his strength seeped into me.

I lifted my hands to rest on his forearms and squeezed. I didn't want to go through surgery again or ever, but if I had Charlie by my side, I'd do whatever I had to.

"Day after tomorrow." Daddy heaved out a sigh. "We gotta be in Laredo at six that mornin'. But we'll have you home by sundown."

There wasn't much I could do other than accept it. "All right."

Daddy came around the counter and kissed my cheek, and then he clapped Charlie on the shoulder before walking out of the room.

"We've got this, Sarah." Charlie had all the confidence in the world.

Faith that could move mountains. "I could use one of your mustard seeds."

10

SARAH

"The surgery went well, and her stats look good." The doctor's voice was clear, but I doubted I'd remember anything he said; everything was hazy. "The nurses are going to watch her for a bit, but once the sedation wears off, she should be good to go home."

I nodded and hoped to God someone else was listening. My head was swimming, and I wouldn't retain anything. Daddy and Charlie were here; surely, they were taking notes. My eyes kept drifting closed, and I'd snap them open to find Charlie grinning at me like he thought it was cute.

"I'm going to write her another prescription for oxycodone and one for an antibiotic. Use the oxycodone as needed for pain. The antibiotic is twice a day for ten days. It's just a precaution, but infection is a risk we don't need to take."

I just wanted him to stop talking and let me sleep. I could read a bottle when I got home; I didn't need a rundown on pain meds and prescriptions. I'd done this before. I took a deep breath and pried my lids apart one more time.

The doctor seemed smaller than he was before surgery—and serious. He'd made it through the hard part; I'd come out of surgery alive. He needed to relax, but instead, he wrote on his clipboard, and the movement of the pen was almost as mesmerizing as Charlie's gaze.

"I'm adding some additional notes that Sarah can read over later, but she needs to take it easy the rest of today. Stick to fluids and bland food like crackers. She should be good to eat tomorrow, but don't overdo it. Rest is key. Sleep is the body's way of healing itself."

"What about physical therapy?"

It sounded like Daddy, but I couldn't be sure. And I hadn't heard the doctor's answer.

"—no sexual activity."

My eyes sprung open. I couldn't be any more awake if I'd had ice water dumped on me. Thankfully, neither Charlie nor Daddy paid me any attention. They were both focused on the conversation with the surgeon. Nevertheless, heat rose in my cheeks, and I was certain I'd blushed. *No sexual activity*—he had no idea. It was laughable. Not that the man had any idea that I was a still a virgin. Sex was one thing on the list of "don'ts" that I *didn't* have to worry about.

Dr. Hammond turned his attention to me now that I appeared to be wide awake. "I'll see you in my office in a week. Do you have any questions?"

I shook my head, afraid to speak. Nope, I was still reeling

from the instruction given to my father and—whatever Charlie was to me—for me not to have intercourse. Randi would have asked if that included all sexual activity or only penetration just to make everyone uncomfortable. I wanted to forget it had ever happened.

"Then that's about it." Dr. Hammond smiled, tore off the prescriptions, and then handed them to Daddy.

The pain medication and sedation kept me pretty well pulled under for the next couple days. I had dozed in and out on the way from Laredo back to Mason Belle, and I couldn't remember how I'd gotten inside the house. When I woke in my bed, I had to assume Charlie had carried me. What I didn't want to know was who had changed my clothes and put me into pajamas. It only took me a few seconds to realize my bra had also been removed, and I cringed when I thought about the panties I had on. I wouldn't be winning any hearts with cotton briefs.

"Hey, sunshine." Charlie knocked on the doorjamb and waited in the hall.

I winced when I tried to push myself to a sitting position, and in two strides, he was at my side.

Charlie propped me up with pillows and made sure I was comfortable. "You must not have heard the part about taking it easy."

I scoffed. "Oh, I heard it. I hear it all the time. I'm not sure how much easier I can take it." Lying in bed was about as laid back as things got. And based on my current pain levels, there was definitely no flight risk.

He loomed over me with his hands on his hips. It was funny how intimidated I would have been by his stance six months ago, but now I realized that broody look demonstrated Charlie's concern. "How are you feeling?"

The age-old question no one really ever wanted an honest answer to. "All things considered, I'm okay." I smoothed the blankets over my legs. "I don't think I can spend much more time in this room, though."

I hadn't really been awake much, but I also hadn't been out of my room since the surgery, not even to take a shower. I didn't want to think about what my hair must look like. Times like these, I wanted to wring my sister's neck for disappearing.

"What are you doing here?" It wasn't that I was unhappy to see him, but I wondered when his family was going to demand that he pull his weight at Twin Creeks. Ranches didn't have extra hands, and Charlie had missed a ton of time since my accident.

Charlie laughed and sat down on the edge of the bed. "I'm not going to take offense to that." His eyes glimmered, and I wanted to kiss his perfect lips. "Austin and I were helping your dad with a new fence by the barn. Your dad went out to get some lumber, so I thought I'd come to check on you before he got back."

I could get lost in his eyes, and there were other parts of him that I wanted to lose myself in as well. I shook those thoughts from my head but didn't stop myself from admiring his rugged jawline and the bit of scruff that came from his not shaving. "So, tell me. What's going on out in the free world." I grinned.

He made himself comfortable on the bed next to me and fluffed up a pillow behind him. When he crossed his ankles, then his arms behind his head, I tried not to laugh. "Well, I don't want to get you overstimulated, so try to contain yourself."

I crossed my heart.

"I woke up this morning and made breakfast."

"Oh yeah? What'd you have?" The thought of Charlie in the kitchen was its own weird form of aphrodisiac.

"Waffles—okay, they were Eggos, but I brewed my own coffee."

I gasped, put my hand on my chest, and batted my eyes in an overdramatic fashion. "Oh, tell me more."

He licked his lips and narrowed his eyes. "I took out the trash."

"This is starting to get good."

"Austin was supposed to meet your dad this morning to help with the fence, so I tagged along."

"So, I owe a bit of gratitude to Austin for the company today?"

He shrugged. "Not too much. I was coming anyhow. He just gave me an excuse to do it earlier."

That admission sobered my silly thoughts, and I stopped giggling, although I couldn't stop staring. I'd never had a man want to spend time with me, and I wasn't sure how to welcome the attention when it wasn't centered around doctors' appointments or physical therapy. I was awkward at best, but Charlie didn't seem to mind. If he did, he never said anything or made fun of me. He just leaned over and brushed his hand over my forehead, sliding my disheveled hair from my face.

"I'm not so sure Jack likes all the time I'm spending with you." His eyes flicked over my face. "You would tell me if he were secretly plotting my death, wouldn't you?" His voice was hard to discern, and there was a hint of a twinkle in his eyes that countered his tone.

I couldn't tell if he if really believed that or if he was just playing with me, but I leaned more toward the latter; Charlie had to know Daddy thought he and Austin hung the moon. "No," I said. "I would continue to make you guess."

He leaned in close, so close I could feel the warmth of his breath against my lips. "That hurts, sunshine." The faint scent of his sunscreen mixed with the smell of cattle and cologne created a scent unique to one man. Heat radiated from his body, and I had to restrain myself from running my hand up his arm.

My gaze flitted from his to his mouth and back. The pull toward him was magnetic, and the desire to taste his lips was almost too much to resist. I wanted to feel his arms wrapped around me as he pulled me in close. The need to touch his skin, caress his taught muscles—I wanted his body pressed to mine.

My thoughts raced along with my pulse, but Charlie didn't move. He had to sense the tension I did, but it wasn't a bad feeling. Foreign, but definitely good. He tipped his nose against mine, all while holding my stare. It was gentle and sweet, but his eyes were wild. I wouldn't have the faintest idea what to do, but if Charlie took the lead, I'd follow without hesitation or regret.

I licked my lips, and the bottom one got stuck on my teeth. When it released, it brushed against his. God, I wanted more—craved more. I tilted my head to invite him in. Electricity traveled between us even without a physical connection. I could hear the sizzle and feel the spark.

My lips parted, but I didn't quite make a sound. I closed my eyes and lifted my hands to the hard planes of his chest. His shirt was soft, but nothing could have hidden the rigid muscles underneath. I slid my palms up to his shoulders, wishing he'd return my affection. I was seconds away from losing my nerve.

Just as I was about to cough on him to force us both back, his mouth finally met mine. His lips were firm until they parted, and then the heat was stifling. It stole my breath, and then his tongue found mine, and the rhythm was perfect. Each swipe sent tingles between my legs, and my nipples pebbled.

My heart pounded, and the rest of the world slipped away. Nothing else existed outside of the two of us. As if I were a pro, I raised my hand to the back of his neck, and he did the same. The deeper the kiss became, the more electricity danced down my spine. Each touch awakened a part of me I hadn't known existed. I was alive in a way I'd never been, and I wondered if this was what drugs felt like.

Then as quickly as I'd found a groove, he switched it up. I felt a sense of loss as soon as he moved away. But he hadn't gone far. Charlie looked at me and then kissed my jaw, my throat, the dip between my clavicles. I swallowed hard when he sought my permission to continue. He shifted on the bed and began to unbutton my pajama top, placing a sensual kiss on my skin with each one he undid.

Just as he reached the final button, I took a deep breath and held it. My body was riddled with scars from the accident and multiple surgeries. I'd had more stitches and staples than any one person should, and those battle wounds had left marks that appeared angry and painful. They were far from beautiful, and my body was nowhere near perfect.

His gaze flitted up, and I wondered if he had realized what he'd started and now wanted to back out. Yet that wasn't at all what I saw when my eyes met his. Charlie's chest heaved, and I finally let go of the air I'd held and hoped he couldn't feel my erratic pulse.

With care and tenderness, he spread my top open and exposed my marred skin. I didn't glance down; I knew what I looked like. What was once a creamy, smooth surface now looked like a battlefield. Charlie dropped his gaze and one by one, he kissed every mark. I took deep breaths each time his lips met a battle wound, and I attempted to relax, but having Charlie Burin this close kept me in a constant state of arousal.

The mattress dipped as Charlie moved the blankets and situated himself between my thighs. And when he dragged his fingers from my knee to my waist, my cotton shorts bunched at the top of my thigh. He squeezed my hipbone just a bit and then grazed my side over my ribs until his thumb rested under my breast, and he hovered over my body.

Our eyes met, and he pushed down, bending at the elbows, to seal his mouth with mine. As naturally as breathing, my hands went around his back, and I stroked his spine. My legs spread to get closer to him, and his hips pressed against me. I gasped at the size of his erection against me. That slight intake of air brought Charlie's attention back to my face. His ears were tinged red, and his cheeks were flushed. His top lip curled into the most seductive grin I'd ever seen, and I wondered if he was as awestruck as I was. That grin turned into a smirk, and Charlie dipped his head.

My back arched off the mattress when he took my breast into his mouth, and I saw stars as he cupped them, kissed them, sucked them. His tongue swirled around my nipple, flicking, teasing, and then he nibbled.

My core tightened and warmed. I tugged at the hem of his shirt, but he weighed too much for me to accomplish anything without his assistance. I wanted more, needed him closer. But most importantly, I had to have him naked. It was irrational and completely out of character, but my heart had wanted Charlie since we were kids. Now my body had finally caught up, and it was just as insatiable in another way.

"Off." I panted, grabbing his shirt, and my chest heaved.

He sat back on his haunches to oblige and stripped away his shirt. He tossed it to the floor without ever losing focus. I stared at his bare chest and his rippling abs. I couldn't get enough of his strong arms and broad shoulders. And more than once, I wondered why he was here. Charlie Burin could have any girl in town, yet he'd chosen me.

His Adam's apple dipped in his throat when he swallowed, and there was the slightest bit of hesitation. If I didn't know better, I'd think he was nervous. His nostrils flared when he took a deep breath, and the muscles in his chest flexed. Charlie reached down and hooked his fingers into the waistband of my shorts and waited for me to nod. Something about that gesture comforted me. Charlie could have taken whatever he wanted. He had to know I wouldn't resist. Instead, he asked for permission.

They glided over my thighs with ease, and then my panties followed. If Charlie were bothered by cotton bikini briefs, I couldn't tell it by his pupils dilating or the way he licked his lips. He pushed my knees apart, exposing my most private parts, and I watched as his head disappeared and he stretched out on the mattress. I wasn't at all prepared for his tongue to part my folds and jumped at the touch, but he wrapped his arms around my thighs to keep me still, and with the next pass, a moan slipped past my lips that could have taken the paint off the walls.

Warm, wet, soft. I had no idea what he was doing, but it sent waves of euphoria rolling through my body. He had me coiled tighter than a spring, and I felt like I would unravel at any given moment. But Charlie took his time and ensured I'd never enjoyed anything more. I couldn't pry my lids apart, and my fists clenched the sheets underneath me. I wanted all of him, but I didn't want him to stop this to do something else. It was too much and then not enough.

By the time he'd made the decision for me, I realized it wasn't enough. He kissed me, and I tasted myself on his hot, needy mouth when his tongue begged for entry. His hips rocked against mine, and he slid one hand under my butt, squeezing it for leverage. There was something gentle in his firm touch. I could feel his arousal through his jeans. They were rough against my sensitive skin but rough in the best way.

I broke away from his kiss to catch my breath, and he used the opportunity to remove his pants. He stood next to the bed, and my head lulled to the side to watch. It was brazen, and I probably shouldn't have, but Charlie didn't seem to mind. His toed off his boots, and then dropped his jeans and his boxers. They hit the floor with a heavy thud, or maybe that was my heart about to explode. I tried to keep my eyes from going wide at the sight of him naked before me, but when Charlie threw his head back in laughter, I knew I'd missed the mark.

He climbed back onto the bed, and I spread for him without request. Charlie accepted the invitation and made himself comfortable.

I shivered when he leaned down, breathing on my neck. His erection tickled my stomach, and I was lost with what to do.

"God, you're beautiful, sunshine." His whispered words were felt, not just heard.

Charlie's forehead leaned against mine, and he held my

eyes. My head warred with what to focus on—the loving way he gazed into my soul or his hot head that throbbed at my entrance. As he pushed himself inside, I worried I'd be too tight. He was well-endowed, and I was a virgin. Despite how much I wanted it, or just how ready I was, I wasn't certain he'd be able to get it in all the way.

I considered saying something, but my need choked off my words. Charlie didn't know I was a virgin. He might have assumed it, but he didn't have confirmation. And if I said anything, he'd stop for fear he'd hurt me. And I *wanted* him. I wanted *all* of him. My fingers dug into his sides, and my arms shook with adrenaline. Deep breaths in and out. But Charlie's focus hadn't left me. He watched my eyes with an intensity I'd never seen. I spread my legs to encourage him—as wide as possible—and he let his hips do the work.

I doubted he'd ever had to muster this type of self-control with another woman. He couldn't just flip me around or toss me over his shoulder. Charlie had to handle me with care, and somehow, he knew exactly how much. He put just enough weight behind his thrust to keep the pressure constant, getting deeper and deeper.

When he stopped, I felt the physical barrier he'd reached. I knew what it was, but it hadn't dawned on Charlie which only served to confirm that he didn't know he had taken my virginity.

But I didn't want him to stop. "More." That one word held more meaning than Charlie realized, and yet it was so softly spoken, I'd barely heard it myself. It had rushed out on a whoosh of air, but I didn't know how to express what I wanted any other way.

Still halfway inside me, he lingered with his lips pressed against mine, nibbling on my bottom lip. I ached for more, but my whole body was wound up with tension. He'd done this before; I was a novice. But without confessing that, I had to wait it out. And Charlie seemed to delight in torturing me.

He trailed kisses down my neck again, his breath a heated slip of air against my skin. "Relax, sunshine." Murmured words had never sounded as seductive as they did coming from Charlie's mouth.

I willed my body to relax, letting my arms go slack and my hands drape loosely against his sides. And when I exhaled a long sigh, he pushed through, burying himself inside me.

My breath hitched, and my eyes squeezed shut. The blinding pain nearly ripped me in two.

And Charlie hadn't missed any of it. He brushed my hair away from my face. "Look at me, Sarah."

I shook my head and took several deep, cleansing breaths. When I finally faced him again, fear etched lines of worry around his rugged features.

"Did I hurt you? Was it your back?"

My entire body trembled, but I wasn't certain what from. It could have been the emotional overload, the fullness I felt, the barrier he'd just torn through, or sheer electricity. Since I'd never done this, I had no idea what was normal, but I got the impression that this was *not*.

He started to pull away, to get up.

"Don't go."

"You have to tell me what happened. I don't want to hurt you, Sarah."

When I didn't immediately answer, he made up his mind to end it. I clutched his back with both hands, trying to stop him. "I've never done this before." And with that confession, I let go. My body went limp under him.

But instead of retreating, he pushed back into me when he settled down. "You're a virgin?"

I shrugged. "*Was.*" Because technically, I wasn't anymore.

The fear and worry softened into love and affection. "Why didn't you tell me?"

"Not really something I wave around." And I'd always wanted to give it to Charlie. That might have been naïve and foolish growing up, but I was glad I'd waited.

Relief and warmth washed over me as Charlie began to rock his hips back and forth. He watched my eyes until they closed, and then I felt his forehead against my shoulder and his breath on my neck. I sighed, closing my thighs around his hips and rolling against him. Every sensation was new, more sensitive than the last. Each glorious inch took me, changed me, made me as our bodies became one.

The pressure started to build, and my core tightened. Charlie wasn't brutal, but he was powerful. As he pushed his weight into me, he hit a spot with each thrust that made me want to cry out. It was so much more intense than any orgasm I'd ever given myself, and it hadn't even peaked. God, I wanted more, but I didn't know what else he could give.

"I'm getting close." He breathed into my ear, and I realized *that* was the more. Charlie's pleasure was what I needed to send me flying.

"Yes, please." Nothing I said even made sense, but it drove Charlie.

He dug his hands underneath me, clutching my sweaty body to his. He ground against me, pushing me into the mattress. My bed frame hit the wall with the shift of his body boring into mine. He thrust faster, harder.

I couldn't think.

Everything happened so fast, and no matter how much I wanted to slow it down to savor the experience, I couldn't stop my climb.

I was so close.

Everything crashed into me at once. Pleasure rolled me in waves, one after another, knocking my world off-kilter. I still didn't want him to stop or even slow down. I wanted to ride the feeling out for all it was worth. Another crash, another swell. And as it started to taper off, I whimpered at the loss, but Charlie held me close.

The whole world around me spun, and I couldn't catch my breath. Charlie pushed his hips into me one final time and let out a grunt next to my ear. Warmth surrounded me, and I realized he'd found his release inside me the way I had him. I loved the sensation of his weight on top of me, knowing what we'd just done. It was the most intimate act two people could share, and I'd just shared it with Charlie Burin.

He slicked his hair away from his face and stared down at me with that big, beautiful smile. "*That* was amazing."

I had to pull him down by the neck to kiss him. "Yes." I held his face in my hands. "It was."

"I love you." Those three words coming from his mouth meant the world, mostly because I believed them.

I trailed my fingers through his hair still damp with sweat and pecked his lips once more. "I love you, too."

11

SARAH

It was a beautiful day, although that was true of most days in Texas. But today the heat wasn't quite as sweltering, and a nice breeze flowed. That light wind carried the smell of Mason Belle with it, and one thing I'd learned to appreciate after months of captivity was the thing that reminded me of home. Hay had a distinct aroma just like freshly cut grass, and the cattle were unique as well, but it was home-cooked food that lingered on a breeze and the honeysuckle that made my heart sing. Because those were the smells of my childhood. The only thing that made them any better was experiencing them at night when I could see the lightning bugs in the fields.

The sun had already started to dip in the sky, and the temperatures had dropped to bearable, in fact, it was a bit cool. I'd grabbed a jacket on the way out to Charlie's truck, although I doubted I'd need it. I was just so excited to be moving more on my own that I found myself wandering for no particular reason at all, which typically resulted in my getting overly tired, but the alternative was sitting in a wheelchair which I refused to do. My gait might be ugly, and I might be slow, but I could move on my own, and I did.

Charlie helped me down the stairs as soon as he saw me on the porch, and the haze in his eyes told me he was tired. He was trying to balance work at Twin Creeks, my appointments, and time with me, and his body was paying the price.

"Are you sure you wouldn't rather go to a restaurant?" I didn't want him to feel obligated to take me out. "Or we could stay at home and watch TV. Just hang out. You've been working outside all day." I couldn't watch his expression since I had to focus on the stairs. It took far more effort to walk; each step was a thought that no longer came naturally.

"No way. It's a gorgeous afternoon, and I want to get you out of the house. Plus, the sun's going down." He let me go at the bottom of the steps so he could open the truck door. "I don't really have any desire to share you with a restaurant full of people, and my mom made fried chicken." That was all he had to say; Jessica made the best fried chicken in town.

Even though I was a bit more mobile than I had been in months, I still wasn't terribly comfortable being around people, which Charlie also knew. My movements were so slow and rigid that I made a spectacle everywhere I went. I'd grown up in Mason Belle, and I hated having people look at me differently than they always had. Charlie swore it was him that people gawked at because no one in town could believe he'd landed a date with a girl so out of his league. I'd rolled my eyes every time he'd said it, but I loved that he did everything in his power to unload that burden from me. Charlie didn't just stand by my side physically; he had my back always. And even if someone did have the nerve to say something to or about me, there was no doubt in my mind that Charlie wouldn't hesitate to deal with it. But I'd rather just not face that, and he knew it.

He drove out to a field passed his parents' farm, and I knew where he was going before we actually got there. Twin Creeks had been named that for a reason. There was a creek that ran through Cross Acres and another from the opposite side of the Burins' farm, and in the backmost part of their property, the two converged. It had made their soil rich and their family wealthy. That spot had always been where Charlie and Austin had held parties in high school, and when their family had large gatherings, it was always where the creeks merged. There was a huge tree that grew right where the rivers created a *V* that provided an umbrella of shade. I'd been there several times in my life—just like the rest of Mason Belle's residents—but never with Charlie.

Charlie turned off the two-lane country road and onto a dirt path that was nothing more than tire tracks through a pasture. They existed all over the county, and the locals knew where they went and who they belonged to, but an outsider would never find one. He maneuvered the truck with ease over the beaten path and drove right out to that huge tree. The spot was a bit overgrown, and I could tell no one had been out here in a while. I wondered if the last time the field had been used was the night before my accident. As soon as the argument I'd had with Miranda over where she'd been that night popped into my head, I shut it down. I refused to go down that road. Nothing good ever came of it. Dwelling on it didn't bring back my sister, and it didn't change what I'd been through.

I waited for Charlie to come around to help me down. I could get out on my own, but it was easier with assistance, and I really liked having his hands on my hips as he lifted me from the seat. My feet were a little unsteady when they reached the grass, but he never wavered until he knew I had my bearings. It was as unspoken as everything Charlie did. He sensed my needs and always met them.

"You good?" He had already moved one hand to grab the picnic basket from the back seat, but his other still rested on my waist.

I nodded, and he pecked my lips. It was as natural as the clouds that floated through the sky. They didn't ask for permission from the sun; they just existed together. Heat and shade. Light and dark. Yin and yang. Without one, the other didn't work.

Charlie used my limited mobility as a reason to keep his hands on me at all times. At first, I'd just thought he was being the Southern gentleman his mom expected and raised him to be. But as time had gone on and we'd gotten closer, he'd known I didn't need as much help. Then after the first time we'd had sex, it was constant. If I were in arm's reach, Charlie had a hand on me. Never in an inappropriate manner. I couldn't describe it as anything other than protective and maybe even territorial—like he'd claimed me. Secretly, I loved it; outwardly, Daddy hated it.

I giggled every time Daddy growled or issued Charlie a warning with one word, "son." Daddy loved Charlie—Austin too—like he was his own, but he didn't know what to do with the relationship that had blossomed between Charlie and me. Austin and Randi had just always been. There was never a time they weren't together, even as kids. So, they were just a given. Since I'd never dated, I wondered if Daddy thought I'd always be single. Thankfully, his desire to see me happy outweighed his urge to strangle Charlie.

Charlie took my hand and carried the picnic basket in his other. Life moved slowly in Mason Belle, and I was grateful Charlie was never in a hurry, at least not when he was with me. He had patience that rivaled Job's. And today was no different.

"You want to sit under the tree?" He let me go to set down the food. As he opened the lid, I noticed that not only had his mom packed food, but she'd included a blanket.

Charlie unfolded the quilt and spread it out on the grass near the trunk of the massive oak. The water trickled around us, and I thought this place was heaven on earth. I didn't know of a spot that was more beautiful and serene in all of Mason Belle. And once Charlie had our picnic situated, he held out his hand so I could take a seat.

Charlie sat at the base of the tree and leaned against it. Before I could blink, he had pulled me between his legs and wrapped his arms around me. Leaned back against his chest, I could watch the birds in the sky and the clouds move with the wind. The leaves rustled above us and the water around us.

He twined his fingers with mine and played with them in front of us. For the most part, mine had all straightened out as they'd healed, but they still got sore when it rained or if I was cold. I could tell where they'd been broken, but I didn't think Charlie cared.

I tilted my head back on his shoulder and peered up at him. I wondered if it would ever become normal to see him show up at my house or have him hold my hand or kiss me, or if it would always feel like a dream that I'd wake from and realize it had never existed. I took the time to appreciate every detail about him any chance I could. Because I knew better than anyone just how quickly things could change.

He shifted to see my face—cradling me—and chuckled when he realized I'd been staring at him. "You hungry, sunshine?"

"Not overly." That wasn't exactly true. I wasn't ready for food, but I wished Charlie would feast on me.

I pulled him down by the back of his neck to bring his lips to mine. It took so little to coax Charlie into affection, and I loved that I never had to ask or tell him what I wanted. One kiss was all it took, and he picked up from there.

Today was no different. As gentle as the breeze around us and as peaceful as the water, Charlie's touch warmed me like the sun. With his mouth on mine and his hands in my hair, the world around us faded. I didn't worry about getting caught when we removed our clothes, and I didn't consider anything outside of us when he made love to me under that tree. He devoured my cries of pleasure and filled my ears with groans of his own. And when he'd taken me to the highest place possible, we fell over the cliff of ecstasy together where the two creeks became one.

I laid there nestled into Charlie's side, thinking life could never get any better than this. His fingers traveled languidly down my back and up my side, and I drew invisible patterns on his chest. When Charlie pressed his lips to my forehead, my stomach growled—loudly.

Charlie's chest rumbled with laughter. "Still want to tell me you're not hungry?"

I pushed up and reached for my shirt, and Charlie rolled over to grab the rest of our clothing. By the time I'd gotten dressed, he had put on his shorts and was down on his knees in front of the picnic basket. With each move he made, shuffling things around, his muscles flexed. His skin was kissed by the sun, and I enjoyed watching him as much as I did TV.

He pulled out a Tupperware container of fried chicken, a bunch of homemade biscuits, grapes, and several other things I couldn't see next to him. There was a bottle of tea and another with lemonade.

"Your mom went all out, huh?" I tried to catch my hair and tie it into a ponytail as the wind pushed it into my face. "It smells delicious."

Charlie shook his head but didn't lift his gaze from inside the basket while he continued to rummage. "There's something missing."

"Looks like Jessica thought of everything." I opened the container of chicken and unwrapped the biscuits. "Whatever it is, we don't need it." I giggled when he kept digging around. "Charlie, come sit with me and eat."

I picked at a piece of chicken while Charlie emptied the basket. He was a man on a mission, and I wouldn't stop him if he wanted to keep searching. It was obvious when he found whatever he'd been digging for. But instead of a smile on his face, he appeared nervous. He stood with his hands together and took the few steps that separated us. I had stopped pulling the meat off the bone and chewed as he approached, with a piece of skin in one hand and a bone in the other.

And then I nearly choked when he got down on one knee and rested his arm on his bent leg. His fingers unfurled one by one to reveal an open, black box. I couldn't decide what to focus on, him or the diamond the sunlight kept catching. I opted for Charlie.

He cleared his throat and sweat beaded at his forehead. "Sarah." His Adam's apple dipped as he swallowed hard; meanwhile, I sat stunned. "Something inside me came alive the day I walked into your hospital room and found you crying. A part of me I didn't know existed opened, and you seeped into my heart and filled me to the brim. And every day since, I've fallen more in love with you. You're my best friend, and I want you to take my last name."

I gasped and covered my mouth with the chicken leg still in my hand.

"Will you marry me, sunshine?" His voice trembled as if he feared I might say no.

We hadn't talked about marriage or even a commitment, but there wasn't a single hesitation when I said, "Yes."

His eyes went wide. "Yes?"

I nodded, and tears filled my eyes. "Yes, I'll marry you."

He took the piece of chicken and the skin from my hands and flung them into the field. I watched the bone fly and then turned back to him. Charlie placed the ring on my finger and grabbed me by the back of the neck. His kiss said everything he couldn't. It was filled with passion and love, and I had no doubt Charlie Burin had never kissed another woman the way he just did me. I felt it from my lips to my toes.

He cupped my jaw in his hands and stared longingly into my eyes. "Sarah, I can't wait for you to be my wife." His cheeks were flushed, or maybe it was just the sun, but either way, it was adorably innocent and perfectly Charlie.

I extended my arm to peer at the ring he'd put on my finger. It was simple yet elegant. A round solitaire with a plain white gold band that suited me to a tea. "It's beautiful, Charlie." I glanced up to see his smile and then back to the ring. "Daddy is going to go crazy." I shook my head as I thought of how my father would react.

"He already knows."

My face fell, and I dropped my hand. "What?"

"He gave me his blessing."

It was a tradition I hadn't expected any man would ever follow, not in this day and age, but it was exactly what I would have wanted had I gotten to pick. "Thank you."

I threw my arms around his neck and buried my nose in

his neck. My tears stained his shirt. In one afternoon, Charlie had managed to make every childhood dream I had come true. I'd always fantasized about getting married, but the older I got, the less I believed it would ever happen. And the man who'd always stood at that altar, waiting for me, had always been Charlie Burin. But never in that dream had I imagined him to be eager to take those vows.

It took a couple of weeks for the reality of the engagement to set in. I'd felt like a celebrity around town with all the congratulations and people asking to see my ring. I couldn't go to the gas station without a girl I went to high school with asking how I'd roped Charlie. I took it all in stride until Chasity—Randi's best friend—reminded me that my little sister wouldn't be around to be my maid of honor, and I didn't have Mama around to help me plan. That wasn't really how any of that conversation had taken place because Chasity wasn't a mean girl; nevertheless, that was the end result. Truth be told, Chasity was heartbroken her best friend had up and left without so much as a goodbye, and I think she'd hoped I might know how to reach her.

The only problem was, I didn't. Daddy said he didn't know where she'd gone—which I found odd, but when I tried to dig, he got angry—and I didn't know where to look. I'd become obsessed with finding my little sister. Come hell or high water, Miranda Adams would be at my wedding.

There was just one problem with that. Randi didn't want

to be found, and I wasn't much of an investigator. Charlie probed Austin, and my understanding was that it had resulted in a fistfight. None of Randi's friends had heard from her, either. It was like my little sister had just vanished into thin air. Social media was a bust. She'd never had a cell phone, so that was a no-go. And there were far more Miranda Adams in the United States than I'd ever dreamed possible.

I'd happened upon a background check website and finally gave in and paid the fee. It had been worth the twenty dollars because it yielded results. There were three Miranda Adams with her date of birth which meant I'd narrowed down her location to Utah, New York, or Idaho. I couldn't picture Randi in any of those places, but I'd found her on a law firm's website. There was no mistaking that it was her, even though she appeared so different. It wasn't just the professional way she was dressed in the photograph; it was the sadness in her eyes. Her spark was gone. And I didn't think that had come from working in Manhattan.

This was important to me. It also might be a way to mend whatever fences had been destroyed the day I'd been hit by that tractor-trailer. I sat at the kitchen table with my phone clutched in my hands. My fingers shook, and I was afraid I'd break the glass with the force I held the device. Every sound around me was amplified as I sat, stuck in my head. The living room fan whirred, Daddy worked the horses outside, and the grandfather clock in the hall ticked off the minutes as I sat there, wasting time.

The screen door banged shut, and with the clatter came

Charlie. "Hey, sunshine." He kissed my forehead, and I wrapped my arms around his middle. His skin was warm with the heat of the sun, and there was sweat on his forehead. Even with the occasional cool breeze, it was still hot as the devil's breath in Texas.

He pulled open the refrigerator and reached in to grab a pitcher of tea. "Still working up the courage to call?" Charlie moved around our kitchen like he lived here; I loved that he was that comfortable in my family's house.

"Something like that." I sighed and set down the phone. "I don't know what to say."

He took a long drink from the glass he'd poured and then wiped his brow with the sleeve of his shirt. "You could send her an invitation in the mail."

That was a lovely idea, except I didn't have anything other than her work address, and that was not how I wanted to reunite with my sister. I wasn't delusional enough to believe there would be some kind of perfect, happy reunion, but we were family. Whatever had driven her away, we could figure out. I just wanted her to come home. I wanted her here.

I'd built it all up in my mind because I simply couldn't understand how she had just up and left Mason Belle, and I didn't even want to think about what stole her away from Austin. There was more to whatever had happened, but I'd been in a coma, and no one would tell me crap. Now I was too afraid to call, too afraid of what Randi might say.

"Babe, what's the worst that could happen?" Charlie

needed to find something else to do other than bother me. His comfort wasn't helping.

"She could say, 'Fuck you, Sarah.'"

"All right then." He chuckled at my outburst and likely my vulgar language. "She could say that. Or she could just say, no. Either way, you're expecting both, so neither would be a shock. And since *no* is the worst that could happen, why not just call?"

I buried my hands in my hair and pulled at the roots. The deep breath I took didn't calm my voice quite as much as I'd hoped it would. "I don't know, Charlie." I sank down into my chair, hating that I was even in this position.

Charlie wouldn't understand because there was no question about his brother or his mother being at the ceremony. Jessica had practically helped plan the entire thing since I didn't have anyone else.

He sat down his glass and came to my side to squat at my side. He pulled my hands from my hair and then tipped my chin to look at him. "Sarah, I know you want your sister there. The only way to make that happen is to call the number."

He was right. The wedding would happen regardless of whether Randi attended. At the very least, I wanted her to know that I was getting married. If she chose not to come, that was on her, but she couldn't make the decision without the information.

Charlie searched my eyes and kissed my lips when he saw my resolution. "If you need me, holler. I'll be in the barn helping Jack." He took a couple of steps backward and winked at me. "Love you, sunshine." And then he exited the same way he'd entered.

The bang of the door startled me every time I heard it. Someone needed to fix that dang thing.

I took a deep breath, touched the numbers on the screen, and hit send. The phone rang twice on the other end before someone picked up.

"Eason McNabb."

I had no idea how I'd managed to get a man on the phone. I'd thought I had Miranda's direct number. My heart plummeted into my stomach. "Oh," I breathed into the phone. "May I speak with Miranda Adams?"

"May I tell her who's calling?"

"Sarah." There was a pause on the other end. "Adams. Her sister." I'd added the last part, hoping it would give weight or credence to my call and get me patched through.

"Hold on. I'll see if she's available."

The music that came through the phone was the only thing that kept me from thinking I'd been hung up on. If Randi were really that upset, I wouldn't put it past her to take the call and then disconnect.

"Sarah?" Her voice was laced with fear, but I didn't know why she'd be afraid to hear from me.

"Hey." I kept my voice upbeat to sound cheerful. I knew it grated on her nerves, but I needed her to think things were as normal as possible. "You've been hard to track down. It's good to hear your voice."

"Yeah..." She struggled to form a complete sentence. "Good to hear from you, too. Is everything okay?"

I didn't really know how to answer that. Life in Mason Belle was great, except that my little sister wasn't there, and I wanted her to come home.

"Oh yeah. I'm sorry. I didn't mean to worry you. I just couldn't find any other way to reach you. Otherwise, I wouldn't have called you at work." It was now or never. "Look," I moved my finger across the tabletop, tracing the grain in the wood. "I know you're busy, and we can catch up soon. I just thought that maybe you'd think about coming back down to Mason Belle."

She didn't so much as breathe into the phone, so I pulled it away from my ear to see if the call time was still running. "I can't right now, Sarah. Things at the office are really busy," she stammered, and I could tell she was trying to come up with viable excuses without flat out saying she didn't want to. Maybe she'd just been caught off guard. "I've got a lot going on here, and— I just don't know if that would be a very good idea."

"Why not?" I had no clue why she'd decided to leave, but she could just as easily make the decision to come back. I didn't bother to tell her that; it would just erupt into an argument the way it always had. "You're always welcome back home."

"I'm not—" Exasperation creeped into her tone. "I can't. I'm not really in a position to explain anything, but I really can't do this. It's just not—"

"It's a special occasion." I rushed the rest of what I had to say so she couldn't cut me off without my getting it out. "I'm getting married." It wasn't the eloquent announcement I'd prepared in my head, but it delivered the same message.

More silence. I'd never thought of tension as a tangible thing until now. "You're getting married?" Randi didn't try to mask the surprise in her tone. "I um...okay. Who?"

"Charlie Burin."

She'd missed out on so much. "Wow." She sounded like she didn't know what to say. "How did, I...congratulations, Sarah."

"Please, Randi."

"I can't. I'm sorry." She wasn't going to elaborate, but I wasn't going to let it go that easily.

I'd spent too much time searching for her not to give this my best shot. "Why not?" I didn't care if I sounded desperate.

"I just can't." She was like a parrot repeating the same thing. "Look, I have to get to work. Call me anytime." She rattled off what I assumed to be her personal phone number, and I scrambled to find something to write on before I forgot it.

"Let me give you the information, at least. That way if you change your mind—" The phone clicked, and the line went dead.

I stewed for a moment, but the flash of anger did little to cover up the hurt underneath. There was no good reason why Randi couldn't swallow her pride and come home for the wedding. Sure, she'd have some explaining to do with Daddy, but in my mind, that was a small price to pay not to miss your only sister's wedding. And if she didn't want to face Austin, then she shouldn't have up and left with no explanation. Regardless of her reasoning, she was an adult. She'd made the decision to run away, and she'd have to be the one to man up and come home. Instead, Randi planned to do what Randi had always done—play to her strengths. Stubborn and selfish, she'd miss the most important day of my life.

12

CHARLIE

"Sarah, you need to go to the doctor. This isn't normal." She'd been sick since she'd gotten in touch with her sister. For any other woman, depression might not be an issue that caused that great a concern after only a couple days, but with Sarah, it was always something that kept me on high alert. And when the vomiting starting without a fever or any other symptom, I insisted she see a physician.

Her body had started to lock up on her, and she had a hard time walking. She was stiff and uncomfortable, and I hated seeing her unable to move. "You're overreacting, Charlie. I'm fine." She rolled her neck to face me. "Don't you have work to do at your parent's house?"

I did. More than I'd ever catch up on, but Sarah was and always would be my priority. Twin Creeks could wait, and there were other men there to help. They'd been making do without me since Sarah's accident; another day wouldn't hurt. "Sarcasm doesn't suit you, sunshine." I jerked my head toward the porch. "Come on. I've already called the doctor's office. They're going to work you in." I could see her formulating an argument, but I wasn't having any more of it. "You can either do this the easy way or the hard way, but regardless, you're going."

She rolled her eyes—which I'd never seen her do—and pushed out of the chair. "I hope I puke on your shoes, Charlie Burin."

I'd deal with that if it happened. Right now, I needed her in the truck. When I tried to help her down the stairs, she swatted me away with a pissy look that made me want to laugh. Sarah was harmless, and she loved me to the moon and back. I wasn't the least bit worried about her being mad —not about this. "I'll take my chances."

I opened her door and stood back. "You going to hop up there yourself, or would you like some help?"

Sarah narrowed her eyes and put her foot on the running board. I didn't give a shit if she wanted my help or not; I wasn't adding broken bones to her list of ailments today. But she didn't fight me off when I grabbed her hips and helped her in. She did, however, push me back and close the door without letting me give her a kiss. She pouted through the passenger window, and I didn't hide my humor. Damn, I loved that woman. Everything about her was a mixture of sweet and sassy, although no one but me ever got to see the sass.

We went to one of her doctors in Laredo and sat for almost an hour before Sarah was called back. They'd left me sitting in the waiting room while they pulled her back for a urine sample and blood work. I hadn't expected the nurse to come to the door and call my name, and when the lady gave me a forced smile, I wondered what the hell was wrong.

I followed the nurse down a maze of hallways that I didn't think I'd ever find my way back out of until she stopped in front of an exam room. She tapped on the wood and then entered. Sarah sat on the edge of the exam table with tears in her eyes, and her arms wrapped around her stomach.

"Sarah?" I bypassed the nurse and the doctor in favor of getting to my fiancé. I cupped her cheeks in my hand and tilted her head. "What's wrong?"

She glanced at the nurse and the doctor, who both promptly exited the room, and I heard the door click shut behind them. Her face was as white as a sheet, and the whole scene scared the shit out of me.

"Talk to me."

She licked her lips and swallowed past a lump in her throat that almost seemed unmanageable. "We're going to be parents." Her chin trembled, and I wondered if I'd heard her correctly.

"Parents?" My mind couldn't even process the word, much less comprehend the implications. My initial instinct was to be happy, but there had to be a reason Sarah looked so miserable.

Sarah glanced down at her belly. "I'm pregnant."

I laughed and put my arms around her to pull her against my chest. "That's incredible." I stroked her hair and then pulled her back. "But why are you crying?" I tried to wipe the tears from under her eyes, but they just kept coming.

"Do you even want kids?" Her brow furrowed, and it dawned on me that we'd never talked about it. We'd never really even talked about birth control because I assumed she was on the pill.

"Of course, I do. Were you worried I wouldn't?"

She chewed on her lip and nodded.

"Are you not excited?" It didn't matter if I were ecstatic; if Sarah didn't want to have a baby, this could take a real turn for the worse.

She used the back of her hand to dry the tears, and her shoulders jerked as she regained control of her emotions. "Of course, I am. But we don't live together. We're not even married, Charlie. Whose last name does a baby get? What kind of example are we setting?"

I chuckled and kissed her forehead. "Only you would be worried about what kind of example you were setting for an unborn child." I tucked her curls behind her ear. "Those are just details, Sarah. We'll work them out. The only thing that matters is whether or not you're happy with the news."

"I'm thrilled, well, now that I know you're not upset."

I hadn't intended for it to happen, but it's not like either of us were eighteen, either. I'd take as many babies as Sarah would give me. "Short of making you my wife, there is nothing I want more than a daughter who looks just like you."

"What if it's a boy—"

There was a knock on the door, and again, no one waited for a response before they came in. The doctor and nurse we'd run out rejoined us and shut the door behind them. The nurse stood at the computer, and the doctor took a seat on the stool.

"I assume this is dad?" The doctor smiled at me while directing her question to Sarah, who nodded. "Hi, I'm Dr. Carroll. I understand today's news is a bit of a shock, and after looking at your charts in the hospital file, I understand why. I wanted to give you some information about your options with regard to the pregnancy."

Sarah looked like someone had slapped her. "My options?" She glanced to me and then back at the doctor. "What sort of options are we talking about?"

"Well, your pregnancy is high-risk." The doctor tried to be as gentle as possible, yet somehow, that made it worse. She glanced at me like she needed back up and then flicked her attention to Sarah. "Your circumstances are very unique, Sarah." She danced around whatever she had to say like a ballerina. "Pregnancy is very hard on the body, particularly the spine. Your back is already delicate, and the added weight could do irreparable damage. You're not even a year out from the accident and are still in regular physical therapy."

Sarah got paler the longer the doctor spoke, and I didn't like how any of this sounded.

"And if, somehow, you make it through the pregnancy without complications, delivery could prove detrimental to the baby and you." She delivered the news with poise coupled with a firm edge. She didn't leave room for any kind of argument.

Sarah sat up straight and swallowed hard. "What kind of complications?"

The doctor flattened her lips and gave Sarah a sympathetic glance. She clasped her hands and sat them on top of her clipboard in her lap. "Spasms, breathing difficulties, hypotension. Women with spinal cord injuries above the T6 are susceptible to autonomic dysreflexia, as well." She was sympathetic, that much I could see in her expression. "Sarah, you're already at a high risk for pressure ulcers, anemia, and urinary tract infections. Pregnancy is just going to exacerbate all of those risk factors."

The nurse stepped forward and handed Sarah a tissue. Sarah's bottom lip quivered, but she hadn't melted down.

I didn't understand most of what was even being said. Yeah, I understood the words but not the actual implication. "Worst case scenario, what could we be facing?" I needed to know the bottom line.

"Paralysis. Possibly death."

Sarah wouldn't look at me, not that I had to see her eyes to know what she was thinking. It was written all over her face. I was certain it matched my own. In less than a few minutes time, I'd gotten the best news of my life and then had it torn away just moments later. My heart sank, and I wanted to put my fist through a wall.

My head spun. I wasn't a gambler, and I certainly wouldn't risk Sarah's life. I didn't care what was at stake.

"Sarah, I know this is a lot to take. I also know it's a

choice no woman ever wants to have to consider, but you have to take your health into consideration," the doctor said. "If you were further out in your recovery and there had been a plan in place, we would be having a different conversation. But between the pelvic trauma you endured, the spinal cord injury, and the continued surgeries since, I just don't think your body can handle pregnancy or childbirth."

I noted that Dr. Carroll hadn't said what she did recommend, although the answer was on the pamphlet in her hand. She gave the brochure to Sarah, who stared at it with tears clinging to her jaw, and she wrung the life out of my hand as I took the seat beside her.

"Do we have to make the decision today?" Sarah's voice was hollow or maybe even haunted. If she hadn't held my fingers with such a tight grip, I would have wondered if she was even still conscious.

Dr. Carroll hesitated and then shook her head. "You don't have to decide anything right now. In fact, I encourage you to go home and do some research to make the best decision for you and your husband. Based on your bloodwork, your HTC hormones indicate you're still fairly early in the pregnancy, so you have a little time to make a decision." She acted like there was an actual choice to be made, but I kept my mouth shut.

"Is that something you'd do here?" Sarah nearly choked on the question, but I guessed it had to be asked.

"No. We would refer you to a specialist either way. There are several options this early on. Although the longer you wait, the fewer choices you'll have."

Dr. Carroll had been as empathetic as any one person could be, and if I were in a different situation, I'd applaud her for her candor and her decorum. She'd just delivered some of the worst news I could imagine any couple receiving with gentle grace. But praising her wasn't my current priority.

She handed me the paperwork and then leaned in to squeeze Sarah's free hand. "If you have any questions, feel free to call our office." The doctor met Sarah's eyes, and a look of understanding passed between them. It appeared as if Dr. Carroll wanted to say something—sorry, maybe—and instead gave Sarah a smile.

The nurse followed the doctor out and let the door close behind them. The ominous click of the latch unleashed Sarah's emotions. I felt it happen before I realized what was going on. I stood as Sarah collapsed into my side. I'd barely caught her when she went limp. I'd never seen her—not even the day I found her in the hospital—look as small and vulnerable and defeated as she did curled against me.

Through an unimaginable accident, the most grueling physical therapy possible, and her sister leaving, all I'd ever seen Sarah do was fight and survive. She'd come out stronger than before, so I knew she'd survive this.

But damn, this was going to be hard.

∿

I'd brought Sarah back to my house instead of taking her back to Cross Acres. This was something we needed to discuss privately, and I didn't want to risk anyone else weighing in or overhearing. This was one of those things we may take to our graves, and I didn't want to put Sarah in a position to have to defend her decision. I thanked God we hadn't gone to the doctor in Mason Belle where we'd have to face anyone we knew.

She'd collapsed onto the couch once we'd walked in the door but hadn't spoken since, and I hadn't pushed her. "I can't do it."

We'd been home for over an hour, and I think all either of us had thought about since we'd walked in the door was the decision in front of us and what the doctor had said.

Her bright-blue eyes were rimmed red and puffy from crying, and I wanted nothing more than to hold her and comfort her, but she'd kept her distance. "There's no way I can terminate a pregnancy, Charlie." Her chest lurched as she swallowed a hiccup.

"Sarah," I reached across the couch, but she denied my embrace. "I know this is hard. It's impossible to wrap your mind around."

"It's wrong."

We'd both grown up in church, and we'd both heard the same sermons and been taught the same lessons. "Sarah, this isn't a matter of just not wanting a baby. You aren't considering it as a form of birth control—"

Her eyes narrowed, and her brow furrowed. "But aren't we?"

I knew where she was going with this, and I wasn't interested in being the voice of reason. If she wanted to argue the biblical stance, then we probably should have considered the same point of view on pre-marital sex. Neither of us had an issue with that, and it happened all the time. But I wasn't fighting principles here. I was only concerned with Sarah's life.

I exhaled through my nose and made sure I could speak without emotion in my voice before I opened my mouth. One of us had to stay rational through this, and while it was my child, too, Sarah was the one who had to carry the baby. "We both want this baby. We didn't know it, but that was evident as soon as you told me. I was a little surprised since you're on birth control but excited just the same." I scooted closer to her on the couch and took her hands in mine. "Sunshine, this isn't our only chance, but if I lose you, then none of it matters."

"It *is* our only chance." All she'd done since we'd left was cry, and I knew this wouldn't be the last of it. "Once this is done, it's done. The doctors are going to want to make sure this never happens again by accident or on purpose. They can make it so that I never have babies, ever." She'd gone from quiet to irrational, and she shook like a leaf in front of me. "Once they take this baby, that's it. And then I won't have anything, and *you* won't have anything. You won't want —" She snatched her hand from mine and covered her mouth.

I had to approach this gingerly. "I won't *what*?"

She shook her head, but I didn't have a clue what ran through her mind. At this point, it could be anything; she was so worked up. "You don't want to marry a woman who can't have children." Sarah turned away, but not seeing her face didn't hide her sobs.

Her statement was like a stab to the heart. She hadn't meant it personally, but it was hard not to take it that way. She'd felt the same way about not being able to walk after the accident. Whether it was right or wrong, women had roles in ranching communities. It wasn't an easy life healthy. Add any type of ailment or disability to it, and it became exponentially harder. Sarah had been right when she'd said men in Mason Belle wouldn't take a wife who couldn't help because she became a burden—not that any of them would have ever admitted that or put it that way. And children went hand in hand with that mindset. Kids worked alongside their parents; as soon as they could walk, they were in the fields or helping with animals, not to mention, there was just a huge sense of family in this small town.

I got up and moved to the floor in front of her so she couldn't avoid my stare. "Do you think the only reason I want to marry you is to have babies?" It was ludicrous since we'd never even discussed kids before today.

"I know you want them—even if it's not today, eventually —and if I can't give them to you, then you should be able to find a woman who can." Sarah looked like she was on the verge of throwing up. "I wouldn't blame you, Charlie." She was as sincere now as when she told me she loved me.

"There are lots of women in better condition than I am that can help you at Twin Creeks and give you a family. I know how difficult it is to be with me, and that's likely never going to change. I'll be in and out of doctor's offices for the rest of my life, but it won't be to welcome your son or daughter into the world...." She was losing it. Her breaths were rattled and anxious, and if she didn't get it under control, she would hyperventilate or pass out.

"Sarah, please look at me."

It took her a minute, but she finally met my eyes. I had to force back the roar that tried to rip through me at the sight of her pain, staring back at me. I wanted to keep her safe, to do everything I could to make this easier for her.

I stroked her curls away from her cheeks and behind her ears. Somehow her hair always got crazy when she was upset. "I love you. I love you more than I can even put into words. And it has nothing to do with whether or not you can carry my children. I didn't ask you to marry me so we could change the population number on Mason Belle's welcome sign. I asked you to be my wife because I don't want to do life without you. We are going to get through this—together. I don't want you to think for one second this changes how I feel about you or alters our future. I'm not going anywhere."

She sniffled and nodded, her eyes never leaving mine. At least she was listening to what I had to say.

I didn't care what anyone else would ever have to say about this choice or what their feelings were on the matter; Sarah was my only concern. "I know this is your body, and whatever decision you will make, I will honor, but..." I swiped my thumb under her eye as a lump formed in my throat that was hard to talk around. The thought of losing Sarah was more than I could bear, but I didn't know how to tell her that without sounding like I was leading her in one direction or the other. "You're the most important thing in the world to me. I want you to be happy, but I wouldn't survive losing you." God, I hoped she saw the truth in my eyes. My throat was raw, and my voice cracked. "I'll do anything I can to give you what you want, but please don't put yourself in danger."

She didn't say anything, but I didn't see any malice or anger in her expression or her eyes, just undeniable sadness.

"Once we get through this, I'll do anything you want. The doctor said things would be different after a year, and we could plan this with a specialist. Hell, I'll buy you a baby if it comes down to that. I just can't lose you."

I didn't wait for her to concede or even acknowledge me. I didn't care if she wanted me to hold her or not because I needed to know she was safe in my arms. I swept her off the couch and into my embrace. It didn't take me long to reach my bedroom, but when she came to her decision, it would be bad. I was here for the long haul, and I needed to have her close. We wound ourselves together under my blankets, and there, I refused to let her go while she fell apart.

Her tears continued long after the sun went down. I cried with her whether she realized it or not. I cried for her pain and the decision she had to make. I'd never been through anything like this and prayed to God I'd never be faced with it again.

"You are all that's holding me together," she whispered into my chest long after I'd thought she'd fallen asleep. "I don't know if I can do this, Charlie."

I stroked her hair and kissed her forehead. There was no easy way through this, and maybe I was selfish as hell for wanting her over a child I'd never met, but that was how it was. "Do it for me. We can try again when you're strong if it's that important to you, but please don't risk your own life. No baby should have to brave the world without its mother, and I'd be useless without you."

I held her impossibly close, hoping she'd heard my plea. "You're the only thing in the world I give a damn about, Sarah."

"I'll make an appointment."

It was the worst victory I'd ever won. Regardless of which way things had gone, I lost something. I was just thankful it wasn't Sarah.

~

Less than a week later, we were on our way to Laredo to have the procedure done. Thank God none of this had taken place in Mason Belle; everyone in town would know every detail of what we were going through. As it was, it had been hard to keep Jack from sniffing around, and I hated lying to him about where we were going and why. But my loyalty was to Sarah, not her dad.

The ride there had been quiet, and when we finally arrived, we sat in the parking lot for a long time. We were early, and I knew Sarah wouldn't want to be inside any longer than she had to, so I put the truck in park and left the air running. I hadn't really known what we were getting into and worried that we'd face protestors, but this appeared to be just like any other doctor's office.

"You okay?" It was a stupid question that I already knew the answer to.

She stared at the entrance of the office and flattened her lips in disapproval. "Just thinking." Her chest heaved, and she took several ragged breaths as she shook her head. "I can't do it."

We'd made it this far, but as much as I'd hoped for smooth sailing so we didn't make this any worse than it had to be, I'd known it wouldn't be that easy. Sarah wasn't just fighting a war in her head; this was a moral battle that she didn't believe she'd survive. I worried about losing her to the baby, and she worried about losing her to her.

"Sarah..." I didn't have to tell her what I thought because she already knew. Her name spoken as a plea said everything I couldn't.

Tears streamed down her cheeks, and her stare remained on the front of the building. "I just can't." Her head barely moved from side to side, but it was just another confirmation of her saying no. "I love you, Charlie. I want to be around for you, but I—" Her knuckles turned white as she gripped the sides of the seat. "I can't do this. I need you to turn around."

I was about to lose my shit. I ground my teeth together and took a deep breath to maintain my composure. "Turn around? And go where?" It was a good thing the steering wheel was firmly mounted, or I might have ripped it out of the dash with the adrenaline that pumped through me. "Back home? Then what? You can't avoid the doctor forever, Sarah, and no matter where you go, they're going to tell you the same thing. We screwed up. You weren't ready to get pregnant. Don't punish us both for that mistake."

"There are specialists here in Laredo." Her voice was so soft I wouldn't have heard it had the radio been on. "We have options."

"Jesus." I ran my hands through my hair and pulled hard at the roots. "Do any of those options guarantee I'll still have my wife at the end of this?" That wasn't fair, but I didn't care.

Her shoulders rounded as she drew into herself. "I'm sorry, Charlie."

I wanted to tell her I understood. I wanted to comfort her. That I knew the decision wasn't easy. But damn, I was so angry I could spit nails. She didn't have a clue what she was risking, what she was putting on the line—and for what? There were no guarantees she or the baby would survive this. I wanted to slap myself for telling her I'd support her decision. In the long run, I thought she'd make the educated choice and follow the doctor's recommendations. Yet it seemed as if none of that mattered and neither did my opinion.

Sarah wasn't the only one with access to the internet. I'd done my own research—none of this was good. There was nothing I could do, and arguing wouldn't get me anywhere. Sarah had made up her mind.

I put the truck in gear and backed out of the parking space. Words burned the back of my throat, and I fought against letting them fly. She knew it. I could see her staring at me from the corner of my eye, waiting for the shoe to drop. When I didn't open my mouth, the silence lingered which was best for us both. I didn't want to snap at her, and I couldn't guarantee that I wouldn't.

It was like watching a train barrel toward her going eighty-four miles per hour and knowing I'd never reach her in time to get her off the tracks. She was willingly putting herself in danger and didn't seem to care.

My heart slammed in my chest, and I struggled to keep my breathing normal. Every part of me wanted to scream, beat the shit out of something—I needed a release. But none of that happened over the forty-five-minute drive back. I was met with nothing other than silence.

I didn't trust myself to speak when I pulled into Cross Acres, and I didn't open my mouth when I stopped in front of the house and waited for her to get out. The fact that I didn't go around to help her down said more than any carelessly worded sentence could have. She wasn't in danger of falling; she could manage just fine on her own. And I was prepared to let her. Before she hopped down, she peered over her shoulder, giving me one last chance to say my peace, and my lips stayed sealed. There was nothing to say. She'd made our choice, and I had to find a way to live with it.

As soon as I saw that she was safely through the door, I pulled the truck around the circular drive and out through the iron gates. Once I knew there was no chance I'd be heard, I let out a blood-curdling yell that finally allowed my heart rate to return to normal.

~

The last two weeks had been tense anytime Sarah and I had been together. We couldn't have a conversation without the baby situation coming up, which made being around anyone else rather difficult. Neither of our parents knew, and I hadn't even told Austin. I'd read more about spinal injuries and pregnancy than I ever cared to, and I was convinced, now more than ever that we needed to wait until Sarah was stronger.

But at this point, we'd missed the appointment for the termination, and now Sarah had her heart set on an OBGYN in Laredo who claimed to work miracles. The last time I checked, Jesus was the only man who'd walked on water, but the one time I'd made that statement it had erupted in an argument I never cared to repeat.

So, we'd left Mason Belle early this morning to get to Laredo on time. There was a wall between us that I couldn't figure out how to tear down, and I hated it. I missed my fiancé. Being around her these days just wasn't the same. Sarah had always been headstrong, and this had proven no different. Once she'd decided on something, nothing would make her back down. The silent treatment hadn't even gotten under her skin, not that I intentionally played that game. I just hadn't wanted to say something I'd regret, so until I was certain I could keep my mouth shut, I hadn't called.

When she called two days later, it wasn't to tell me that she'd reconsider or that she was sorry. It wasn't her wanting to discuss the situation. She'd called to ask if I intended to take her to the specialist in Laredo, or if she needed to break the news to Jack and have him go.

It should have pissed me off because she should have known what my answer would be, or maybe that was exactly why she'd said it. She was the love of my life, and whether I agreed with her decision or not, I had no intention of not standing by her side.

Even now, when being by her side meant going against everything I'd begged her to do, I squirmed in my seat. The one thing I could say for this guy was he hadn't played around. He'd consulted with all of Sarah's doctors and painted a grim picture. Sarah's "miracle worker" wasn't quite sure he could turn the water into wine.

Dr. Nesbit laid out every detail of every possible complication that could and likely would arise. And then he—her savior—suggested she consider termination and try again when her body was stronger.

But she remained rooted in her decision. Sarah refused to terminate, and she acknowledged all the risks. She wore him down faster than she had me. And by the time he got ready to leave the room, Dr. Nesbit had agreed to take her case.

He had been my last hope, and he'd failed to seal the deal.

13

SARAH

There wasn't a lot of time to plan a wedding if I wanted to have one before I started to show. Thankfully, just like with everything else in Mason Belle, when a need arose, the town pulled together to make it happen. This was no different. Without Mama here to plan, several of the ladies stepped up, and Charlie's mom stepped in. There was nothing like a wedding to make me love or hate my future mother-in-law. Thankfully, Jessica and I clicked, and she filled in all the gaps that my mother had left.

I'd never dreamed of anything over-the-top, but I still wanted elegant—simple. I'd grown up in a small town, and we just did things a certain way here. Charlie and I had debated between Cross Acres and the tree where the rivers came together at Twin Creeks. Ultimately, we decided on the spot at the Burins'. There was just something so fitting about having our wedding where two vessels met and became one, and I loved that tree.

The unfortunate part of living in a smaller than small town that hadn't really been modernized over the last couple of decades was that we had to go to Laredo for everything. I managed to squeeze in visits to rental companies and dress shops between doctor's appointments and physical therapy, but it was taxing. I'd never felt exhaustion like the kind pregnancy brought on. Couple that with what I already felt post-accident, and there were days I did good to hold my eyes open until sundown.

"You about ready to go, sweetheart?" Daddy's voice came from down the hall, and I could hear his approach.

I checked myself in the mirror one last time and wondered if I'd wake up from this dream before or after Charlie committed his life to me. The sunlight from the window caught on the random crystal woven into the lace on the bodice just enough to make it sparkle when I moved. I stared at the dress and hoped Charlie loved it as much as I did. It was understated and classic, timeless and elegant, and somehow, it managed to hide the majority of my scars. The girl who'd done my hair had worked miracles, and I couldn't even tell where the pieces had been shaved after the accident.

My eyes glistened with tears as I stared at myself in the reflection. This was the closest I'd come to looking like the me I was before the accident. No one could tell that I'd been pieced back together more than once in the last year, and for that, I was grateful. I loved the idea of not looking like a patchwork quilt in my wedding photos. It might be vain, but it was one day, and I wanted it.

"Sarah?" Daddy knocked on the doorframe and waited in the hall.

I turned to face him. "Yes, sir." I nodded and bit my lip.

He stepped toward me and took my hand. Lifting it over my head, he spun me around to take in the details. "You're beautiful."

I kissed his weathered cheek and pulled back to look at him. A smile lifted my cheeks, and I'd never been more proud. "You clean up pretty well yourself."

"I need to get you to the Burins'." Daddy stuck out his elbow, and I wound my hand through it. He escorted me out of our house for the last time and into the truck to take me to my future husband.

Daddy stayed quiet on the ride to Twin Creeks, and all I could do was try to envision what I was about to see. Jessica and I had talked about it, but since I wasn't the one there supervising the work, I didn't really know what to expect.

When Daddy turned down the dirt road to where the two creeks met, every truck in Mason Belle blocked my view. I had no idea who had orchestrated the parking, but they'd done an amazing job. Perfect rows lined the field with an aisle up the center. All I could see was the top of that tree, and I knew Charlie waited underneath.

My breath caught in my throat, and when Daddy parked and put his hand on my shoulder, I didn't try to stop the tears from falling. Never in my wildest dreams had I expected this. I didn't have a clue what I'd find when Daddy took me down that aisle, but I knew that it would be met with love because that's what this town did. Without Mama and

Randi, they'd pulled me into a giant hug of support. And I'd be surprised if there was a single resident who wasn't here.

Daddy got out of the truck and came around to the passenger side to help me down. I straightened my dress as I stood next to him, and when he closed the door, the sound of birds chirping and the water flowing and the leaves of that great oak rustling were music to my ears. Daddy took his cell phone out and made a call to let someone know we were here. And then he tucked the device back in his jacket and again gave me his elbow.

He kissed my forehead and patted my hand resting on his forearm. "I couldn't have asked for a better man for you, Sarah. Remember where you came from and know that home isn't a place."

I nodded, unable to speak. Any more tears would ruin my makeup, and I hadn't brought anything with me to do any touchup.

"I love you, Sarah Anne."

As if Daddy's words had queued the start, an acoustic guitar joined nature's sounds, followed by another. And when I took my first step into that aisle created by rows of trucks, there were three playing, and the tree where Charlie had proposed came into full view.

And so did Charlie.

Daddy didn't offer to let me change my mind. He didn't provide a getaway route. Instead, he squeezed my hand and said, "I've never seen a man love a woman the way he does you."

And he was right. And it was all written in Charlie's

expression. He had trimmed his shaggy hair and shaved, the tux was—well, hot. But it was the grin that took over his features that told me just how perfect he was for me. His eyes sparkled a brilliant green, and I thanked God that I got to spend the rest of my life with this man at my side.

Charlie took my hand from Daddy after they exchanged whispered words and a clap on the back, and then Charlie did what Charlie always does. He kissed my forehead. "God, you're beautiful." He didn't whisper. He didn't hold back.

And I knew he never would.

Everyone in attendance heard Charlie's proclamation, followed by our vows. And when we sealed our promise with a kiss, they cheered as loudly as they had when Mason Belle had won the football state championship.

As we walked back down the aisle as husband and wife, I scanned the crowd for the one person I'd hoped beyond all hope would surprise me. But Miranda wasn't there. I had thought she might make a grand entrance— Randi style—right before Daddy led me between the rows of chairs. That she would appear, and I'd see her out of the corner of my eye. She'd flash me that snarky grin of hers before taking a seat in the front row. Or maybe she would show up in the middle of the ceremony, and I would see her taking a seat in the very back row. Or that she'd possibly come up to me afterward, and we wouldn't have to say anything—we could just hug, and all would be forgiven. Anything would have been welcome. Even appearing at the reception, having missed the ceremony entirely because her cab ran late or her flight was delayed...

I would have accepted any excuse. I just wanted my sister to be at my wedding.

But when we reached the end of the chairs and started through the rows of trucks, I knew she wasn't going to be. It was devastating, but there it was laid out in front of me. I could do nothing other than accept the facts. It was heartbreaking. But in the end, it was Randi. She'd left Mason Belle of her own will, and this was no different. She marched to her own beat and played by her own rules. She didn't want to do anything that would require her to face the turmoil she'd left in her wake. That clearly extended to me as well as Daddy and Austin.

Miranda Adams had chosen to miss the most important day of my life. I would not allow her to ruin it as well. So when we reached Charlie's truck, and he opened the door, I turned into him, threw my arms around his neck, and kissed him like no one was watching.

His hands slid down my sides and around to the small of my back. When he cupped my butt in his palms and pulled me roughly against his body, I reluctantly tore myself away from his mouth.

"I don't think anyone needs to see us consummate our marriage." I felt the heat of a blush on my cheeks, and Charlie roared with laughter.

"Probably not, sunshine. Let's get to the house and change so we can come back and enjoy the reception."

And that's what we did back at his house. He left his tux, and I left my wedding dress in exchange for outfits that were more suited to the Texas heat. I had no idea how we'd changed so quickly, but Charlie looked just as edible in jeans and a T-shirt that hugged his chest in all the right ways, and I loved the sundress he'd picked out for me.

When we got back to the field, I hopped out of the truck, and Charlie came to take my hand. I got one step from his side before he pulled me back and into his embrace. Pressed front to front, I stared up between the distance that separated our height and into his pretty green eyes.

"You are the light of my life." He told me. "Thank you for marrying me." He met my mouth with his in a tender kiss. "I hope this is the best day of your life, sunshine."

"It is." Those two words had never been more true. There was nothing more I'd ever wanted in life than to be with Charlie. "I always wanted to be a Burin." I grinned against his lips as I spoke.

"There's my girl." He swept me into his arms and carried me bridal style back into the thick of the party that was now in full swing.

Tables and tables of food had been set up while we had changed, along with a makeshift dance floor. The guitars played music that made people want to move, and beer flowed as freely as whiskey. I had no idea where it had all come from or how Jessica had transformed this field in the time we were gone. I just knew that our guests were having a good time, and I was absolutely in love with the man who'd just asked me to dance.

Charlie took my hand in his and led me into a simple dance. It was nowhere near the same pace as the people around us, but he was more focused on paying attention to me than he was on keeping up with the crowd. We were lost in the world of being newlyweds where nothing could separate us. Between well-wishes, dancing, and food, the evening gave way to the night.

I found myself standing under that giant oak in the same place Charlie had proposed. I'd managed to slip to the outskirts of the crowd while Charlie mingled with friends. I listened to the sounds of the water and the music as I watched the fireflies dance in the fields, and I wondered if life could ever get any better.

Then my husband's arms wrapped around me from behind and pulled me back against his chest. His lips fluttered over my neck, peppering kisses down my throat. "You ready to go home, baby?"

I smiled and thought, yes...it was about to get infinitely better.

Charlie and I had gone to Gulf Shores for a quick honeymoon. We enjoyed the beach for a couple of days and then came back in time to make my first appointment with the specialist. It was the first ultrasound, and the doctor wanted to get it done to figure out just how far along I was. My best guess was about twelve weeks, but with all the risk factors involved, Dr. Nesbit wanted as exact a date as we could get. I hated that I was subjecting myself to more doctors' offices and appointments, but at least this had a prize at the end.

A nurse had led us into an exam room and instructed me to hop onto the exam table. I wasn't going to be doing any hopping, but with a little effort and Charlie's help, I got situated just before the ultrasound tech came in.

She dimmed the lights and introduced herself. "I'm Amy. It's nice to meet you." She had me lift my shirt and then tucked a paper sheet into the waistband of my pants and draped the remainder of the paper down my legs.

Charlie sat at my side, and we both watched as she squirted warm gel onto my stomach. I swore there was already a tiny bit of a bulge, but Charlie said I was crazy. He was probably right. The poof was probably from eating more and putting on weight versus pregnancy. Nevertheless, Amy put the probe in the goo and smeared it around on my skin with one hand while she lit up the screen on the other.

"You can watch the television on the wall so you don't have to crane your neck." And then she pointed a remote, and the TV came to life.

As soon as the machine came on, a whoosh filled the room followed by an electronic thump. My hand tightened around Charlie's as the shapes started to form in front of us. I glanced over to see a smile tilt his lips upward and wished I could capture the awestruck look on his face as he stared at his child on the screen. I knew he wasn't thrilled about this, but it wasn't the child he didn't want; it was the possibility of what could happen to me that he didn't want to face. But seeing his expression now, I had to wonder how different things would be when we left here. The baby was no longer a possibility; it was a reality. It was in front of us—not that I could decipher what I saw just yet—and it was as much a part of him as it was me. Charlie would have to come to peace with this on his own terms, but this was one step closer to heading that direction.

I watched as Amy measured things on the screen, and I could hear her clicking on the keyboard next to me. She hadn't said much, and when I looked over, the lines in her forehead and her marred brow had me asking questions.

"What's wrong?"

Charlie's grip on my fingers tightened, but he didn't speak.

Amy took a deep breath and forced a smile to her lips. The lines on her face smoothed away, and when she faced me, there was an air of surprise. She moved the wand on my stomach and pointed to the screen. I watched as letters appeared on the left side—Baby *A*. She moved the wand to the other side of my stomach, clicked again—Baby *B*.

My jaw dropped, and all the air left my lungs. "Twins?" My heart skipped a beat—or maybe five—and when it resumed a steady strum, I managed to drag in a ragged breath.

Charlie's eyes were wide, but his mouth remained sealed. I needed the lights on to see his face better because he wasn't giving anything away, and I couldn't tell what he was thinking.

"If you look right there—" she dragged an arrow up a dark line—"they're in two separate sacs. So, they aren't identical, but yes—twins." Amy then pointed out different parts of each baby's anatomy, printed out some pictures, and made us a disc of the ultrasound—all of which she gave to my husband.

Meanwhile, Charlie still hadn't said a word.

"Dr. Nesbit will be in shortly to talk to you." She wiped the gel off my stomach and tossed the paper drapes into the trash. "Congratulations." And then she flipped on the light and shut the door.

That ominous click didn't bring Charlie out of his haze; however, the arrival of Dr. Nesbit in the room did. Charlie hadn't let go of my hand, but his grip had gotten increasingly tighter, and now the muscles in his forearm flexed, and his jaw ticced. I swallowed hard and waited for Dr. Nesbit to speak.

He sat on the stool and propped his feet on the metal ring beneath the seat. When he clasped his hands between his thighs, I braced myself. "This makes things infinitely more difficult." Dr. Nesbit didn't once look at Charlie; he stared directly at me. "The strain of one baby on your spine was going to be a challenge. Two could prove catastrophic."

I didn't dare look at my husband, and I didn't know what to say to the doctor. All I could do was watch Dr. Nesbit's lips move. I'd already heard what he had to say the last time we were here. Now the trouble had doubled, and I didn't know what to think. It was like our decision was being challenged again.

"Are you listening, Sarah?" Charlie finally decided to speak, and I hadn't heard a word that had been spoken past those first two sentences.

I shook my head. "I'm sorry. I'm just a bit overwhelmed."

Dr. Nesbit kept talking, and I tried to focus on what he said, but it was disjointed at best. "Texas law..." His voiced teetered out. "Abortion up to twenty weeks." I watched the spit collect at the corner of his mouth. "A few weeks to decide." He stared at Charlie, and then he finally got my attention. "The longer you wait, the harder this will be. Your body just can't hold up to this kind of stress, Sarah."

Charlie stood, and the next thing I knew, I was standing, and Dr. Nesbit had his hand on the doorknob. They said goodbye, and I followed Charlie to checkout. There I stood lost in my head when he took my elbow in his hands.

"Babe, do you have your insurance card with you?"

"Huh?" I stared at him blankly.

"Your insurance card. The one they had on file isn't working."

I didn't even have my purse. I shook my head. "I didn't bring my wallet. But my insurance hasn't changed."

The lady looked at me with a sympathetic glance. "The carrier says the coverage isn't active."

"That's not possible. I use it all the time." I went to doctors' appointments several times a week. *Someone* would have pointed out that my insurance wasn't paying the bills. Although I hadn't received any bills from anywhere.

"Baby, all of those visits would have been covered in the accident." Charlie had thought through this better than I had. "What about the last visit? We were just here a couple of weeks ago."

She typed on the keyboard and stared at her screen. "Dr. Nesbit doesn't charge for the initial consultation."

Charlie had lost his patience with all of this. He wasn't rude, but he wasn't going to stand here debating the issue any longer. "How much is today's visit? We can just file a claim from home, right?"

"Of course. I'll print off a receipt for you to use. Once you get it straightened out, just give us a call, and we'll run the verification again. Today's visit is two-hundred and fifty dollars."

I nearly gagged. Instead, I swallowed the bile that rose in my throat and took my husband's arm to keep from falling over. He led me out to the truck and helped me inside. I watched like life was in slow motion as he rounded the hood of the truck and then joined me in the cab. He started the ignition, but he didn't put the truck in gear.

He stared straight ahead, and more than once, I opened my mouth to speak. But if there was one thing I'd learned about Charlie since we'd been together it was pushing him didn't help a situation. He blinked slowly several times, and then he licked his lips. When he started to shake his head, I braced myself for whatever thought was coming. "You can't go through with this." There was no emotion in his tone—it was hollow and lifeless.

"What do you mean?"

His irises were nearly brown when he turned his gaze on me. "This pregnancy. You can't risk your life." His knuckles went white, the longer he clutched the steering wheel.

I stared at him, not knowing what to say. I was terrified before we'd walked into that exam room. I worried every day that I'd made the wrong decision, but I'd kept the faith that

God would take care of me—of us. I tried to block out the possibility of what dying really meant or what kind of burden being paralyzed would place on Charlie, especially with an infant. That had been with the notion of one baby. I couldn't fathom or even conceive of what kind of drain I would be to Charlie if I survived. There was no way one man could take care of a wife and two babies and a farm on his own.

"I don't know what to do, Charlie." My voice sounded as broken as I felt.

He shifted in the seat and took my face in his hands. Green started to ebb its way into the brown the longer I stared into my husband's eyes. "Baby, think about the strain this is going to put on your body. I didn't want you to take the risk with one—but two? It's just not worth..." He was losing his composure.

Charlie dropped his hold on my jaw and sat back in his seat. I watched as he ran a hand through his hair and then down his face. This was going to get worse before it got better, and I braced myself for what was about to come.

"Damn it, Sarah. Think about it. If one baby had the power to leave you paralyzed, then what damage will two do? I don't think your chances of making it out of this pregnancy unscathed are very good, and I'm starting to wonder about the possibilities of you even making it out alive."

I started to protest. I opened my mouth to fight back. But nothing came because I had no valid argument. Every part of keeping this pregnancy going was putting my life at risk, and it wasn't just me that had waded into the water. I had

Charlie to consider as well, and all the people who would be affected if something happened to me.

Charlie's lids slid closed, and he took a deep breath. When he opened his eyes, he centered his focus on me. "I can't make it without you. I don't want to. You're the most important thing in the world to me, and this is just too big a risk right now. We can figure it out down the road when you're strong, but God, please don't take this chance now."

"Charlie..." I uttered his name on a breath and a plea. I wasn't fighting for or against. The truth was I no longer knew what was right or wrong or at what point my life became more valuable than others. But I was afraid to die, and I already knew I didn't want to live paralyzed. I'd faced that fate and fought tooth and nail to overcome it.

"I want to beg you to think about it, but Sarah, I don't think you need to dwell in this any longer than you already have. The decision isn't going to get any easier. Dragging it out isn't fair to you." He took a deep breath and stared me in the eyes, holding my attention so I understood the seriousness of what he was about to say. "This isn't going to end the way you want it to. I know that sucks. I know that's unfair. But Sarah, there is no second chance if you die. If you terminate, we have options. We can try other things. Adoption. A surrogate. Hell, the black market. I don't give a shit what it is. But if you're not here, none of it matters."

He'd said all he had to say, and I knew there wouldn't be anything to add. I also knew that he was right, regardless of how much I hated to admit it. I was too weak to walk this path—physically and emotionally. I didn't have the strength to roll the dice and hope the odds were in my favor.

Tears fell when I blinked, and as they ran down my cheeks, I admitted the words I hated to say. "I know."

"Baby, you have to know I'm telling you this because I love you. It's purely selfish; I get that." He captured my cheek in his hand, and I leaned into the warmth and security of his touch.

My emotions continued to leave tracks on my cheeks, and I finally conceded. "I know I can't go through with it. I'll schedule..." I choked on my own words. "I'll call the doctor and..."

He tipped his forehead to mine as his hand slid around to the back of my neck. "We'll get through this." He took my hand in his and brought it to his lips. "I promise I won't leave your side, baby. You're not alone. And when this is over, we will grieve together, and then we will find a way forward together. But I need *you* for there to be an *us*."

I took a deep breath, trying to calm my racing heart and soothe my raw soul. I felt like I was going to throw up, and my emotions were a whirlwind inside of my head. I had nowhere to put them. Electricity burned inside me with no way to get out, and nothing about that was good. I felt like I was being burned alive and couldn't escape the flames, not even to yell.

I didn't want to do this, and I knew he didn't want me to have to do it. But there were times that life left no choices except death. And this was one.

He sensed my ache, the turmoil, the pain. There was no

doubt he felt a version of it himself. I wasn't naïve enough to believe this was any easier for Charlie than it was for me. I'd seen the way he looked at that screen, and I saw the way he looked at me. He was burning in a pit of his own flames.

He let me go and turned the key in the ignition. But before he put the truck in gear and pulled out of the parking lot, he leaned over the console to kiss me. "I love you, Sarah. And I promise, we're going to be okay."

"I love you, too."

I trusted him to make that true, but I could barely breathe.

14

SARAH

The number was typed in, and I held the phone between both hands. Each time the screen dimmed, I'd touch it to bring it back to life, but I'd yet to press call. I'd battled this war in my mind non-stop since we'd left Dr. Nesbit's office. The only part of me that wanted to do this was the part of me that wanted to live. The rest of me argued vehemently with myself.

Death terrified me almost as bad as living a life without mobility. Charlie was right. I knew he was right. Everything he had said, sitting in the parking lot at the doctor's office was spot on. But that didn't stop the images of two heads and two little spines popping into my mind. Prior to the ultrasound, the pregnancy was a notion—it wasn't a child. Now it wasn't just a child; it was two. They were very real and very much alive inside me.

But as soon as I'd resigned myself to telling Charlie I couldn't go through with it, I thought about what it would be like for them not to have a mother. I knew that pain, and I wouldn't wish it on any child. I didn't want to abandon my children, and there was no guarantee I wouldn't. In fact, there was a high probability that I would.

I stared out the kitchen window to see Charlie in the driveway. I loved the way he moved. Watching his tanned arms flex and the muscles in his back go rigid made my mouth water. It also reminded me of how I'd ended up in this situation. I couldn't resist my husband's shirtless body or his charms. I loved him with more passion than I'd believed possible, and I wanted to spend the rest of my life with him. I also wanted that to be longer than the next six months.

I shifted my attention back to the phone and pressed the green button. I chewed on my lip as the line rang and I waited for someone to answer. The girl who'd told us about the insurance issue answered the phone just before it went to voicemail.

"Thank you for calling Dr. Nesbit's office. This is Megan. How can I help you?"

I took a deep breath and hoped my voice didn't fail me. "Hey, Megan. This is Sarah Burin."

"Hey, did you get the insurance situation sorted?" Her voice was far more cheery than mine, but it was safe to say, she wasn't facing the decision I was, either.

I hadn't spent much time thinking about the insurance situation. "No, not yet. I was calling to schedule an appointment."

"Is this for an office visit or our surgery center?"

The lump in my throat made every word more difficult

to speak than the last, and trying to clear it did nothing to help. "I assume the surgery center."

"Let me just pull up your file..." Her voice drifted off, and I assumed she realized what I would be doing in their facility on my next visit. That joyful demeanor she'd answered the phone with was now nowhere to be found. It had been replaced by a melancholy similar to my own. "I assume sooner rather than later would be best?"

"Yes." It was the best I could do at answering.

She set the appointment, gave me a list of instructions, and by the time I hung up, I was dizzy from the pace at which everything happened.

In a few days, this would all be over. Charlie would be relieved, and my life would be safe, at least from pregnancy. But I wondered what other repercussions we'd face. I wondered if I would ever forgive myself for taking two lives. I wondered what this would do to our marriage. The list of questions was a mile long, but at the end of the day, I just hoped it didn't change the way Charlie and I saw each other. I hoped we came together in our grief and didn't allow it to rip us apart. And I prayed that I didn't blame him for a decision I had just made.

My mind wandered to the procedure itself. I was grateful that I wouldn't be awake, but I worried about the pain the babies might feel. I couldn't stop myself from thinking they already knew my voice. I could only hope they didn't know fear. I tried like crazy to shut down my brain, and when I wasn't successful, I went to my husband.

No sooner had I stepped onto the front steps than his

attention turned toward me. I'd never know if it was the expression on my face or the tears that dripped from my jaw that brought the fortress of his security. Either way, he'd wrapped his arms around me, and without question carried me inside with my face buried in his neck.

Charlie cradled me in his lap when he sat on the couch, but he didn't say a thing. No couple should ever have to face this choice, much less this soon after getting married. He didn't have words to fix it, so he didn't try. He just held me and stroked my head. Every once in a while, he pressed a kiss to the top of my head, yet he didn't speak. Charlie recognized my pain and his need to shoulder it.

When my tears had finally subsided, Charlie didn't move to get up. Instead, he shifted on the couch, stretching us both out with my head still on his shoulder and his on a pillow. And then he pulled a blanket over us and held me close. I drifted off, but when I woke to use the restroom, Charlie was wide awake. His eyes were puffy and bloodshot, and I knew he hurt as much as I did—even if he hadn't been able to tell me.

Reluctantly, he let me up but held my fingers until the very last second, and when we separated, something in me snapped. And then it started to fester until it took root and started to grow.

Charlie had remained relatively quiet for the last two days. We both knew nothing would ever be the same, yet we weren't talking about it. Neither of us admitted it out loud. Now, walking into Dr. Nesbit's surgery center, the wound had festered until puss poured from it. It was infected, and it had the power to kill us. I kept trying to tell myself that this would all start to go away once we got through today, but it was a lie. Nothing would ever right this decision. The wrong could never be undone.

He had held my hand as we made it through the parking lot. It was still dark out, and dew glistened on the flowers near the door. I'd managed to get the first appointment of the day, and while this wasn't an abortion clinic, I was worried that everyone would know why we were here. My shame was amplified by the cover of night, and the drops of water on the grass only reminded me of things that were made anew...every day. If only I had faith the size of a mustard seed... I sighed and cast my gaze toward the ground, unable to take in any of the beauty God put before me. It was a painful reminder that I didn't trust Him. That I believed he'd made a mistake, and that I, as a human, had the power to undo what He set forth. And since I was too weak to acknowledge His power, I refused to acknowledge His grace or His mercy.

Each step Charlie and I took forward was another in the path of selfishness. This was more than just guilt. There was conviction, and I was forcing it out. I'd been chosen as these children's mother, and yet, here I stood, telling the Almighty He'd made a mistake.

My heart pounded beneath my sternum as we stepped up to the desk. I couldn't hear anything Charlie said to the girl I'd never met. Megan wasn't on this side of the facility, although I was grateful she wasn't here to witness my weakness despite the fact that I barely knew the girl.

He took the clipboard and pen while still holding my hand. Then he took me to a seat in the waiting room to complete the liability and financial forms. Mindlessly, I'd signed my name to the first, and I nearly gagged at the last. I really should have dealt with the insurance issue before we'd come here, but I couldn't bring myself to handle any more reality than I currently had on my plate.

My hands shook as did Charlie's when I handed him the forms to sign after me. He could pretend all he wanted that he was strong, but the quiver in his signature said otherwise. The question became, were either of us strong enough to turn around and not do this. Could I face the possibility of losing it all to protect my children?

"Mrs. Burin?" A woman in scrubs stood at the open door to what I assumed was the surgical area.

Charlie stood and took the clipboard to the desk. He reappeared in front of me—where I still sat rooted in my chair—and held out his hand. I glanced at the lady who waited and then up at my husband whose eyes were the darkest brown I'd ever seen them. They were laced with sorrow and remorse—and the deepest pain I'd ever seen in another person's eyes.

I couldn't do this.

I *had* to do this.

I took his hand and closed my eyes. And there in the waiting room, I prayed that God would give me the strength to pull off what I was about to do. I had to cleanse the wound that had grown between us, and it wasn't going to be easy.

They weren't born, but they were mine. And if I went through with this, I'd be no better than my own mother who'd left us for her own selfish reasons without ever looking back. But I'd be damned if I could live with that decision. I doubted I would make it through this pregnancy unscathed and maybe not even alive. But at the end of the day, regardless of what happened, I wanted my husband to be able to look our children in the eyes and tell them I had loved them enough to die for them. Because that's what mothers do—they choose their children over themselves.

I couldn't do what my mom did. Years of memories flooded my mind in an instant, all those years Randi and I had spent together without Mama. Most of them at odds because I should never have been forced to assume that role in her life. I wondered how different our relationship would have turned out had she not abandoned us. Maybe we wouldn't have fought. Possibly we could have been friends. It's almost certain that had Mama not left, the accident wouldn't have happened.

There were a lot of *maybes* spinning around in my head. More uncertainty ate at my soul than ever had in all my years on earth. But the one thing I wasn't uncertain about was this.

I stood and placed my hands on Charlie's chest. I could feel the life of his heart under my fingertips, and I knew how much love was housed there. "I can't do this, Charlie."

He glanced over his shoulder at the nurse still waiting for

us to join her, and when I peered at her, there was understanding in her eyes, not impatience. "What are you talking about, Sarah?" He had lowered his voice to try to keep our conversation private, but I doubted this wasn't something the employees hadn't heard before.

I didn't miss the irritation in his hiss or the confusion in his eyes.

One arm rounded my lower back to pull me against his front while his other hand captured my jaw. He stared into my eyes, and I saw the depth of his emotion as if it were my own. "Sunshine, I know you're scared, but we've been through this. I'm not going to leave your side. You're not alone in this." His eyes searched mine when his fingers tucked a tendril of curls behind my ear. Charlie did everything he knew to reassure me from the tone of his voice to the way he touched me, but it wasn't about him.

I couldn't see the staff behind me, and thankfully the woman at the door busied herself with the chart in her hand, even if it were just for show. I appreciated her attempt at giving us privacy when we had nowhere to go.

"We need to go home, Charlie." I wanted to look away, to find anything other than his hurt to focus on, but if I were taking this stand, I had to do it with the conviction I'd felt in my heart since I'd gotten up from the couch that day and felt our thread snap.

"Sarah, please don't do this...."

I took in a deep breath and prepared myself for the hardest words I'd ever have to say. I moved my hands from his chest to his jaw and lifted onto my toes to press my lips to his. Tears pooled in my eyes and then passed down my cheeks. "I can't do this. I'm not *going* to do this."

Defeat etched his brow, and his shoulders slumped. "You knew this was going to happen, Sarah. It's normal to have second thoughts. You came here prepared for that. We've talked about all of this."

I stroked my thumb over his cheekbone and hoped that in time, he would understand my choice and maybe respect it at some point. "If I do this, I'm no better than my mother. This is selfish, just like every decision she made with regard to Randi and me."

"And you don't think it's selfish to make this decision alone? What am I going to do with two kids if you don't make it through this?" His tone had gone from compassionate to bitter, but I understood his fear.

"I'm not going to have this argument here, Charlie." I pulled back to put space between us so I could head out the door. "I'm more than happy to talk until exhaustion knocks us over, but we can do that at home."

He put his hands on his hips, and his face hardened into an expression I'd never seen on him. "Sarah, they aren't going to let us keep going back and forth. And they're likely going to charge us for today regardless of whether we stay. Prolonging this isn't going to make it any easier, and making this trip time and again is only going to hurt more when you finally acknowledge that you can't have these babies." Charlie ran his hand through his hair and then scrubbed it down his face. "Just take a deep breath, and think about what you're doing. This doesn't make sense."

"What doesn't make sense is thinking that we can just end this pregnancy with no recourse. How can you have watched that ultrasound and not believe that your children have heard your voice? They've felt your love—even if it's just the love you feel for me. I won't do it, Charlie." I sighed and tried to appeal to the part of him that adored me. I softened my tone and tried again. "You believed in me when no one else did, Charlie."

His eyes flashed to mine, and there was a hint of understanding there.

"Believe in me now." I took his hand, but he didn't squeeze back. "It's just a mustard seed."

He shook his head, snatched his hand away, and muttered under his breath. "And hell is just a sauna." Without looking back, he took long strides toward the entrance and knocked over a chair in his wake.

I apologized to the nurse and the woman at the desk and asked her to send me a bill. She nodded but said nothing, which I appreciated. By the time I'd gotten outside, light had started to break through on the horizon, and even with as much turmoil that currently existed in my life, I knew I'd made the right choice.

Charlie was in the truck and had it idling. He hadn't helped me in, but I didn't expect any different. He was scared, and his worry manifested in anger. He didn't speak to me as we drove back to our house. He didn't open my door when we got there, either. Once we got inside, he stomped off down the hall, and I dumped myself on the couch, exhausted. It wasn't even eight o'clock, and I was already exhausted.

The door slammed down the hall, and I realized then just how upset Charlie was. I ran my hand over the small bump on my stomach and hoped a day would come soon where we'd moved past this.

15

CHARLIE

Not once in my life had I ever experienced rage so strong that I had to force myself to keep my mouth shut and then isolate myself to temper it. But that was exactly what I'd felt driving back from Dr. Nesbit's office. I forced myself to drive the speed limit. I refused to let a word slip passed my lips because nothing I said would be nice much less loving, comforting, or supportive. Sarah was being reckless and irrational, and I'd be damned if I could keep from telling her just how selfish I believed her actions to be.

So, when we'd gotten home, I left her in the living room and made my way to our bedroom. While she thought she was doing the noble thing, she hadn't considered what life for those kids would be like without her. I'd resent the hell out of them for taking her from me. It might be a dick move, but it was the truth. She hadn't thought about us at all in making her decision, only her guilt. Sarah wasn't the one who'd be left to clean up the mess she could leave behind.

That would be me. And I didn't want to raise children without my wife. I didn't want to be a single dad by choice. I wanted my wife at my side, and if that meant we never had kids, then so be it. I didn't give a shit.

I wanted to break shit. I needed to put my fist through a wall. Yet there was no outlet for my aggression, and everywhere I looked in our bedroom, there was nothing but happy crap that further pissed me off. I didn't want our wedding pictures to be the only occasion we got to share together. I wanted holidays and birthdays—years of memories framed in our home. Her choice started a clock, a countdown to the inevitable. She'd put a timeline on our marriage and might as well have asked for a divorce.

I threw myself onto the bed and stared at the ceiling. The fan wasn't even on to hold my attention. I laid my arm over my eyes and willed the thoughts to stop pummeling my mind. I couldn't take the idea of losing her, and that was all I could see. There was no way around it. Even if she survived, what kind of life would she have in a wheelchair? I'd seen what that did to her. I'd witnessed it not all that long ago, yet somehow, it seemed to have slipped her mind. Maybe she'd forgotten what had brought us together in the first place, but I'd never forget the defeat that weighed her down that day I found her in the hospital.

I stared at the ceiling for hours and then out the window, but nothing came to me. I didn't find peace or resolution. The only thing that happened was my heart no longer threatened to beat out of my chest, and my head didn't pound with the force of a thousand drums. My entire body was heavy, including my mind. And as the sun dipped behind the horizon and evening stole the day, I knew I couldn't hide in our bedroom anymore.

When I opened our bedroom door, the house beyond was unusually quiet. It didn't take me long to find my wife. The sound of dishes in the kitchen alerted me to her location. She hadn't heard me coming and had her back to the door. I leaned against the molding, watching her make dinner. She'd pulled her hair back, but a group of curls had fallen from her tie. She kept using her forearm to try to keep it from her face because her hands were covered in flour.

She startled when she turned and saw me from the corner of her eye. Her white palm met her chest, and I was certain it would leave a print right between her breasts. Any other time that would have humored me. Today it just hurt.

"You scared me." Sure enough, when she grabbed a kitchen towel, all five of her fingers were clearly outlined on her shirt. "Are you hungry? I'm making fried chicken." She was digging deep if she thought food would solve this issue. Not even fried chicken was a salve for this wound.

"You could have talked to me before you blindsided me with your decision."

She took a deep breath and moved toward the fridge. "It wouldn't have changed anything."

"Why didn't you go through with it?" I needed an answer, something better than whatever crap she'd spouted off at the surgery center. I had to have something that made a lick of sense.

She set down the milk and faced me, leaning her lower

back against the counter. "Because, I'm not going to put my needs over that of my children."

"It's not you putting your needs before theirs. It's you making your health and life a priority. If you don't take care of yourself first, you won't have to worry about your children's needs because you won't be a mother if you die."

She unballed her fists and clutched the counter on both her sides. Her knuckles went white, and she pressed her lips in a firm line before responding. "And what if I don't die, Charlie?"

"Even worse. Are you prepared for a lifetime of paralysis? Because you sure as hell weren't when I found you at Anston on the verge of a breakdown at the thought of never walking again." It was harsh, but I had to pull out the big guns here—she wasn't listening to reason. "You're going to hate every second of being confined to a wheelchair. Have you thought about what it will be like not to get on the floor to play with your kids? Or being unable to pick them up? You won't be able to do anything with them a normal parent would do. Is that the life you want to give them?" I could feel my lip turn up in a snarl, and I didn't recognize my own voice as it ripped through the air in accusation.

She pushed off the counter, and in a few short steps, our bodies were less than an inch apart. Fire raged in her eyes, and her chest expanded with each heated breath she took. "Don't you dare!" Sarah poked me in the sternum without taking her eyes off mine. "Don't you put that on them or me. You can't predict the future, and you certainly don't determine my fate."

"No, but you sure as hell don't mind determining mine."

"What's that supposed to mean?" She blanched and took a step back.

This had gotten completely out of hand. I knew it; she knew it; yet neither of us stopped it. "They're going to hurt you!" I couldn't fight the animosity that poured out, nor could I bring myself to lower my voice. "Bit by bit, they're going to tear your body apart. With one, I was willing to concede, to give it a shot despite multiple doctors telling you not to proceed. But I saw the look on Dr. Nesbit's face. You're committing suicide, and I don't understand why when you have choices." His hand found his hair and then dragged his face, contorting his otherwise beautiful features. "Do you have *any* idea what twins do to a healthy body?"

"Spoken like a man who will never be faced with the decision," she snapped.

Jesus Christ, she was delusional.

"Have you thought about this at all? I mean beyond as far as your personal involvement?"

She crossed her arms over her chest and looked at me like I was stupid. "Of course, I have, Charlie. It's all I've thought about."

"So you've thought beyond leaving me without you? You've thought about what two kids will feel like never having known you?"

She nodded like there was nothing she hadn't considered.

I kept hammering on. "What about your dad? Have you thought about what it will mean to Randi? You're so hell-bent and determined not to be like your mother, but wouldn't your choice be doing the exact same thing to them? You'd be no better than the woman who walked away from you and your sister. She made a choice, and you're making the same one—just for different selfish reasons."

She blinked twice, and her mouth fell open. Sarah quickly closed it and pulled her lip between her teeth. I'd gone too far, and now she fought off tears. She turned away but not before I caught her flushed cheeks heated with anger. But she didn't say a word. Sarah stepped back to the counter and resumed what she'd been doing.

I should apologize, but I don't. "I'm just trying to get you to see things from my point of view, Sarah. I love you, and the thought of not having you this time next year is more than I can handle."

"I know, Charlie. You are so bent on my seeing things from your perspective that you refuse to consider mine." Her shoulders rose when she took a deep breath and then fell when she exhaled. "My decision is made. Like it or not, I'm not terminating the pregnancy. I hope that at some point, you'll stop being mad and consider another side of things. But if you can't, then that's something you'll have to find a way to live with. In a few short months, you're going to be a father, Charlie, and no amount of arguing is going to change that."

I rubbed my face with both hands, wishing I could pull my hair out and that it would solve this problem. "You aren't being reasonable. You're allowing your emotions to dictate our future instead of using the brain God gave you to consider what I have to say. If you'd just listen to me for a minute—"

She threw the knife on the counter, wiped off her hands on the towel, and spun to face me. "Oh, I've heard every word, loud and clear."

Before she had a chance to say anything else, I recognized that I'd lost this battle. I still should have apologized, yet I still didn't. Instead, I took the coward's way out. "Let me know when you're ready to have a rational conversation not controlled by your hormones."

Her bottom lip trembled, and I was well aware I'd done that, too. I couldn't continue this. It wasn't getting us anywhere except further apart. I stormed out of the kitchen, grabbing my keys as I went. I slammed the front door so hard I wouldn't be surprised if it cracked the glass, but I didn't look back. When I reached my truck, I pulled hard on the handle, then threw myself inside. I didn't have a destination; I just knew the longer I stayed here, the more damage the two of us would do to each other. Regardless of how angry I was, I didn't want to hurt my wife. I loved her so much that I didn't want her to hurt herself. And that was the part of this she was missing.

～

"No offense, Charlie." When Austin spoke like that, I knew we were about to fight, and when guys fought, it resulted in punches being thrown not just insults. My little brother had bulked up in recent weeks with all the work he did at Cross Acres, but I still had a solid two inches, twenty pounds, and six years on him.

I had been in the process of pulling a shard of metal from the thick rubber of my work boots. I didn't know how it had gotten there; I only knew it pissed me off every time I took a step, and if I weren't careful, it would find its way into my heel. I looked up at him from where I sat when he spoke but didn't say anything in return. I just wrenched the pliers I held and tugged on the boot again.

Austin sat down at the table. "When are you going back?"

I finally yanked the damn shard free from my shoe and tossed the pliers onto my parents' kitchen table. Then I stared at the hole left in my boot like it held some significance. "I don't know what you're talking about. I go by the house every day—more than once—to check on her." Just because I hadn't *talked* to my wife didn't mean I was a total dick who'd left her to the wolves. Right or wrong, I needed space and time to process the choice she'd made for us both.

"It's been two weeks." Austin folded his arms over his chest.

It had only been thirteen days, but I wasn't going to point that detail out to my little brother. He'd kept quiet for the most part. Austin had his own issues to deal with, namely Randi's disappearance, and we hadn't talked about my marriage or what had me sleeping at my parent's house for the better part of a fortnight.

He tipped the kitchen chair and rocked on its back legs while he stared at me. "I'm talking about the fact that your wife called yesterday, and you refused to pick up the phone. We won't mention that you're sleeping in your old room when you have a house of your own just down the street with a beautiful woman in your bed."

I glared at him, but still, I said nothing.

"You won't talk to her; you might as well talk to me. Mom and Dad aren't going to let you hide out here forever. Honestly, I'm surprised they've let you stay at all." He raised his brows like somehow, he'd become the mature one in the last two weeks.

I shrugged. "We had a fight." I wasn't stupid enough to believe anyone in my parents' home believed it was that simple. I also knew my mom wouldn't tolerate my walking out on my wife, even if it were just temporary; she'd given me a wide berth, but that gap was fast closing.

"That's what you said—two weeks ago. And man, I love having you around, but not, however, at the expense of your wife. So, I'm back to wondering why you're still here. So, you can either talk to Sarah, talk to me, or face Mom and Dad." And there it was—Austin was the messenger.

"Austin," I said. "You're nosey as hell."

Austin's stubbornness matched mine. "Charlie, you need to get whatever's bothering you off your chest and go home."

I didn't have to tell him shit, and I knew that. But he was right, sooner or later, something had to change. Austin was the easier choice, but Mom and Dad would find out soon enough if I couldn't get Sarah to see things my way. As it stood, she hadn't budged on her stance, and each week that ticked by was seven days closer to no longer having an option. I settled back in my chair and crossed my arms over my chest to match his stance, and then I took a deep breath, preparing myself to acknowledge what no one but Sarah and I knew.

"Sarah's pregnant."

The chair he'd been leaned back in fell forward with an ominous thud. I'd never seen Austin stunned into silence, but there it was, and it wasn't pretty.

"With twins." I added that in for emphasis, and then I let it sit for a second.

Austin marinated in my words, but I knew he didn't really understand the severity of his sister-in-law's being pregnant. For any other couple, it would be a cause for celebration. My parents would go crazy knowing Sarah wasn't just giving them one grandbaby but two. But our situation wasn't normal, and it sure as hell wasn't a reason to be over the moon.

"Her doctors don't think she can survive the pregnancy. We've been to a specialist who has consulted with her orthopedic doctors and physical therapists, and no one has anything good to say. We've been advised by more than one physician to terminate the pregnancy." I leaned forward with my hands on my neck and tried like hell to rub away the tension. "Two weeks ago, we had agreed to it. *We.* She made the appointment. We went to the surgery center. They called her name." That day played on repeat in my head like a horrible rerun I couldn't get to stop. "We were in the lobby, and she just up and changed her mind. Said she couldn't do it."

I took a breath to see if my brother offered any sort of support, but he kept his mouth shut and waited for me to continue. Of course, the one time I wanted his opinion, the one time I felt certain he'd have my back, he sat silently staring at me.

"It's like she can't face the reality of what's going to happen. Or maybe she doesn't care. She's not thinking about what it's going to do to her family or me if we lose her."

"Maybe she thinks she doesn't have any options."

I shook my head. "Uh-huh. I've given her options. The doctors said when she was further out from the accident and her body was stronger that we could try again. I suggested adoption or a surrogate. Hell, I offered to buy her a baby, Austin. I keep telling her I'll do anything she wants, but I can't lose her."

He cocked his head to the side like he was considering something, although I had no idea what until he finally spoke. "Have you asked her why?" He held up his hand when I started to answer. "And really listened?"

"Something about her mother and Randi. Hell, I don't know. She isn't making sense, Austin. She's thinking with her hormones instead of her brain."

"I hope to God you haven't said that to her."

My grimace must have confessed that I had because Austin slowly shook his head, and I could tell he wanted to call me a dumbass even though he didn't. Instead, he leaned forward with his forearms on his thighs, and his expression got tight. My brother was a laidback guy until a year ago when all this shit had happened with Sarah and therefore

Randi. It had changed him, and I wasn't certain it had been in a good way. We didn't talk about it—ever. His girlfriend was a topic that was strictly off-limits, which was also the only reason I believed he'd understand my desperation to make my wife see my side. He knew what it was like to lose someone in the blink of an eye, and Austin would never recover from Randi's choosing to walk away from him.

His nostrils flared, and anger flashed in his eyes. "Charlie," he said, "if I were sitting any closer to you, I'd smack you upside the head right now."

"What?"

"You're a selfish bastard." His mouth hung open, and I'm sure mine did the same. "It isn't Sarah who's being unreasonable; it's you." His eyes went bloodshot as he fought emotion. There was a lump in his throat he didn't seem to be able to swallow past. He tried, anyway.

I wasn't accustomed to seeing this kind of reaction from my little brother. Since had Randi disappeared, all he'd dealt the world was anger and a lot of quiet weeks. Austin didn't talk much; in fact, he had gone days without so much as a word in her absence.

"Austin, are you okay, man?"

"No." He shook his head. "Yes, I'm fine; I just can't believe you. Do you have any idea what I'd give to be in your shoes right now? I was blindsided by Randi's leaving. There's not a day that goes by that I don't miss the hell out of her. But if I'd had the choice, and she was going to leave anyway, I would have *killed* to have a piece of her still here after she was gone. But she's gone, and I have nothing."

I stared at my little brother, regretting I hadn't been around more recently. I knew he'd been hurting, but I didn't have a clue just how much. And while I didn't think Austin wanted to be a single father, I got the sentiment all the same.

"Sarah's going to be gone one day, too, man. It's a miracle she survived that crash."

"I don't want to think about my wife dying, Austin."

He ignored me and kept going. "You don't get it. She doesn't have to die, Charlie. She could just leave. Hell, who knows, the way you're acting, she might; I damn sure wouldn't blame her. But to have a piece of her—a piece of both of you—that was created in love, that's everything good about who you two are—you can't *buy* that. It's priceless. You keep saying that you will, but you have no guarantees, and an alternative isn't the same. And you won't know the difference until you've lost everything."

Austin got up and stormed to the fridge. He pulled out a beer, but I didn't bother lecturing him on underage drinking. I didn't even bother to raise a brow in question. I had enough of my own problems; I'd let my mom deal with Austin.

"Damn it, Charlie. You're my brother, and I love you, but I wish you weren't so stupid sometimes." He took a long pull from the bottle in his hand and stared me down like he hated me.

I'd never seen my brother so worked up. And I hated to admit that I had no idea he'd been this affected by Randi's absence. It made sense; I just hadn't paid attention. He'd lost his best friend, his girlfriend, and his soulmate in the blink of an eye, and he didn't have the first idea why.

I pushed back from the table and turned my chair to face Austin. "Are you okay?" I'd just asked that question, but it bared repeating.

"I'm fine, but you aren't going to be. Get your head out of your ass, Charlie, or you're going to wake up one day and realize what I'm saying is true. Only it'll be too late for you to do anything about it."

"So, you think I should just let Sarah risk her life? I should just tell her everything's going to be okay? And pretend like I'm not going to lose her in a handful of months?"

He nursed the bottle in his hand, and then he finally answered. "You don't have to lie to her, but you can support her. She's made the decision. The question is: Do you want to be in the picture or not? Do you want to have those months if that's all that's left? Or do you want to be the bastard who walked out on his wife and kids? At least, if you're by her side and something *does* go wrong, then you get to keep a piece of her in your life. I'm not saying Sarah isn't important or that her life is worth less than the babies'." He finished the beer and tossed the bottle into the trash with a clatter. "I'm saying, you need to make a decision. You need to decide whether or not you want to have this part of her. But from where I'm standing, you'd be a fool not to grab hold of whatever part of Sarah you can keep."

I hated to consider my little brother might have a point, and I sure as hell didn't want to admit it to his smug ass. "When the hell did you grow up?"

"The day Miranda Adams walked out of my life."

That was as real as it got, and if I weren't careful, I'd face the same fate long before this pregnancy was over. If I didn't get my head out of my ass, I'd lose my wife to my ignorance and fear. "I'll call her back."

Austin kicked the leg of my chair as he walked by. "Do better than that, shithead. Go home. Your wife misses your dumbass." He smirked at me, and I knew his lecture came from a good place.

"Yeah, yeah, yeah. Will you tell—"

"Mom and Dad will be fine. But yes, I'll let them know you opened your eyes. I will not, however, tell them your wife is pregnant. Mom is going to flip." Austin clapped me on the shoulder as he left the kitchen.

I retied my boot, and then grabbed my keys and stuffed my wallet into my back pocket. He was right. Sarah deserved more than a phone call, and I'd resort to groveling if push came to shove.

When I got into my truck, I didn't bother trying to run through what I'd say when I got home. I figured the less rehearsed, the better. Sarah deserved honesty, and that didn't come in any other form than an apology.

I parked the truck in the driveway and noticed none of the lights were on. Her car was here, so I was fairly certain she was as well, but it would serve me right to have to hunt her down after disappearing for nearly two weeks. She'd known where I was, but that wasn't the point. I wasn't at home with my wife, and that was all that counted.

The front door was locked—we never locked the doors. And I felt like an ass for her not believing she was safe in her own home. I stuck my key in and turned the deadbolt. Silence met me on the other side, but I could see the flicker of the television in our room.

I didn't want to scare her, and I hadn't so much as sent her a text that I was on my way home. "Sunshine?" I called out into the darkness to alert her I was here. "Babe?"

When I peeked my head into our bedroom, I found her on her side asleep. One hand was under her head and the other cradled her stomach—our babies. I stripped off my shirt, kicked off my boots, and then slipped out of my jeans. In nothing but my boxers, I climbed into bed behind her and eased my arm under her neck and my hand underneath hers on her belly. Her fingers naturally laced with mine, and she murmured something as she stirred.

"Charlie?" She rolled into me and gradually opened her beautiful blue eyes.

I tucked her hair behind her ear and kissed her forehead. "I'm sorry." Because that was what it all boiled down to. "For everything."

She let out a heavy sigh, and I expected her to close her eyes. Instead, she opened them wider and placed her hands on my bare chest. "I can't do that again, Charlie."

I knew what she meant, but I also knew she was going to say the words, and I dreaded hearing that I'd let her down.

"If we have a fight, you can't just leave. We're married. We stick it out. We hash it out. We argue. Whatever we need to do. But we don't leave. And we sure don't do it for two weeks."

I didn't point out that it had only been thirteen days. It

wouldn't help my case. "You're right. I'm sorry. I promise. Never again."

She searched my face and then placed a sweet kiss on my lips. "I love you, Charlie."

"I know you do, babe. I love you, too."

16

SARAH

I knew pregnancy was going to have a lot of ups and downs, but no one was really good at telling me what to expect. I was having large and small complications, not to mention continued insurance issues that I finally gave up on and took to Daddy. He swore he'd get it taken care of and that he'd gotten behind on payments while I was hospitalized. The next time we'd gone to Dr. Nesbit's office, Daddy told me it had all been handled, and when I called Megan, she confirmed that the bills were taken care of.

I had come close to getting mastitis. One of my milk ducts became blocked, but it formed a cyst on the side of my breast instead, which eventually drained and left behind a painful mark that was deep enough to scar. And as the doctors had predicted, the further along I got, the more strain the additional weight put on my spine. Everything I'd been warned about plagued me, but it was the ongoing blood pressure issues that had raised the red flags and set off all the warning bells.

I now spent as much time in Dr. Nesbit's office as I did with my physical therapists—not really, but it felt that way. I was sick of the weekly visits, but they weren't going to cease anytime soon. Nothing was getting easier; instead, it was getting infinitely harder.

"You're measuring on track for twins."

Charlie had gotten to where he questioned everything the doctors and nurses said as if there were hidden meaning behind it. "Is that a good thing or a bad thing?" It was a legitimate question since nothing held the same weight for me that it did for other pregnant women.

He moved his head back and forth, considering his answer. "It would be good for anyone else. It's good for the babies. It's hard on Sarah's spine and organs. Obviously, we never want the fetuses to be underweight or malnourished, but in your case, smaller would be a blessing."

"I feel the added pressure of every pound." It was true. "Standing up and walking have become quite the chore and leave me totally out of breath."

The doctor sat on his stool and stared at me. "Any headaches? Difficulty breathing?"

"Headaches, yes. My face gets flushed, and I have to lie down. They're nearly unbearable."

Charlie interjected. "She's short of breath, too.

I waved him off. "I'm carrying around a giant fishbowl in front of me with two huge goldfish vying for equal space. Of course, I'm winded. It's a workout to walk down the hall. I've got two other people with me."

Dr. Nesbit attributed both issues to my on-going blood pressure problems, especially the headaches. "I think we're at a point that we need to consider bedrest. We can reevaluate it at each appointment, but you need to be kind to your body, Sarah. And other than incubating those two babies, your life is on hold for the foreseeable future."

I wanted to argue, but I knew it wouldn't get me anywhere. There was a reason Charlie insisted on coming to every appointment. He knew I'd leave out critical pieces of information, and if he were there, then he could ensure he enforced them all. This would be no different, and I cringed inwardly even thinking about how overboard he would go.

Charlie had also learned that I had a hard time following my instructions letter by letter, so he made certain to have it spelled out so there was no misunderstanding. "What exactly does *bedrest* mean...specifically?"

Dr. Nesbit chuckled. He'd gotten to know us both better in the time we'd spent with him, and he appreciated Charlie's candor and his questioning. "Exactly what it sounds like. Off your feet, in bed or on the couch on your side, not your back. Limit your physical activity as much as possible."

I closed my eyes to keep either man from seeing me roll them, and when I opened them, they both stared at me. "So television and potty breaks? What about a wheelchair?"

"More or less. But you don't have to ruin your mind with reality TV. You can switch it up with a book or a conversation here or there. Just no grocery shopping, running errands, cooking dinner..." He looked down at his clipboard. "Or working on a ranch. And no great amounts of time in a wheelchair, the pressure is too great on your spine." He winked, and this time I rolled my eyes so he didn't miss it.

"Yeah, I've been out bailing hay." I can't even see my toes, but whatever.

Dr. Nesbit clapped Charlie on the shoulder and chuckled. "You've got your work cut out for you, son." Then he directed his attention back to me. "If the pain gets to be too much, you can take acetaminophen, but that's about it. The best thing you can do is stay off your feet and keep the pressure off your spine."

I nodded because there was nothing else I could do. Tylenol was worthless when it came to warding off pain, and I wondered if anyone actually benefited from it. It wouldn't even dull the aches I already dealt with, and it wouldn't touch the heartburn that kept me up or the constant nausea. These two little demons wanted to make sure I felt pregnancy at every turn—or kick—and I was fairly certain they were prepping me for what life with two infants would be like once they arrived.

We said goodbye for the week, made our appointment for next week, and I waddled out to the truck. Before too long, Charlie would need a forklift to get me into the cab. Once I was safely buckled in, I set my hands on my stomach and slid them down the front. I was ready for this to be over. Thankfully, there had been so many little issues that kept cropping up along the way that I'd managed to block out the major issue at the end of the road. Terror hadn't set in because I was too busy dealing with present-day to worry about delivery.

Even when Daddy or Charlie's parents talked about the what-ifs, it didn't really sink in. I'd been listening to that kind of chatter behind my back since the accident, and it had almost become a way of life. I saw the looks they all gave me —they sucked at hiding their concern. But I'd proven doctors wrong once, and I aimed to do it again. I'd made my choice knowing the consequences and the risks, and nothing would please me more than raising these kids into adults. The only way I could do that was to ride this out, bide my time, and do exactly what the doctor recommended.

I probably should have been worried. I probably should have been concerned about the pressure Charlie could face. But my heart was at peace with my decision, and I believed I'd been blessed with this pregnancy...even if no one else felt the same way.

That wasn't fair. After Charlie's two-week stint at his parents' house, his entire attitude had changed. Whatever Austin had said to him the night he came home had completely jerked him out of his plight to force termination. He still worried. And he did everything the doctors told us to. But if he still saw this as a death sentence, he hadn't voiced that again. Now, he talked to my belly, and he rubbed shea butter all over my stomach. We'd picked out cribs and furniture and all things baby with the idea that two of us would be sharing the parenting duties. And that was how I had to look at things.

I knew nothing would ever be the same again once

Charlie apologized, but it was no longer the fear of losing him or his losing me. It was the fact that we had two little girls to get ready for, and Charlie didn't have a clue what to do with that.

~

"Charlie..." I tried to keep the panic out of my voice, but I could feel the sticky moisture on my thighs and under my bottom. My voice climbed with every passing second and syllable out of my mouth. "Charlie!"

Charlie stirred in the bed next to me, but he hadn't fully woken up. I had my hand resting firmly on my stomach, but each wave of pain brought tears to my eyes. I didn't want to press too hard because it hurt, but as I cradled my belly in my hands, I worried that if I let go, my insides would come falling out. My head was pounding, I couldn't catch my breath, and I would have sworn someone had sliced me open and the babies were going to deliver themselves.

The third time I called his name, Charlie's eyes fluttered open and then suddenly became alert. "What's wrong?" He sat up, now wild-eyed, searching my face and reaching for me. "Sarah?" He threw back the bedspread and then turned on the lamp. His ruffled hair fell into his face, and I noticed his cheek was red and wrinkled from the pillow until the blinding pain raced through me again.

"Everything hurts." My voice cracked as I tried to maintain my composure. "My body feels like it's on fire and like someone took a knife to my gut. I can't move, Charlie." I lost the last bit of resolve I had when he came around the bed and moved my blankets.

There was blood everywhere. My water hadn't broken; I was hemorrhaging. It looked like massive amounts of blood. If my pain level was any indication of just how much, it was a gruesome scene.

"Baby, we've got to get you to the emergency room." He didn't wait for me to respond when he picked up the phone.

I didn't know if he'd called 9-1-1 or somebody he knew in town. When I heard him give them the address, I was fairly certain it had been emergency services. I writhed in pain on the mattress, knowing there was no way I could get up. And when anyone tried to move me, it would be agonizing.

When Charlie disconnected, I didn't have any idea what was going on, but I trusted my husband. Minutes seemed like hours under the most excruciating pain I'd ever endured. But when I heard the sirens in the distance, I held tight to Charlie's hand and prayed.

"Baby, I have to go let them in. I'll be right back."

That meant I had to let him go, and I as did, I lost my hold on consciousness as well. I'd drifted in and out, never really sure where I was at that point until the sirens would flood my ears, and I wanted to block out the noise. Every time I tried to cover my head, my arms were met with resistance, and I couldn't move. I could hear Charlie talking, but I couldn't see him. And as quickly as we'd been moving, we'd suddenly stopped. I closed my eyes to swallow back the pain of the bumps as the paramedics took me out of the ambulance.

Stars and then hospital lights passed over my head. I felt like I was going to vomit, but I couldn't keep a hold on reality long enough to worry about turning my head.

"She's aspirating."

"Get that damn mask off her face."

"I need some help over here."

I didn't recognize any of the voices, and the one I needed to hear wasn't around. "Charlie?" I hadn't heard myself, so I doubted anyone else had either.

The lights over my head were so bright that I closed my eyes to fight the sting. Nurses talked around me; things stuck me; alarms went off. And through it all, the only time I could find Charlie in the midst of the chaos was as he was dragged away. But when I tried to reach for him, my arms were still bound, and my voice didn't find him. I couldn't do this without him. I had to have him, and if he stayed behind, he'd never find me. I sobbed and choked.

That thought raised panic. The nurses tried desperately to calm me down, but at some point, a rush of cold ran up my arm, and I assumed they'd injected something into my IV. Before I completely lost hold, I wondered if this had been it. If that was the last time I'd see Charlie. If I'd ever wake from this. Or had this been what I'd been warned about?

But before I could think any more about it being the end, darkness took over.

17

CHARLIE

The nurse had practically dragged me away as they prepped Sarah, for what I wasn't sure. Another woman joined the lady who'd pulled me away from my wife, but I only heard bits and pieces of what she had to say as she shoved paperwork at me.

"Mr. Burin, I know this is a lot to take in, but the babies aren't going to wait. I need you to sign the forms."

I nearly dropped the clipboard and pen as I tried to form a sentence. "Wait? What do you mean? Sarah's nowhere near her due date." By nowhere, I meant weeks...like eleven or twelve of them.

The nurse who had pulled me away gave the one who'd joined us a sympathetic glance before she turned remorseful eyes to me. "An emergency C-section is the best hope for all of them."

I couldn't swallow.

My throat had completely closed, and I was struggling to even breathe.

The worst that could have happened was happening, and I was stuck in the middle of it—alone. I stared at the paper in my hand and then looked back at the women waiting for my reply. My eyes filled with tears as the reality of losing her took shape. The notion had always been there, but it hadn't really taken root. I'd believed she'd survive. I'd convinced myself the doctors were wrong. Yet, here I was in a living hell of our own making, facing the devil without my wife at my side. And I was terrified.

I took a deep breath, knowing that every second that passed was one I kept a doctor from doing what he or she could to save my wife. "Do whatever you have to do to save my wife first."

The nurses both stared at me, and then one nodded her understanding and dashed off the way we'd come. I didn't care what they thought of me. They didn't know Sarah, and I didn't know the babies. I couldn't do this without her. I didn't want to. I couldn't think about loving them when I was blinded by my love for her. Maybe that was the difference between a mother and a father, or maybe I was just a selfish bastard.

I scrawled my name on the bottom of all the forms without reading a damn one. It didn't matter what any of them said; I would have sold my soul, standing in the emergency room and never looked back. I didn't give a damn what it cost or what they had to do to make it happen. I'd live at my parents' house or in a cardboard box as long as Sarah was with me.

And then I took a seat in one of the many plastic chairs to wait. The ER was like a ghost town, ominous. The sterile smell and lack of color nearly drove me insane as I sat there listening to the beat of my heart pound in my ears.

"Mr. Burin?"

I lifted my head from my hands to find the nurse who'd given me the paperwork standing in front of me with a cup of coffee. She held it out in offering and took a seat at my side.

"Is there anyone I can call for you? It might be good to have a family member with you while you wait." Her eyes were a pale blue, kind. They softened the longer she held my stare.

I wondered if she knew something that hadn't been shared with me and was trying to prep me to have someone there when I fell. God knew, I would fall. Hard. "Have you heard anything about her condition?" It didn't answer her question, but I needed to know.

"I haven't heard anything since they took her to the operating room." She took a deep breath. "Your wife is in critical condition, Mr. Burin, but we have an excellent team of doctors. She's in good hands."

I nodded and sipped the coffee she'd brought me. "I'll call her Dad."

With a tentative smile, she stood and started back toward the nurse's desk. "If you need anything just let me know."

If I needed anything, she wouldn't be able to help me.

No one would.

But that wasn't something I could focus on right now. I needed to call Jack and my parents. I dreaded both calls, but after making them, I couldn't recall anything that had been said. They were shocked and short, yet beyond them agreeing to meet me here, I couldn't remember a thing.

I didn't think it was humanly possible to get here as quickly as Jack arrived. He came barreling through the door like a bull in a rodeo with no regard for who he tore through in his wake. His face was beet red, and his chest heaved like he'd run here from Cross Acres instead of driving.

I stood when he got close—more out of habit than intention—and braced myself for whatever came my way. I wasn't expecting it to be Jack's arms closing around my shoulders or the fierceness of his embrace. It was rough. It was desperate. It was terrified. And when he finally released me, I looked into the eyes of a father who feared the same outcome I did. But he didn't voice it.

"Have they said anything?"

I crossed my arms and anchored my stance. "Not much. Just that they're doing everything they can." I didn't add "to save *her*" because no one ever needed to know that had been my instructions to the staff. I'd take that secret to my grave if I lost any of them. "There wasn't really time to talk before they took her to surgery, and the nurse doesn't know anything new."

Jack was a man of few words, and tonight was no different. We stood there both lost in our own thoughts when the nurse who'd brought me coffee came back and touched Jack's arm.

"Can I get you anything?" she asked, but he shook his head. "Mr. Burin, I know it's not a great time, but I need to get some information from you to get your wife into the system."

I dropped my arms to my side, and just as I was about to follow her back to her station, my parents flew through the door in the same disheveled descent that Jack had.

Jack turned to see what I was staring at and then clapped my arm. "You see to your parents, son. I'll take care of the other."

I should have argued with him. I should have told him it was my responsibility. I should have done a lot of things. Instead, I stood there like a little boy and let my mom hold me like she did when I was a kid. My brother stormed through the door and gave me a chin lift while my mother cried on my shoulder. He knew. We didn't have to share words for him to understand. Austin had felt the pain of his soul being ripped from his body just like I was now.

He stood back while my parents rattled off questions that went unanswered. When Jack rejoined us, my mom and dad turned their attention to him, and Austin stepped up to me. He didn't try to hug me to make me feel better. For a long time, he was just silent. We took seats while the other three yammered on, neither of us saying anything. I was numb, and Austin wasn't stupid.

Austin didn't look at me when he finally spoke. He was leaned forward like I was with his forearms on his thighs and his hands clasped between his knees. He stared straight ahead, into the same void I'd been lost in for however long this hell had been burning. "It's too early, Charlie."

I bobbed my head and croaked, "Yeah."

And then my brother did something that blew my mind. He reached over, put his hand on my shoulder, bowed his head, and he prayed. Austin wasn't bashful in his request, nor did he care who heard him beg God to let me keep my wife and my children. But it was when he pleaded with God that if that prayer couldn't be answered that He give me the strength to make it through whatever the next few hours brought—*that* was when I lost my composure. Because Austin knew as well as I did, the first would take a miracle, and the last would take mercy.

By the time I trusted myself to lift my head without falling apart, I glanced at the clock and realized I'd been here less than an hour. If I couldn't endure an hour wondering whether I'd see my wife again without being in sheer agony, there was no way I'd survive losing her. I didn't want to.

I pulled on my hair and scrubbed my face, wishing that action would bring me some sort of relief. It did not. "Jesus. How long does this take? I thought C-sections were fast." I stood and started pacing.

"Sweetheart, maybe that's a good sign." My mom tried to rub my back, and I shrugged her off. "Can I get you something?"

I spun around, teeth bared. "My wife. Do you think you can make her materialize? Maybe you could rewind time about seven months? Or maybe one of you could have helped me talk some sense into her so we weren't standing here having this very conversation?"

My dad stepped between my attitude and *his* wife. "Son, that's not fair—"

I pushed against his shoulders. "No!" I shoved my old man again. "What's not fair is that she could have prevented this!" I took a step forward and rammed my palms on his chest, moving him backward. "What's not fair is that I may lose her!" And on my fourth lunge at my father, he grabbed me and pulled me into him. "What's not fair is that I'd take her place right now. This very second, I'd leave this world so she could stay. I'd give up everything to give her those two girls." I sobbed into my father's shoulder, unable to stop the anger and the hurt and the devastation that poured from my mouth.

My dad held me tight, not letting me move until I gave up the fight. "Charlie, there's never been a day in your life that you've been alone, and this ain't no different. There's no room in this story for a quitter, son. And you don't know the ending, yet." He spoke to the side of my head, low enough that no one else could hear him, but strong enough that I knew he'd help carry me until I could stand on my own.

"Mr. Burin?"

Three Burin men turned toward that voice. My dad let me go, and my brother stood. Together they flanked me, preparing for my fall. I couldn't move. I stood rooted in place, knowing whatever came next out of that stranger's mouth held my fate.

She approached us when we didn't answer her call. "Which one of you is Sarah's husband?"

I lifted my chin, but words failed me. I didn't wipe the tears from my eyes or dry my cheeks. I didn't give a shit how weak I looked. The next sixty seconds were the most important of my life. My lungs burned with the breath I held, and time seemed to stand still.

"The babies are in the neonatal intensive care. Your wife is still in surgery."

I stared at her. I needed more of an explanation, but I couldn't bring myself to ask for one.

"Would you like to see your daughters?" Her eyes shined with something I couldn't discern.

And that strength Austin had prayed for washed over me. I nodded and took a step forward. I didn't look back at my parents, Jack, or my little brother. I followed the nurse to meet my children—my daughters.

She didn't speak on the way up the elevator, nor when we stepped off into what I guessed was the maternity ward. I stayed a pace behind her with each door she went through and each room we passed. And when we got to wherever we were going, she stopped and had me scrub my hands and put on a paper outfit over my pajamas. I mimicked everything she showed me or did, and seconds later, I stood next to an incubator.

They were perfect. Tiny, but perfect. Their little hats were too big for their heads and their diapers nearly swallowed them, but they had ten little fingers and ten little toes.

I hated to see the tubes and didn't want to know what they were for. All I wanted to know was if they were safe.

I jerked my head toward the girl I'd been following around. "Are they okay?"

She looked up at me with a smile. "They've got a fight on their hands, but their chances are really good." Then she tilted her head toward the small openings in the side. "You can touch them. Talk to them."

And that's what I did. I didn't know when she left my side, but I wouldn't have cared if she'd stayed there as long as I did. I wanted to scoop them into my arms and protect them from the world—that instinct was so strong it was hard to fight. For a moment, it was strong enough for me to forget why they were up here without their mama. For just the briefest blip in time, I only thought about how lucky I was that these two creatures had been safely delivered into my life. In the blink of an eye, I'd fallen so hard, so deeply in love with these two girls that I would never recover. They owned my heart in a way my wife didn't touch.

As I gazed down through the plexiglass at them, I wondered if this was what she felt like when she saw them on the screen that day during the ultrasound. She had a physical connection then that I couldn't fathom. Now, just touching their delicate skin and feeling the heat radiate off their tiny hands, I couldn't imagine my life without them.

They were precious and perfect...and *mine*.

～

There was a knock that startled me. There wasn't anyone in the NICU other than the nurses, and none of them spoke. It was the middle of the night, and the hospital was fairly quiet. This ward was dead silent. The babies didn't cry, and other than the machines that beeped or pulsed around me, there was nothing.

I glanced over my shoulder to find the nurse who'd brought me up here, and the shine in her eyes wasn't nearly as bright as it had been when she'd asked me about meeting the girls. So I waited for her to speak.

"Sarah's out of surgery. We'll be moving her to recovery shortly."

I didn't know what to do. I couldn't take the twins with me, but I couldn't stand here, either. They were too little to be left alone, and I couldn't be in two places at one time. I glanced at the incubator and then back at the lady in scrubs, unsure of what the right decision was.

"I think your family would like to see your little girls." She read my mind, and I wanted to hug her. "Would you like me to bring one of them up?"

I nodded. I was about to give my daughters my attention when I caught her before the door closed. "My brother. Austin."

She tilted her head to the side and considered me. Then she smiled and nodded. When the door closed, I realized that likely wasn't protocol. It should have been a grandparent since it couldn't be their mother, but Austin had been right. Whatever happened, I needed these pieces of Sarah and me...living, breathing evidence of the way we loved each other.

"How's it going?" Austin's voice came from the doorway.

I looked up and gave him a weak smile as he walked in. I'd never been so tired in all my life, and I was quite certain I looked like hell, but I was glad to see him. "Is it possible to have my best day and my worst rolled into one?"

Austin took the few steps to join me, and wordlessly, he peered through the acrylic at his nieces. "Charlie, man..." He shook his head but didn't take his eyes off the girls. "They're..."

"Perfect?" I beamed.

He shrugged and cocked his head to the side. "I was going to say tiny, but yeah." Austin chuckled, and it was the first bit of levity I'd felt in hours. He kept staring and finally asked, "How'd I'd get to be the lucky one up here first? Mom was beside herself that you asked for me. I almost didn't come so she could."

I raised my brow at my brother.

"Luckily for you, the nurse intervened and said you'd specifically asked it be me. Otherwise, you'd be standing next to Jessica Burin while she gushed over your kids. So what gives?"

I shrugged, unable to find words to express anything I felt.

"You okay, Charlie?"

Parts of me were; parts of me weren't. "I'm scared as hell, Austin."

"Sarah's in recovery. Your girls are in the best hands possible. You've got this."

But I didn't know if that were true. There were so many unknowns, and I couldn't even see the majority of them. Right now, three lives hung in the balance, and I needed every one of them to pull through. "What if I lose her? I don't know shit about being a dad much less to girls."

"You're not going to lose her." Austin had far more confidence than I did. He also wasn't directly involved in any of it. He loved Sarah, but he wouldn't grieve her the way I would. He took a deep breath and let it out on a heavy sigh. "Charlie, she's tough. That woman has been through hell and back. I've never met anyone with the resilience she has, and she wants nothing more than to prove all the doctors— and you—wrong. She'll make it through this just to say I told you so."

I chuckled and ran my hand through my hair. "God, you're probably right. I'll never live this down." It wasn't funny, yet it totally was.

"And Charlie, you're going to be a great dad. When that nurse came to get you, there was zero hesitation about where you needed to be. I can see it in your eyes now. You don't want to leave them regardless of how much you want to go to her."

"I don't have a clue what I'm doing."

"No one is ever ready to be a parent, not even a mother. Just breathe, man. You'll figure out the rest as you have to. And right now, you have to go see your wife."

It was harder than I could have ever imagined to leave

my girls under my brother's watch. I swallowed past a lump in my throat that threatened to cut off my air supply.

"Charlie, seriously. I can watch two babies in an incubator without supervision. But even if I couldn't, there are like ten nurses wandering around in here. And I'm quite certain Mom will find a way up here before I find mine back down."

"Thanks, man." I had my hand on the door when I finally answered my little brother's question. "Hey, Austin?"

"Yeah?"

"I picked you because you told me to pick them." I angled my head toward the girls, and I saw the recognition in his eyes. "I know it hurt when she left, but I don't know what I'd do without you."

Sarah was on the hospital bed, barely conscious. As soon as I saw her, the high I'd felt in my daughters' presence deflated. There was no color in her complexion, her hair was matted to her head, and she looked like she was one wrong move away from breaking in half.

"She's lucky to be alive." The nurse tending to my wife gave me a tentative smile. She might be tenured at dealing with these situations, but I was far from a pro. "We lost her during the surgery."

"What?" I understood the words she'd said, but I didn't get the full weight of what they meant in the context of my wife.

"She's lucky you guys got her here when you did. Another couple of minutes and I don't want to speculate what might have happened."

"You lost her?" My mind still hadn't grasped hold of that idea.

The nurse nodded. "She flatlined." The woman stared down at Sarah like she knew her, and as if her still being here brought her personal satisfaction. "Right after Baby B was delivered. It was like she held on to make sure they were safe." She glanced at me. "But the doctors brought her back."

I wasn't sure if this lady fully grasped what she was saying to a patient's husband. While I was grateful that skilled hands had brought my wife back to me, the thought of her dying on an operating table was more than I cared to remember.

Sarah had died. Those words were a heavy weight on my shoulders. Although she was alive now, I was quite certain she wasn't out of the woods. Hell, she was barely breathing. Despite the steady beep of the monitor on her heart or the cuff that regularly inflated, she was weak. The number might not show it, but I knew it.

I hadn't *almost* lost her.

I *had* lost her.

"Don't tell her. Or our family." I hoped my eyes conveyed the severity of what I felt. "No one needs to know that. Least of all my wife or her father."

"Of course. I'll make sure to note her chart. But if *she* asks, Mr. Burin, no one will refuse the information."

Sarah wouldn't ask because Sarah wouldn't care. The

only thing that would matter to my wife was that her children were alive. It had been more important than her own life. She wouldn't care about the details of the story, just the ending.

As the nurse left, Jack arrived. I had no idea where my parents or Austin were, but I could assume that at least one of them was with the girls. I trusted Austin knew I didn't want them left alone, and no one could spoil a child like my mother. It wouldn't matter that she couldn't hold them; somehow, she'd manage to find a way to coerce the nurses into giving her grandchildren special privileges. I shook my head and smiled at the thought.

"Hey, son. How you holding up?" Jack looked as bad as I was sure I did. This man had endured more than any father should have to in the last year between Sarah and Randi.

I took a seat next to Sarah's bed and held her hand. "Hanging in there. You?"

Jack pulled up a chair on the other side and did the same. "Well, I got two beautiful granddaughters that I can't wait to hold." Then his gaze dropped to his daughter, and nothing more needed to be said.

Silence lingered between the two of us comfortably. Watching Sarah breathe was about as much as either of us could manage. I was exhausted but afraid to fall asleep, and I couldn't speak for Jack, but I'd say he was there, too. Irrational fear rose in me that if I nodded off, I'd lose her while I slept, and I refused to take that chance.

"You need some rest, Charlie. You ain't gonna be no good to nobody if you can't hold your eyes open."

I shook my head and put my chin on my arm attached to the hand that held Sarah's. "I've got too much on my mind to rest, Jack. Two babies in NICU and a wife in ICU—it's a lot to process."

"Hmm."

I stroked Sarah's hair and willed her to wake up so I could see those beautiful blue eyes. Just a glimpse would calm my worry. "We'll figure it out. I can find a way to make more money. As long as I've got her and the girls, the rest is just details."

"This trip ain't gonna come cheap." He was right about that, but I couldn't put a price on any of the lives of the Burin girls—my girls.

Jack sat up and stared at me until I met him eye for eye. "You need to focus on your wife and kids, Charlie. Being gone all the time ain't gonna benefit any of 'em. She ain't gonna bounce back from this quite so quick as another woman would. Her body still ain't healed from the accident. Now she's been cut from hip to hip and got a bad back. That don't work for a new mama with two infants."

I got where he was coming from, but that didn't change anything. "It's my responsibility to provide for them, Jack. I'll do what I have to do." There weren't enough hours in the day to work at Twin Creeks, help Sarah, take care of twins, and work a second job, but I'd figure it out.

Jack took off his hat and set it on the mattress at Sarah's feet. "Let me help you, Charlie."

"What?" I didn't know what Jack was proposing, but men—Southern men—had pride.

He sucked his teeth and took a deep breath. "This is between you and me. You ain't never to breathe a word of it to your wife. I need your promise on that."

"I don't even know what we're talking about, Jack." I chuckled and shook my head. I swore the old man was starting to show signs of losing it.

The scowl on his face told me just how serious he was, and it stilled my laughter. "Just assure me that no matter what I say, you don't go discussin' it with your wife. This stays 'tween us."

"Okay. You've got my word." I didn't want to lie to my wife, but I sure as hell wasn't going to get in the way of Jack Adams and whatever plan he'd concocted in the back of his mind.

"Let me take care of the hospital bills." Jack held up his hand to protest, not letting me get a word out. "I'll cover whatever the insurance doesn't."

Jack Adams wasn't hurting for money, but it didn't feel right that he should pick up the tab for our kids—for our accident. I'd never call them a mistake, but they weren't planned. My kids were my surprise responsibility.

"I can't let you do that. She's my wife. They're my little girls."

Jack swallowed, and I watched as his Adam's apple bobbed in his throat before he spoke. "There's a lot you don't know, and even more I hope Sarah never finds out. I ain't aimin' to discuss the ins and outs. I'm just tellin' you; I owe it to her."

I didn't have any idea what he could possibly know that

made him feel this sense of debt toward Sarah, but I had to imagine it had to do with her mama running off. It had changed the course of Sarah's teenage years and subsequently her life.

"Jack..." I shook my head, determined to refuse his offer.

"It's already been done, son. I'm just trying to give you the courtesy of tellin' you I did it."

"How?" It wasn't like I couldn't undo whatever magic he'd worked in the billing department.

The old man wasn't going to budge, that much was evident in his stern expression. Nor did he have any intention of sharing the details with me. "You're a new father." Jack wasn't telling me anything I didn't already know. "And I hope you never go through what I have. I don't want you to ever feel the hopelessness that I have, thinking that each time I walk out of a hospital room is the last time I'm going to see my daughter alive. It ain't a good place to be."

I couldn't imagine. This had nearly killed me, and Jack had not only endured this, but he'd almost lost her in a car accident less than a year ago as well.

"Your daughters are the most beautiful and precious things you'll ever have. You'll wanna protect 'em with your life. I let my little girl down. When her mama left, with Randi, the accident—she deserved better, more. I want to do this for her." There was more to this than what Jack was telling me, but I knew the man well enough to know that he'd never give me one more detail than he'd just shared. Whatever guilt he felt, he'd keep it close.

I rubbed the back of my neck, hesitant to give him what

he wanted. "Why don't you want her to know? That's an incredible gift to your daughter. You know she'll want to thank you." *Not that she ever could.*

"Because I know Sarah. She don't need to feel the guilt or the burden of what she thinks I'll be givin' up. Just let her focus on what's important. If she ever mentions it, just say the bills have been taken care of." It was that simple in Jack's mind; clearly, he hadn't thought about the vagueness of that statement. My wife would never let that sit without further explanation. "We agreed?"

Sitting in that room at Anston Hospital, I vowed to secrecy that would be almost impossible to maintain, but it was important to my father-in-law, so I let it be important to me. It met our need. It met his. And it allowed me to focus on Sarah and the girls.

18

SARAH

"Sarah."

My name. But I wasn't being addressed. It took me a minute to come around, and I had to fight against the grogginess that wanted to keep me under. I blinked several times, trying to clear the cogs, but when I went to speak, my mouth was dry as a bone. Once I was able to focus, I noticed the number of people in the room.

Daddy, Charlie's parents, Austin, and my husband. I watched them all as one by one, they turned toward me, and it finally caught Charlie's attention. He looked at our family and then back at me, and whatever unspoken words he shared with them caused them to exit with grim expressions.

No. No, no, no, no.

The machine monitoring my heart rate started to beep faster as my pulse ratcheted up. There was no way I'd gone through all of this and lost them, but the looks on their faces and the way Charlie now held my hand, left no room to believe anything else.

I let my hand drift down my side and to my stomach. It was soft, unlike how it had been when Charlie had called the ambulance. And it took me no time to realize how little feeling I had...anywhere. "Charlie." I sobbed his name, but it was hoarse and broken at best.

"Sarah," he cooed as he stroked my hair, and I couldn't stand the idea of being placated.

He held my hand that was covered in tape and tubing, and I did my best to squeeze back, but I couldn't get beyond the crushing weight that had settled in my chest. I needed him to pull me close, to swallow me in a hug, to protect me from whatever words were about to fall from his mouth.

I croaked his name again, but he was as choked up as I was. He leaned over and pressed his forehead to mine, and I nearly came out of my skin.

"What's going on?" I bellowed in his ear.

When he pressed his lips to my forehead, my heart went from racing to a standstill. My breath hitched, and my heart stopped. But he refused to speak whatever he knew. And something wasn't right.

I managed to pull myself together before I totally lost it. "Charlie," I said again. "What's going on?"

"They did an emergency C-section. You had a placental abruption. I don't even know what that means."

I was frantic. "What about the girls?" I didn't care what I'd been through. Clearly, I was alive since we were having this conversation. "They're only twenty-eight weeks."

"Sarah—"

"Where are they? Have you seen them? Charlie, tell me something!" Panic had taken over, and I wasn't sure anything he said would even register.

He nodded. "I've been with them. They're fighters, but they're not out of the woods. They're so tiny, Sarah."

They'd made it. I'd made it. All of us were still here. "What do they look like?"

Tears raced down my cheeks as I did my best to wipe them away. But it was no longer fear because I knew God had brought me my miracles. He had rewarded my faith. My girls—*our* girls—were here and breathing, and I was still alive to see it.

A tear-filled smile lifted Charlie's lips. "They're beautiful." He took out his phone to show me pictures of our daughters. They were as different as night and day, and I didn't know it was possible to love someone I'd never met, but I did. Fiercely.

"They don't have names, sunshine." He nearly choked on his chuckle backed by tears, and I'd never thought I'd love to see tears in a man's eyes.

We hadn't considered names. It wasn't that I didn't want to, but if something happened to me, I wanted Charlie to be able to choose that for them.

~

aneuvering to the NICU had been no simple feat, but I'd been determined to see my daughters as soon as humanly possible. I didn't care how much pain I was in, nor did I care what the doctor's thought about moving me. I wasn't guaranteed today or tomorrow, and there was no chance I'd risk not seeing them, talking to them, touching them. Personally, I thought the nurses conceded just to get me to shut up, and I didn't bother trying to hide my satisfaction when Charlie suggested they make it happen. He'd never seen me overbearing...until today. My mama claws came out sharp and fierce, and I'd protect those girls until my last breath.

Even though I'd seen pictures, they didn't change the magic of the moment I first met my daughters. Peering in at their tiny little bodies, I, too, noticed all the things Charlie had said about their differences. It was the little things like the pulse of one versus the other, the skin tone, the way one breathed, the little bits of fuzz on their heads. They were twins, but even at only a couple of days old, they had their own spirits and personalities.

Kara was the smaller of the two, and she was also the more intuitive. Quiet, introspective if a baby could be. Whereas her sister, wailed—as much as an infant with underdeveloped lungs could. She fought tooth and nail against everything from cannulas to feeding tubes. Kylie was the polar opposite of her fairer sister. But they were both breathtaking.

"Kylie reminds me of Randi." Charlie instantly regretted

his statement, and almost flinched when he saw the words land on me.

I hadn't thought about it, but she was a little replica of my sister, and Kara was more like me. If we'd been twins, I could envision this being us. Except for the part where Kylie always sought out Kara. As if on instinct, she knew she was the stronger of the pair, and some part of her was always touching her sister. "You're right."

I missed my sister. I wished like crazy that she'd concede and come around, but that was a battle I hadn't won—yet.

"Kara is definitely more you and me." He continued once he'd confirmed I wasn't wounded by his first acknowledgment. "I wonder if anyone else has noticed that." Charlie didn't expect an answer; he was just thinking out loud.

Between his parents, Daddy, Austin, and us, these girls would know they were loved. There had been a vigil at their sides since they were born, and that would continue throughout their lives. And I absolutely loved that. For my girls and about my family.

"Would you like to hold them?"

The nurse scared the crap out of me. I hadn't heard her walk up, and the sound of her voice nearly had me out of my wheelchair and into Charlie's arms. They moved like ninjas in this place, and the intense focus of parents on their children made it even easier for them to do.

I clutched my chest, and my heart pounded against my hand. "You scared the daylights out of me."

"I'm sorry. I didn't mean to." She stared at me, but I had no idea what for. Finally, she asked again with my having forgotten there was a question on the table. "Would you like to hold them? Skin-to-skin contact is really good for mama and baby."

My heart now raced for an entirely different reason. I had no idea I'd get to hold them, much less this soon. I glanced up at Charlie with eager eyes, and his softened under my stare. When I turned my attention back to the nurse, she took my enthusiasm as a yes and moved toward the incubator.

"You can drag up a chair." She spoke to Charlie who eagerly searched the perimeter.

Once he found what he was looking for, he pulled it close to me and excitement bubbled in his expression.

Trinity—now that I could see her name badge—had Charlie help me with the ties of my hospital gown, loosening the top. And then, she navigated my sweet, sleeping Kara under the cloth and against my bare chest. Nothing could have prepared me to feel my daughter nestled against my skin. But if I'd thought that was mind-blowing, seeing Charlie Burin nestle Kylie against his chest was out of this world.

I couldn't stop myself from staring. I didn't want to. I wanted to soak in the memories and the love and the blessings sitting in this space. For years, I'd pined after a man who'd never noticed me. A man I'd believed would never see me much less love me. And now, not only did I share a last name with that same man, but the two of us held our hearts and our love for each other flush against our sternums. There was nothing more attractive, and I knew from that moment on, Charlie Burin would always own my heart. And these two little girls, already had us wrapped.

Never, in my wildest dreams, would I have believed that a tragedy as great as my accident could turn into the greatest of miracles and happily ever afters.

But sometimes, it's the journey that makes the destination so worthwhile.

EPILOGUE

SARAH

My sister had missed yet another milestone in my life, and I'd decided I'd had enough. I might not ever win back her affection—although I wasn't sure I'd ever had it to begin with—but there wasn't going to be a day that went by that Randi didn't know I wanted her to come home. The twins had taught me one thing—tomorrow is never a guarantee.

Every two weeks, like clockwork. I called my sister. And anytime something happened in Mason Belle she heard from me then as well. I had a great relationship with her voicemail for several years. I was really good about keeping up with her, but the conversations were strained at best, and I did the majority of the talking. She would grunt or acknowledge that I'd spoken, but she never engaged. Randi never called me or texted me—it was always a reply to my reaching out. But she did reply, and that had to count for something. I ended every phone call with an invitation for her to come home, not just to meet Kylie and Kara, but to meet Rand as well. He'd joined our family two years after the twins, and I knew, if Randi ever met him, she'd fall head over heels for him and him for her. But my sister always declined.

There was no doubt in my mind she'd settled into a nice life in New York. She was practically married to one of the partners at the law firm she worked for, and I had to admit, Eason was a great guy. Sometimes I thought I had a better shot of convincing Eason to come to Mason Belle than Miranda. If she had it her way, she'd never step foot back in South Texas. I just didn't know why. But that didn't stop me from hoping or trying.

I wanted Randi to be a part of my life and my children's lives. I wanted her to be their aunt, even if that just meant she flew down from New York once a year to tell me how much they had grown and bring them presents that made too much noise. She needed that place in our lives as much as we needed her in it. And I wanted her to feel like she could call me at any part of the day and talk to me about anything that was going on in her life. I was certain she'd made friends, and my guess was Eason's family had welcomed her with open arms, but that didn't mean she didn't have roots, too.

I didn't know anything about her anymore. I used to believe I knew all there was to know...that I knew my sister inside and out. No matter how much she annoyed me or how she tried to pull the wool over my eyes, I wasn't as blind as she had thought I was. I also loved her in a way I'd never love anyone else. We fought, sure, and those fights turned out to have devastating consequences. I just wish Randi realized they'd also had beautiful repercussions. That argument, that accident, it brought me everything good in my life. There wasn't a day that went by that I wasn't grateful for the events of that day in June six years ago. Without them, I wouldn't be married to the man of my dreams, nor would I have three gorgeous kids who kept me on my toes.

I tapped my little sister's name in my list of contacts and stared at it before taking a deep breath. Then I pressed the green button and held the phone to my ear.

Surprisingly, she answered. "Hey, Sarah." Not surprisingly, she sounded tired, uninterested, and obligated. It was a tone I recognized and heard more often than not.

"Hey." I attempted to keep my excitement to a minimum because it drove my sister bonkers. It was my defense mechanism when I was apprehensive, and even after years of these calls, I was still nervous making each one. "It's good to hear your voice." And that was the start of the downhill slide.

I sounded like a mother and not her sister. I just didn't know how to make the transition when she refused to assist in building any real relationship. There were days I wished Eason would answer. He was easy to talk to, and somehow, I felt like he appreciated my presence in his girlfriend's life.

"It's good to hear from you, too." There was always an edge to her voice that told me she didn't mean it.

I wondered if this was her professional voice, the one she used at the office to speak to clients and lawyers because it certainly wasn't the laidback ease of Mason Belle that she'd grown up with. And her Southern accent was all but gone. A hint of sincerity might have been present, but a larger part of her answered out of obligation. That much I could tell from one sentence out of her mouth.

Before I could ease into a conversation, Randi cut right to the chase.

"Is there something that you needed?" New York had really done a number on her when it came to cutting through the niceties. Southern charm was no longer part of Randi's vocabulary or demeanor, and I hated to see that go.

I took a deep breath and did my best to keep the happy in my tone. "No, I didn't need anything." I wasn't doing a very good job at hiding my irritation—it wouldn't hurt her to take five minutes out of her day every other week to be pleasant for five minutes. "I just wanted to see how you're doing."

Every call started the same way with slight variations, and they all ended the same, too. I shouldn't have to have a reason to call my sister. "You know Rand's birthday is coming up. Have you thought about coming to see him and the girls?" My kids were typically a safe topic of conversation, but I knew when I heard her sigh on the other end that my light tone had not deterred her eye roll or irritation.

"Sarah, we've talked about this," she said, "repeatedly. Why do we keep having the same conversation? I'm not coming back to Texas." That was the first time she'd made such a resolute statement. Typically, she beat around the bush with excuses that held no weight or merit.

"You have nieces and a nephew that you haven't met. I haven't seen you since the accident." I heard her wince and plowed right through it. "You haven't seen Charlie or our house." I didn't want to give her a guilt trip, although I did want to remind her of all the things she was giving up by not coming home. "Why do I have to have a reason to beg my sister to come home? I just want to see you, Randi...."

"Miranda."

I chose to ignore that name preference. That might be who she thought she was in New York; it would never be who she was in Mason Belle, Texas. *Never*.

"I want to give you a hug and talk to you for more than five forced minutes. There's no reason we can't have a normal relationship. You're a grown woman, and so am I. We aren't kids anymore. We can rebuild our connection, but you have to give it a chance. And that means not answering my calls purely out of duty, and instead, putting forth a little effort."

"I don't know." Randi's resolve was waning, and I could hear the want in her tone. She might not be ready to admit it, but there was a part of her that missed our small town. If she'd tell me what drove her away, I might be able to fix it so she'd come home. "I love you, Sarah; I really do. But I don't think rebuilding is quite the word you're looking for."

I could admit our relationship had been tumultuous, tenuous even. She was a kid. I was charged with her supervision and discipline. None of that existed anymore. We could just *be* if my sister would allow it to happen.

"Then what do you think we should do? This isn't working, and it doesn't feel right. This isn't how a family is supposed to communicate."

She sighed. "I know. I really do. I wish you understood what all happened, but since you don't and you can't, then I just need to watch from afar." She paused, and I wondered if she was finished. "I'm glad you're happy, Sarah. I think it's great that you have Charlie and the kids and that life is all you want it to be. It's just not *my* life anymore. I hope someday you'll understand."

I'd given it all I could today. These conversations were taxing for us both. I didn't have a clue why she needed to stay away—no one did but Randi. And she had decided that wasn't a secret she'd ever share.

"You can call me anytime you want, Sarah. I'll always try to answer."

I took a deep breath. "I just want us to be close again."

There was a pregnant pause. We were not going to be close like I wanted us to be, and I think we both knew that. We hadn't been close since we were both little, since before Mama left. And there was too much that Randi wasn't willing to let go of yet. But I believed in miracles. I had a house full of them. And I was certain Miranda would be one at some point as well.

"Look," Randi finally said, "I have a lunch appointment at one...."

"I'll let you go, but we will talk more soon."

"Okay, Sarah." The tension in her voice was gone, replaced by exhaustion.

I softened my tone to the one I used to use when I whispered to her as we hid in my room at night when we were little to avoid Mama and Daddy hearing us. "Good to hear your voice again." I smiled, even though she couldn't see me as I thought about a time where the two of us were just sisters. "I love you."

"I love you, too." It wasn't heartfelt; nevertheless, I claimed it as a victory.

~

"Sarah!" Panic laced my husband's tone, and I dreaded hearing what he'd come in to tell me.

Mason Belle was in a state of emergency as wildfires tore through the fields, pastures, and ranches all around us. We'd hoped like crazy that they'd blow in another direction, but that wasn't the path they took. For days the flames had inched toward our county and then one by one taken over.

Last night, they'd hit Cross Acres and Twin Creeks, and every available hand had been called up to do everything they could to help, which primarily meant driving the cattle to safety. That was difficult to do at Cross Acres because there were so many more head than on any other ranch around. That many cows required space to even stand much less feed. When Charlie had gotten the call from his dad last night, I'd been woken as well. What hadn't happened was an update since.

Even if my condition didn't prevent me from hopping on

a horse to try to heard cattle, my three children did. And before the night was over, my three children had grown into twelve kids, who were all brought over dead on their feet so their parents could try to salvage and help. At the very least, it occupied my time and made me feel like I contributed something so their mothers could assist their husbands. Land and cows were everything around here, and if I could free up seven moms to save their farms, then I was glad to do it. Unfortunately, it left me waiting for someone to tell me anything.

For Charlie to have left Twin Creeks, either the fires had burned past the family's acreage, or something had happened. The tone of his voice said it was the latter, but I prayed it was the former.

"Sarah?" He moved through the house in search of me.

I dried off my hands from doing the breakfast dishes and called back. "I'm in the kitchen. What's wrong?" As soon as I tossed the towel onto the counter, I turned to meet him. My heart thundered in my chest, and I struggled to breathe, but it wasn't the thick, dark smoke outside the windows that threatened to choke me out.

It was the look on Charlie's face. His eyes were a deep brown, his forehead marred with worry, and his bloodshot eyes swam with unshed tears. He grabbed my bicep, tugging me to his chest. If he hadn't dipped his mouth to my ear, I doubt I would have heard him over the pounding beneath my sternum. "Sunshine, there's been an accident."

I pushed away from his embrace, needing more information than I could garner from those words alone. "What kind of accident?" My voice was as hollow as my aching heart.

He wouldn't have come to me unless he had to. There was too much to do and too many ranches that needed help.

Charlie swallowed, and it took effort. Whatever was on the tip of his tongue was a message he didn't want to deliver. "Jack—"

"Daddy? What's wrong?"

He took every bit of effort he could muster to maintain his composure, but I could see it in his eyes. The bloodshot might be from the smoke; the wet was from his emotion. "Austin just called. He's in the ICU." His chest heaved, even though his voice stayed level. "Austin found him out in the Southern pastures last night when he got to Cross Acres."

"Oh, my God." White noise rang in my ear, accompanied by the staccato beat of a rampant heart. "Is he okay?" Clearly, he wasn't, or he wouldn't be in ICU. "Is...is Daddy...?"

I could see the shadow of doubt that flickered in his eyes. Charlie wouldn't lie to me, but he'd sugarcoat the heck out of something to keep me from worrying. "Austin's there with him now."

"Have the doctors said anything?" My hands trembled along with my heart, and I wasn't sure how much longer my unsteady legs would hold my weak back. I clutched the fabric of my husband's shirt, begging him to tell me what I needed to hear.

He shook his head, and I knew that wasn't good. I didn't have any idea how long Daddy had been at the hospital, but

Daddy's call for help went out around midnight last night, and it was daylight now.

I had a room filled with other ranchers' kids. I couldn't just hop into the truck and race off to Laredo. And I couldn't leave small children unattended. I glanced to the living room and then back to Charlie.

"My mom's on her way."

I sank into his embrace and praised God for a husband with the forethought to send reinforcements. "She doesn't know about all the other kids, though."

He brushed my hair behind my ears. "And she won't care. Go get dressed so we can leave when she gets here." Then he pressed his lips to my forehead.

"I have to call my sister."

Charlie hesitated. "Sarah, are you sure that you want to...?"

"Positive," I told him. "Randi needs to know. I don't care what's kept her away. It's time for her to come home." The words caught in my throat. I refused to admit her attendance might be needed for a funeral, and instead, I focused on the fact that it was the perfect opportunity for healing.

He swiped his thumb across my cheekbone. His hand came to rest on my jaw, and he tilted my head back to meet my eyes. "All right." There was nothing but love radiating back at me. "Call your sister. I'll be waiting when you're ready. My mom should be here soon."

"I love you." I didn't wait for his reply or return his sweet tone. Instead, I dove for my cell phone.

Randi's number just kept ringing. I had hoped she'd

realize that if I were calling at seven in the morning—eight her time—that it wasn't a call to chitchat. She needed to pick up. I closed my eyes and waited. Every second felt like a year, and then I got her voicemail.

I could barely contain my frustration. Tears welled in my eyes, and I ended the call. I tried one more time, and again, I had the same result. I didn't have time to keep trying, so I tossed my phone aside and quickly got dressed. Just as I tied my shoes, I heard my mother-in-law downstairs being greeted by her grandkids. I took a deep breath, grabbed my cell and my purse, and did my best to hurry.

Jessica kissed my cheek, and pity stained her expression. I wondered what she knew. There had been an extra layer of concern in Charlie's eyes that I hadn't unpacked. When he'd barreled into the kitchen, he looked like he'd seen a ghost. His mom shooed me out the door with promises to stay until we got back and each of the twins hugging one of her legs.

Charlie took my hand and led me to the truck. He was silent as I got in, and when he settled himself behind the wheel, he caught my eyes while he backed up. "She didn't answer?"

I shook my head. It would have been more surprising if she had.

"I'm sorry."

My shoulders lifted in a shrug that held far less emotion than I truly felt. I certainly wasn't apathetic to the situation; I just didn't have words to express what I actually felt. We hadn't gotten to say goodbye to Mama. I didn't want my sister to hold that same regret with Daddy. The first hadn't been a choice. This absolutely would. And it would be one she regretted.

I wasn't sure that forty-five minutes had ever passed as slowly as they had on that drive. Once we got to the hospital, Charlie came over to the passenger side to help me out. It still made my heart skip even though I no longer needed his assistance.

Charlie led me inside, not bothering to stop at a nurse's station or reception. I could only assume Austin had told him where they were. And sure enough, when we stepped off the elevator, Austin was there to greet us. I dropped my husband's hand and raced into my brother-in-law's arms.

Austin gave Charlie a half-smile when I finally released him from my death grip. Thankfully, Austin didn't need me to give him words, or Charlie for that matter. He just moved over so we could have two seats beside one another. I tucked myself into Charlie's embrace while he talked to his brother. I didn't hear what either of them said beyond Austin's having no news. I closed my eyes and inhaled my husband's scent. It, coupled with his hold, were the only things in the world that had the power to calm me during the darkest night and raging storm.

~

My phone rang in my purse the next day, and I raced to locate it amongst the crayons and action figures. The second I found it, I saw Randi's name on the screen. I'd blown her up, trying to get in touch with her, and it seemed she'd finally figured out that it might be important.

I grabbed Charlie's arm and gave it a squeeze. "I'm going to go take this." I flashed the phone his way and stood to walk out for privacy. I stepped away from the waiting room before answering the phone.

"Randi?" I tried like crazy to keep the fear out of my voice, but I wasn't successful.

A breathy puff of air rattled against the speaker. "Yeah?"

"You need to come home." My voice cracked, and I lost the fight against tears. "There's been an accident."

There was silence on the other end. I didn't know if she was processing what I'd just said, not interested, or had gone mute.

"Randi? Did you hear me?" My questions were met with more silence. I couldn't even hear her breathing anymore. I pulled the phone from my ear to see that the call was still connected. "Randi! Say something."

She finally spoke, but only one word. "Who?" There was no mistaking the pain and dread she knew the answer would bring.

"Daddy." I had as hard a time talking as my little sister did. "The wildfires..."

"When?"

"Austin found him late Sunday night out in the south pasture."

"What happened?" Her voice was more distant than normal, and I wondered if she really heard anything I said.

Just thinking about what Daddy endured brought a frog

to my throat and tears to my eyes. I couldn't contain the emotion and no longer tried. "He tried to save some cows that fell behind when they moved them to another pasture. He went alone." I didn't touch on the ignorance in what my father had done. Anyone who'd ever stepped foot on a cattle ranch knew how dumb that bold move was. "When Austin found him, he was still conscious. He's not now."

Randi was quiet for longer than I expected, and then finally, she spoke. "Why was Austin there?"

"Seriously?" Gone were my tears. They'd been replaced by outrage. "That's what you're worried about? What about Daddy's condition?" I didn't even try to hide my annoyance as I huffed loudly into the receiver. "Great day in the morning, Randi. You need to get your head on straight and get home."

"Is he..." She struggled to ask whatever was on her mind, and if it were one more question about Austin instead of Daddy, she wouldn't have to worry about coming home. I'd go to New York and drag her butt back to Texas. "Is he going to make it?"

My sister couldn't hide her trepidation, and suddenly, she was the little girl I'd loved so much before Mama had left. The one I used to whisper to in church and play with in the fields.

I released a heavy breath, wishing I could comfort her without thousands of miles between us. "I don't know, Randi. You need to get home."

She didn't fight me. She didn't even argue. She just conceded.

Miranda Adams was coming home to Mason Belle.

The End

(Read Miranda and Austin's story in *Gravel Road.* It's available now on Amazon.com and free with your Kindle Unlimited subscription.)

ACKNOWLEDGMENTS

This one was on those books that I never intended to write, but thankfully, I listened to readers who begged for Charlie and Sarah's story after having read *Gravel Road*. And thus, *Beaten Paths* was born.

So a huge thank you goes out to all the readers who relentlessly pursued this writing of this story. Without your persistence, *Beaten Paths* wouldn't have happened. And shhh, don't tell anyone, but there's another story coming from *Gravel Road* based on your requests as well. Eason and Garrett's story, *Cement Sidewalks* is coming in November 2019!

Linda—and the team at Foreword—thank you for the countless hours you put in behind the scenes to make each release happen. Without your help, I'd flounder. Without your friendship, I'd be lost. You're my sounding board and my vault—thank you!

Kristie—Thank you for the kick-ass cover that so perfectly aligned with *Gravel Road*. Vanilla Lily is the shit, and so are you.

And, as always, thank you to the bloggers who read and promote. Authors—especially me—would be lost without you! xoxo

ABOUT THE AUTHOR

Stephie is a forty-one-year-old mother to one of the feistiest preteens to ever walk. They live on the outskirts of Greenville, South Carolina, where they house two cats and two dogs in their veritable zoo.

She has a serious addiction to anything Coach and would live on Starbucks if she could get away with it. She's slightly enamored with Charlie Hunnam and Sons of Anarchy and is a self-proclaimed foodie.

ALSO BY STEPHIE WALLS

Bound (Bound Duet #1)

Freed (Bound Duet #2)

Redemption (Bound Duet Spinoff)

Metamorphosis

Compass

Strangers

chimera

Beauty Mark

Fallen Woman

Girl Crush

Unexpected Arrivals

Label Me Proud

Family Ties

Gravel Road (The Journey Collection)

Dear Diamond

Her Perfect

53727667R00175

Made in the
USA
Lexington, KY